W9-BOG-734

It's a
Date
(Again)

ALSO BY JENEVA ROSE

It's a Date (Again)

JENEVA ROSE

 Montlake

This is a work of fiction. Names, characters, organizations, places, events, and incidents are either products of the author's imagination or are used fictitiously. Otherwise, any resemblance to actual persons, living or dead, is purely coincidental.

Text copyright © 2023 by Jeneva Rose
All rights reserved.

No part of this book may be reproduced, or stored in a retrieval system, or transmitted in any form or by any means, electronic, mechanical, photocopying, recording, or otherwise, without express written permission of the publisher.

Published by Montlake, Seattle

www.apub.com

Amazon, the Amazon logo, and Montlake are trademarks of Amazon.com, Inc., or its affiliates.

ISBN-13: 9781662512414 (paperback)
ISBN-13: 9781662512407 (digital)

Cover design by Jarrod Taylor
Cover image: © DayArt00 / Shutterstock

Printed in the United States of America

For my thriller readers,
heads-up, there is no murder in this book.
I tried adding one in, but apparently "it's not typical for
the genre."
So prepare to swoon instead—because I'll make your
heart race one way or another.

CHAPTER 1

The first raindrop settles onto my cheek. It's warm despite the cool Chicago air. Gusts of wind blow between the lit-up skyscrapers, rustling my long locks. I spent an hour curling my hair for really no reason at all, and I'm sure it resembles more of a bird's nest rather than the soft, loose ringlets I created earlier. I catch a glimpse of myself in a window of a closed business. Yep. My blonde hair is exactly how I pictured it, and my pencil skirt has twisted 180 degrees clockwise. I swivel it back into place and tie my trench coat closed. Cars and city buses whoosh past me. Horns blare intermittently. Traffic is the sound of the city. I've lived here for a long time, so it's become more like white noise to me. It's comforting—a reminder that I'm not alone.

I breathe in the crisp fall air, savoring it, because I know it won't last more than a couple of weeks. As a midwesterner, the four seasons are like a personality trait to us. We'll brag that we have all of them, gush about our hot summers, our snowy holidays, our colorful falls, and our blooming springs. But we always leave out the fact that they're not divided up even remotely equally. Three months of a hot, humid summer, two months of a rainy spring, two weeks of a heavenly fall, and six and a half months of stone-cold winter. But it's this weather right now that makes it all worth it, even if it is fleeting. It's the short-lived moments where life happens.

Another raindrop hits my cheek. I wipe it away but realize it isn't rain that's streaking my face. It's tears. I'm crying, and I don't even know why. He told me he loved me. I told him I didn't love him back. It's simple. Like a math equation. Two plus one does not equal four. The feelings weren't mutual. It just . . . it doesn't work. But if it's that simple, then why am I crying? Maybe it was the look in his eyes. He was stunned. No, he was devastated, like he had imagined it playing out very differently. Like me saying I didn't feel the same way was never even a remote possibility. He asked me a couple of times if I was sure. I told him I was. I was sure. Wasn't I? He reminded me of the good times we had. And we had a lot of them. But I said no. I said I'm sorry. I said, *I don't feel that way about you.* His shoulders slumped. Tears threatened to spill from his eyes. He tucked his chin in, and his gaze fell to the ground. I immediately felt guilty, or at least that's what I thought I felt . . . guilt. It sat in my stomach like a rock, heavy and all-consuming. Then, he nodded and walked away. That was that. But if that was that, why am I crying? And why do I feel so empty?

I wipe my face with the sleeve of my coat. It makes no difference because they just keep falling, like rain from bloated clouds pushed beyond their limits. They must be coming from somewhere. At an intersection, I wait for the WALK signal to turn. Cars pass by in a blur, and it's not because they're driving fast. It's because I can't stop crying. It feels like I'm viewing the world through glass, unsure of my place in it.

"Hey, miss," a voice calls out. Startled, I turn around quickly to find a large man dressed in faded sweatpants and an old, oversized jacket. He's more than twice my size, or maybe I see him that way because I feel so small right now. His skin is weathered, evidence of a hard life, but his eyes are kind, evidence that he hasn't let the hard times harden him. Pinched between his thumb and pointer finger is a torn piece of cardboard with a message written in Sharpie. It reads, DOWN ON MY LUCK. ANYTHING HELPS. Despite his sign, somehow the corners of his lips turn up.

Without thinking, I reach into my purse and pull out a couple of one-dollar bills. It's the only reason I carry a small amount of cash on me at all times. My friend Maya is always warning me that it's dangerous to give money to others, that I might get robbed or worse in the process. But I always say if it's dangerous to help another person, then my middle name must be Danger. I know the difference between needing help and not needing it can come down to one bad incident or one wrong decision. You can't control whether you need help or not, but you can control whether or not you help.

"It's all I have," I say, extending the dollars and a tender smile.

He glances down at my hand and then meets my gaze. "Then it's all I need. Thank you, miss. Bless you." His grin never falters as he accepts the cash and nods. Just as he's about to turn away, the man stops and squints, doing a double take. "You all right?" he asks.

I wipe at my face again and sniffle. "Yeah." My answer doesn't come out even remotely convincing, but I assume he'll say, "Okay," and be on his way. That's the socially expected thing to do, and it's what everyone does.

He stuffs the dollars into his coat pocket and shuffles his feet. "I'm sorry, miss, but I don't believe you."

I nibble on my bottom lip, trying to stop it from quivering. I don't know what to say. That wasn't at all the response I was expecting.

"No, really, I'm fine." I force a smile. It's a crooked one, though. I'm sure I look like a total mess, complete with smeared mascara, bloodshot eyes, and tangled hair. But my disheveled appearance doesn't seem to faze him.

He presses his lips together and studies my face. "Then why are you crying?"

I shrug and glance down at my shoes. "I'm not sure," I say. I'm embarrassed that I'm crying in front of this man and doubly embarrassed that I can't even explain why it is that I'm crying.

"Deep down you must. I'm Hank, by the way." He extends his hand toward me.

I look at his face, covered in salt-and-pepper facial stubble, and then at his large, calloused hand, complete with neatly trimmed nails. "Hank. I'm Peyton." My hand disappears in his, and we shake.

"Like the football player?"

"Yeah, but after Walter, not Manning. Mine's spelled like Manning because my dad got the spelling wrong, and my mom didn't correct it because she liked it better with an *e* rather than an *a*. But yeah, like the football player . . ." Realizing I'm rambling, I trail off and fiddle with my fingers.

Hank chuckles. "Glad it's after Walter. Especially here in Chicago."

"Yeah, me too." It feels like I'm submerged underwater, so I know those damn tears just keep falling. I wish I could turn them off, so I try to grin through them instead. I must look unhinged right now, but Hank doesn't seem to notice or care. He simply smiles.

Shoving his hands into his coat pockets, he rocks back on his heels. His face turns from jovial to serious. "So, tell me what happened to you tonight. I can't leave you out here crying without at least trying to make you feel better."

I sniffle and clear my throat. "It's nothing. It's silly, actually."

"If it's got you crying, it must not be silly to you."

I break my gaze again, staring down at my feet for a moment before looking back at Hank. His kind eyes search mine, and his brows draw together as though he's really concerned about me. I don't know this man, but I get the feeling he would stand out here all night talking to me if need be.

"Well, a guy told me he loved me tonight."

Hank scratches his chin and makes a *humph* sound. "Sounds awful," he says, sealing his sarcasm with a small grin.

I nod and laugh and cry at the same time. "I told you it was silly."

He flicks his hand. "Nah, there's gotta be more to it. How did you respond to his declaration of love?"

"Well." I lower my chin and wipe at my wet face again, but it feels more like I'm trying to mop the ocean. "I told him I didn't love him back."

The WALK signal turns again, and cars steadily pass through the intersection. We're in a city of nearly three million, surrounded by people—but right now, it feels like only Hank and I exist. A city bus honks as a car nearly merges into its lane. The car swerves back, and traffic continues without a hiccup. I divert my attention to Hank.

"Oh." He raises his brow and runs his fingers down the sides of his jaw. "I see what's going on here."

"What do you see?" I ask, hoping I can see whatever it is he can.

Hank talks with his hands as if he's giving a lecture of some sort. It reminds me of my dad, and I find it both endearing and comforting. "This man told you he loved you. You told him you didn't love him back. Now you're here crying on a street corner. I know I didn't make you cry, or at least I hope I didn't. This beautiful fall night didn't make you cry. That man that told you he loved you didn't make you cry. So it must be what you said back."

A hiccup escapes me like I swallowed something I wasn't ready for—perhaps the truth. I blink several times, trying to make sense of what he's saying. I know what he's getting at, but sometimes you can't see what's right in front of you because you're looking through it.

"I just told him how I felt," I say with a shrug.

"Did you?"

"Yeah." It comes out high-pitched and loud as though I'm trying to convince him and maybe myself too.

"Did that truth come from your heart or your brain?" he asks.

"Aren't they the same thing?"

"Not at all." He lifts his chin. "The heart loves. The brain thinks. And sometimes, the two don't agree. My wife was twelve years older than me when we met. I was twenty-six. She was nearly forty. My heart loved her, but my brain needed some convincing. Damn thing didn't think it was a good idea to love a woman more than a decade older than

5

me. It tried to get in the way. Tried to tell me I should be with someone my own age. Someone that would live as long as I did. Someone I could have a big family with. But the heart wants what the heart wants. I got nearly forty perfect years with that woman. We didn't have children, but we had each other, and that was more than enough. Just like my brain had warned, she did pass before me, around two years ago from cancer. We drained our savings and lost the house trying to keep up with the medical bills, but it wasn't enough." He pulls his chin in.

"I'm so sorry, Hank."

"Don't feel sorry for me. Sure, I'm alone now, but I lived a hell of a good life with her, and I wouldn't change it, not none of it. Even though my brain sometimes tries to make me regret my choices, that love in my heart is so much stronger, and it alone will carry me to my next life. So, to answer your question, Peyton—no, the brain and the heart aren't the same thing." There are tears in his eyes by the time he finishes speaking, and the tears in mine have more than doubled. Now I'm crying for the both of us.

"I don't know what to say. I'm sorry."

"Nothing to be sorry about. I'm an incredibly lucky man. Don't look like it." He gestures to himself with a laugh. "But I am."

"How'd you know the difference?" I ask.

"Between what?"

"Your heart and your brain?"

"Why'd you tell that man you didn't love him?" he asks.

I bite my lower lip, trying to think up a reason, but I'm struggling to find the right answer. *Why did I tell him that?* "Because . . ." I fiddle with my fingernails. They're freshly manicured and painted a light pink.

"Because why?" he presses.

"Because I didn't want to get hurt, I think."

"You think?" Hank lifts his brows. "That don't sound like your heart talking."

"I . . . I didn't want it to end."

"You didn't want it to end, so you never let it start?"

"I . . . I . . . don't know." My head falls slightly forward, and I exhale.

"It sounds like you let your brain make this decision, and your heart is the one crying because of it. Trust me, Peyton, it's better to live with a broken heart than to never let anyone into it in the first place. Mine has been split down the middle for the past two years, but I still have both halves."

Tears escape my eyes in a steady, uncontrolled stream. "But what if—"

"But what if nothing," Hank interrupts. "The heart don't ask what if. The heart just does. Like when I asked you for help. You didn't hesitate. You gave me those few dollars without even thinking. Why?"

"I don't know." I shrug. "You asked for something, and I had it, so I gave it to you."

"That's your heart."

"But that's different."

"Is it?" His brows knit together. "Because I don't think it is. This man is asking for your love. Do you have love to spare?"

"Well, yeah."

"You said you were scared that it might end. That's why you said no. But love is endless. It has no end. Ask yourself, do you love him?"

"I think—"

"No." Hank cuts me off again. "Don't tell me what you think. Tell me if you love him."

"I . . . I . . ." My eyes close for a moment. I picture him in all the ways I've seen him and in all the moments we've shared. I see his smile. It's as bright as he is. His goofy faces that can flip my mood from sad to happy in a nanosecond. His pensive look, reserved for when he's working or listening intently. His laughter that's so genuine and infectious, it makes everyone laugh too. His frown that he lets only those closest to him see. My skin begins to tingle just thinking about him. My heart beats a little faster. I feel a warmness come over me like I'm nestled up by a fire rather than standing outside in the middle of October. And then I picture him not in my life. Like earlier, when he turned and walked away without looking back at me. What if he never turned around again? What if he simply kept on walking . . . right out of my life? A coldness runs through me, leaving me both numb and in pain. My stomach feels empty and sick at the same time. And my heartbeat, it's barely there, thumping just enough to keep me alive but not enough to feel alive.

Realization sets in, and my eyes spring open. "I love him." The words tumble out of my mouth as though they'd been tucked underneath my tongue, waiting to be uttered.

"I know," Hank says with a chuckle.

"But it's too late. I already told him no."

"Nonsense. It's never too late."

"You didn't see his face." I let out a sigh. "I broke his heart. No, I more than broke it, and I don't think there's a way back from that."

A group of twentysomethings walk past us, giving Hank and me a once-over. They whisper to one another and cross the street, glancing back a second time. I refocus my attention on the wise, kind man standing before me.

"That's where you're wrong, Peyton. There's always a way back." He points off in the direction I came from. "Now, go tell that boy you love him."

"But what if—"

Hank holds up his large hand, stopping me from rattling on. "What did I tell you about what-ifs?"

"I know . . . okay." I nod several times, trying to perk myself up enough to follow through. I've built walls so tall around myself, they seem impossible to break down. But if I don't do it now, I'll never see what's on the other side. I have to. I can't keep everyone at arm's length because I'm scared to lose them. I repeat Hank's mantra silently to myself: *It's better to live with a broken heart than to never let anyone into it in the first place.* "I'll tell him. I'll tell him right now," I say.

"Then get." He flashes his teeth and motions for me to go with a flick of his wrist.

"Thanks, Hank," I say, turning on my foot.

"No, thank you." Hank waves me off, and I burst into a full, wobbly sprint. These heels were barely made for walking, let alone running.

"Follow your heart. It'll never steer you wrong," he yells, and I can't help but smile. It's so simple, yet I've never followed it.

At the end of the block, I kick off my heels and choose to carry them instead, fearing I'll sprain an ankle if I continue. Despite the thick tights I'm wearing, I can still feel the cold pavement on the bottoms of my feet, but it doesn't deter me. I've been running away from most things nearly my whole life, but now I'm finally running toward everything I've ever wanted. Right as I come to an intersection, the crosswalk signal lights up. It's as though the city is escorting me to my destination.

I can't believe I told him no. I always do this to myself. Deep down, I must have known I was lying as soon as the words left my mouth, but I couldn't help it. The easiest person to lie to is yourself because you don't question your own thoughts. You accept them as facts, even when they're not. They're just reflections, like looking in a mirror. We see ourselves, but we don't see how others see us. We get a distorted version. My feet slap against the sidewalk. Raindrops fall from the sky—real ones this time. They're thick, cold, and scattered. And then all of a sudden, they burst from the clouds buried in the sky above me.

My phone rings, and I stop abruptly, nearly tumbling over. My hand dives into my purse, scrambling to retrieve it. Maybe it's him. Maybe he could sense I was running back to him. The screen reads, The Funniest Person I Know is Calling. It's Maya. She changed her name to that in my contact list years and years ago, and I never changed it back because it's true. I click "Accept," hold the phone to my ear, and pick up my pace again, running down the sidewalk. I've wasted enough time, and I'm not going to waste any more of it. I'm just a few blocks away from his apartment and the life I should have been living all along.

"Hey," I say.

"Hey girl hey. Wait, are you out of breath? Oh, did I catch you in the middle of s-e-x?" She giggles.

"No. But Maya, I'm done."

"Done with what?"

"I'm done with serial dating, short-lived relationships. I'm done with all of it, Hinge, Bumble, Tinder, and all those other dating apps. I know who I love. I know who I want to be with."

"Are you drunk, Peyton?" Her voice raises. She clearly has the phone pressed firmly against her ear so she can hear me better, analyze whether I'm slurring my words or not. On her end, there's a lot of background noise, loud voices, laughter, and someone speaking into a microphone. She must be at Zanies, waiting to perform, or maybe she just finished her set.

"No, I'm not drunk."

A car blares its horn at me as I run through another intersection. I put my hand up and mouth *Sorry*, and I keep going. Nothing is going to stop me because I've already removed the greatest barrier . . . myself.

"Where are you? Are you okay?" Maya asks, her voice full of concern.

"Yes, I'm fine. I just haven't been seeing clearly. But I can see now. He's my soulmate. He's the one I'm supposed to be with. I love him, and I'm going to tell him right now, before it's too late."

"Who is? Who are you talking about? The consultant guy? That'd be cool. Since he has beaucoup bucks. Or the contractor? He'd come in handy. Get it?" She chuckles. "Ooooh, is it the chef? Maybe he'd meal prep for me."

Another car lays on its horn. Tires screech far too late. I see a set of blinding headlights for only a mere second before I don't see them anymore. A gut-wrenching scream escapes me. My feet leave the ground, and it feels like I'm flying. Maya yells my name through the speaker. There are other screams, but I'm not sure where they're coming from. Glass shatters. More tires screech and squeal. Metal clashes into metal. I can see the raindrops fall from the sky as I fall with them. My body slams against the ground with a thud. Something cracks against the pavement. I'm sure it's my skull.

And then there is no rain.

There is no sound.

There is nothing.

CHAPTER 2

A steady beeping sound rouses me. At first, I think it's an alarm clock. But no, it's too calm and controlled. My eyelids flutter as I try to peel them apart. It feels like they've been glued shut. When they finally open, it's all a blur. I blink several times until my surroundings become clearer. I'm lying in a hospital bed, tucked beneath covers and hooked up to various machines. A small plastic device is clipped onto my pointer finger. An IV needle is stuck in my hand with tape holding it in place. A clear tube is positioned into my nose, emitting a steady stream of air. The ceiling is made up of sterile-white tiles. I turn my head to the right and see an empty chair and two closed doors. In front of my bed, a television hangs on the wall playing some game show. Either it's muted or I can't hear it at all. Beneath the TV is a stand adorned with vases of colorful flowers and propped-open greeting cards.

My head throbs like the contents of it have been scraped out, shaken up, and dumped back into my skull. A slew of questions rattle around my brain: *Why am I in a hospital? What happened? How did I get here? Where is* here? The sound of pen scratching at paper pulls my attention. It's deafening. I slowly turn my head to the left, where the noise is coming from, and find a woman sitting in a chair. Her head is craned forward, focused on the notebook she's writing in. Her dark hair is full of tight curls, streaked with caramel highlights. Her makeup is minimal except for extralong lashes and red-painted lips, as though she knows those are her most bold features. She's dressed in a pair of black leggings, combat boots, and an oversized sweatshirt. She's pretty, but I don't know who she is. I try to speak but only a gasp comes out.

Her head flicks up, and her honey-brown eyes go wide. "Oh, Jesus. You're up." She snaps her notebook closed and jumps to her feet. "Nurse!"

I try to speak again, but I can't. It feels like I swallowed sand. All that comes out is a croaky gasp. When she realizes I can't talk, she picks up a Dixie cup from the stand beside her and brings it to my lips.

"Here. Have some water," she says, tipping the cup. I swallow a couple of gulps and exhale deeply, trying to catch my breath. A fruity, floral scent wafts off her. It's lovely and familiar, but I'm not sure why. She yells for the nurse again.

I struggle to talk. "Why . . . am . . . I . . . in . . . the hospital?" The words come out slowly, quiet, and raspy. I'm not even sure I actually said them out loud.

Her eyes bulge. "You don't remember what happened?"

My head moves side to side only an inch or so in each direction.

"Oh, Peyton." She reaches for my hand and holds it. "You were hit by a car."

"Peyton?" I ask.

She leans in closer and places her hand against my forehead like she's checking for a temperature. I can't feel it, though. There's some sort of gauze wrapped around my head. "Yeah, Peyton."

"That's your name?" I ask.

A bewildered look takes over her face. "No, that's your name. I'm Maya."

"Maya?"

"Nurse!" she yells in a panic, and scrambles toward the door.

Just as she's making her quick exit, a man carrying two Starbucks coffee cups pushes the door open. They collide, spilling coffee onto themselves and the floor.

"Maya!" The man groans, pulling the crushed coffee cups from his chest.

He's tall, much taller than she is, with broad shoulders. His eyes are blue, electric almost. Despite their brightness, he appears tired. His dark hair is cut short on the sides, with a little more length on the top. He sports a five-o'clock shadow. I'm not sure if it's intentional, or he just hasn't had time to shave.

"She's awake," Maya says, pointing in my direction.

He looks to me, and his sharp jaw drops with surprise. Letting out a sigh of relief, he beams, revealing a set of perfectly white teeth.

"Peyton," he says, his voice a mix of excitement and apprehension.

"She doesn't know who she is," Maya whispers. I'm only ten feet away, so I hear it clear as day.

"What? She knows who she is. Right, Peyton?" His gaze never falters as he crosses the room in a few large steps, placing the half-full coffees on the table beside my bed.

I shake my head.

"Do you know who I am?" he asks.

I shake my head again. Maybe if I shake it enough, I'll rattle my memories loose. How can I not know who I am? Tears build up. They're hot and heavy, ready to spill out at any second.

"Nurse! We have a problem," Maya yells.

A tall woman dressed in green scrubs appears at the door. Dark circles cling to the bottoms of her eyes. She wipes her forehead with the back of her hand and exhales. "I'm not bringing you any more Jell-O, Maya."

"This isn't about that." Maya tucks her chin in. "But I would like some more." She points to me. "My friend is awake but you've replaced her brain with a potato because she doesn't know who she is."

"I had brain surgery?" I reach for my head and try to sit up, but my whole body is stiff and tender. It's like trying to bend a wooden board in half.

"I'll get the doctor." The nurse bolts from the room.

The guy with the blue eyes takes a seat and reaches for my hand. "No, no. Ignore her. You didn't have brain surgery," he says.

"Why don't I know who I am?" My bottom lip quivers, and those fat tears spill out.

He holds my hand, and I'm not sure he should be holding my hand because I don't know who he is. But it's warm and comforting, so I don't pull away.

"I don't know," he says with a sympathetic look. At least I think it's sympathetic.

"Who are you?" I ask.

"I'm your friend Robbie."

Oh, he's my *friend*.

"And I'm your best friend, Maya. I can't believe you could ever forget about me." She folds her arms in front of her chest. "Brain injury or not, I'm kind of hurt."

I can't help but laugh. I'm not sure if she's trying to be funny, but she is.

"At least you still have your sense of humor." She cracks a faint smile. "And by that, I mean you find my jokes amusing." Maya walks around the front of the bed and retakes her seat opposite Robbie.

"So, you're my friends?" I ask.

"Yes," Robbie says, trying to smile, but the corners of his lips quiver instead, like he feels sorry for me.

"No," Maya says. "I'm your best friend. Robbie is your friend. I am Robbie's best friend too. But he is my friend. Get it?"

"No," I say. My eyes swing like a pendulum between them.

"Stop, you're confusing her even more." Robbie chides Maya. "And for the record, Peyton is my best friend. You're my friend."

She squints. "Since when?"

"Since you had me heckle you at your comedy set, and I ended up on that bar sports website."

15

She lets out a huff. "That was almost a year ago, and how was I supposed to know someone was recording it and that it'd go insanely viral? No phones are allowed in the comedy club." Maya leans back in her chair and crosses one leg over the other. "It was pretty great they called me 'shockingly funny,' though, right? Even though it was a dig, it skyrocketed my career." She smirks.

"I still get recognized from it." He squints.

"Sorry," she says.

"You're a stand-up comedian?" I ask.

Robbie laughs. "She's funnier than you are, Maya."

"I know that's not a question." She gives me a teasing look.

There's a knock at the door. An older man with graying hair pops his partially balding head in. He wears a guise of determination and a white doctor's coat. A stethoscope hangs freely from his neck. "Welcome back, Peyton. I'm Dr. Hersh."

"Hi, Dr. Hersh," I say.

"I hear you're having some difficulty with your memory." He strolls into the room, carrying a file folder.

"Yeah, I don't remember . . . anything, I think." Thoughts roll through my brain as I try to conjure up memories. But they're not memories that come to the forefront of my mind. They're just names of things that I know, or at least I think I know. Like states. Wisconsin. Illinois. New York. Then I think of animals. Dog. Cat. Cow. I glance around the room, noting the things I see. Chair. Bed. Flowers. TV. Hot guy. Funny girl. Doctor.

"Anything? What's your name?" He studies my face.

"Peyton."

"She doesn't actually remember that. I told her her name," Maya says.

"What about your last name?"

Robbie gives me a pleading look, like he's saying *Please, Peyton. You remember. Just say it.* I glance at Maya. Her mouth sits partially open as though she's about to tell me the correct answer but she doesn't. "I don't know," I say to Dr. Hersh.

"That's all right," he says. "Your name is Peyton Sanders."

He's trying to be encouraging but he's not. There's nothing positive about not knowing your own name.

"What about your friends? Can you tell me their names?" the doctor asks.

"Robbie and Maya."

"We told her those too," Maya says. "What's my last name?"

I examine her face, hoping the answer to her question will reveal itself. A beauty mark sits a half inch above her full lips, a little off to the right. She has high cheekbones, but the rest of her features are soft. Her complexion is a warm beige with golden undertones. I stare into her large brown eyes flecked with gold, but the answer doesn't come to me.

"I don't know," I say, shaking my head.

She sighs and rubs my shoulder with her manicured hand. "That's okay. It's James, by the way. Maya James."

"Maya James," I repeat, trying to commit it to my memory.

Robbie clears his throat. "And I'm Robbie Parker." He pats the top of my hand.

"Robbie Parker," I say.

Dr. Hersh pulls a clipboard from the end of my bed and reads from it before opening the file folder he carried in. He scribbles some notes down.

"How long have I been here?"

"You were brought in four days ago," Dr. Hersh says, briefly watching me before returning his attention to the paperwork.

"I've been in a coma for four days?"

"Yeah," Robbie says. "Do you remember the accident at all?"

I try to think back before I woke up in this hospital bed, but it's all blank like a fresh chalkboard. There's nothing. It's an endless dark tunnel with no light at the end. But I know words and the names of things. Like the stethoscope around the doctor's neck. I know what a car is and what an accident is and what a hospital is and what a friend is. But I have no memories attached to anything I know. I swallow hard. I feel like a brand-new computer being powered on for the first time. The knowledge is there, but there's no context.

"No, I don't remember it."

"What about anything earlier that day?" Robbie asks.

I shake my head.

Maya leans forward in her chair. "Do you remember the ending of *The Sixth Sense*?"

I squint. "No. What is that?"

"Only one of the greatest films of our generation." She lifts her chin. "Ugh. You're so lucky."

"Maya!" Robbie chides.

"What? What I wouldn't give to be able to watch that movie for the first time again." Maya cracks a grin.

"You'd give up all your memories?"

"Maybe." She shrugs. "It's a really good movie."

I think she's being a little insensitive to my situation, but now I really want to watch it.

Dr. Hersh clears his throat, making Robbie and Maya drop their bickering immediately. We give the doctor our full attention.

"Can you tell me what the capital of Illinois is?" he asks.

Maya shakes her head.

"Springfield," I say.

"She knows that but doesn't remember my name?" Maya rolls her eyes, while Robbie shushes her.

"Can you tell me how many planets there are?"

"Nine, if you count Pluto," I say. "But I don't think they count it anymore, so eight."

The doctor nods. "Good." He looks down at his chart again, pausing for a moment before lifting his head. "When you were brought in, we ran an MRI scan to examine for internal injuries. We found no broken bones, internal bleeding, torn ligaments, et cetera . . . so, that's the good news. We also performed a brain CT scan and found a small structural lesion on the prefrontal cortex."

"Oh, great, luckily only your brain took the brunt of the accident." Maya's words drip with sarcasm.

The doctor gives her a disappointed look. "Now, lesions do heal on their own," he says. "But it takes time. The location of the lesion has affected your memory, resulting in retrograde amnesia."

Maya squints. "What does that all mean?"

"It means Peyton has lost her memories prior to the accident, but it's hard to tell how far that memory loss goes back. It could be days, months, even decades. Since you're also unable to remember personal information, it leads me to believe that dissociative amnesia, which is very rare, is also occurring. How long have you all been friends?"

Maya speaks first. "Since freshman year of college, so fall 2009."

"Yeah, around the same time," Robbie says.

I nod but I really don't know whether that's correct. I glance over at Maya, wondering how she and I met in college. Did we have the same class? Were we roommates? Maybe we worked together on campus. I don't know what campus that is, though. I close my eyes tight, hoping I'll be able to find the memories in the dark, behind my lids, or floating somewhere around my brain. But they're not there. When I open them, I look to Robbie. He said we met around the same time too. Probably college as well. It must have been because it seems Maya, Robbie, and I are equally close.

"Is there anything you can remember since 2010, Peyton?"

I move my mouth side to side and shake my head.

"And nothing before then?" he asks.

"I don't remember anything."

The doctor lets out the tiniest sigh and nods.

Maya rubs my shoulder again, and I feel Robbie's hand gently squeeze mine. It's like they're both saying, *It's okay, we're going to get through this.*

"Your amnesia appears to be episodic as well, meaning it's affecting your memories, not general knowledge or language. I understand this is extremely confusing for you since you're missing memories and can't remember personal details. But given your brain scan, your age, and overall health, I believe your condition is temporary."

"How temporary?" Robbie asks.

"It's too early to tell. It's likely that the personal details will come back before the memories. I've seen cases that last a few days, and I've seen ones that last weeks or months."

"Have you seen cases where they never get their memory back?" I hold my breath when I finish asking the question, bracing myself for his answer and wishing I hadn't asked it.

Dr. Hersh nods. "Unfortunately, yes, but I don't believe that will be the case for you."

"Don't believe?" I ask shakily.

Believe. He's a doctor. Shouldn't he know? Shouldn't it be a fact? Not a belief. Isn't what all those years of school are for? To just know things?

"I can't say for certain. I'm sorry, Peyton."

The beeping on the machine speeds up.

"It's going to be okay," Dr. Hersh says. "Just stay calm."

"I am calm, super calm." I force an unsteady smile. The machine betrays me, beeping faster.

"What can we do to help, Doc?" Maya stands from her seat like she's ready to take charge and take action. "Are there foods she should be eating, stuff that's good for the brain? Chia seeds or salmon? Should she exercise? Meditate? I've heard laughter is the best medicine. Would it help if she attended a couple of my stand-up comedy shows?"

Robbie rolls his eyes.

"Obviously, eating well is always a good thing. Avoid any strenuous exercise, just light walks are fine when you're feeling up to it. Avoid drugs or alcohol. The best thing you can do is interact, talk about things that have happened, expose yourself to things you love, activities and foods you enjoy, people you know, places you frequent. All of that can help jog your memories and bring them back to you. I'm prescribing an antianxiety medication, a muscle relaxant, an anticoagulant, an anticonvulsant, as well as diuretics. They'll help with any complications that could occur and will aid in faster healing and recovery."

I can feel the muscles in my face pulling in all directions. He must notice my confusion because he angles his head and gives me an encouraging look. "Don't worry, Peyton." He closes up his folder, returning the clipboard to the end of the bed. "Your nurse will go over the medications with you in greater detail, and since all of your vitals look good, I can discharge you later today as long as you have someone staying with you at least for the next two weeks until your follow-up appointment. If not, I'll recommend that you continue your recovery here."

I nod along, although I'm not entirely sure what he said.

"I can stay with her," Maya says.

"I can too," Robbie adds.

"We can switch on and off." Maya looks to Robbie. "To make sure someone is with her at all times. I'll take days and you can take nights."

Robbie agrees to the schedule. This all feels so weird to me. I have to be watched twenty-four seven by these people. I mean, they say they're my friends, but I don't know them. Heck, I don't even know myself.

"I really don't want to be a burden. I can stay here," I say. A hospital is familiar. I know what it is. It's a place where people get better . . . or die, actually. Maybe that's not the right choice, but I just feel strange, like an alien that's been dropped on a new planet.

Dr. Hersh clears his throat. "I will say recovery in cases of amnesia is better at home surrounded by the people you love. Do you have family nearby?"

I don't know the answer to that. How do I not know if I have family or where they live? "No, she doesn't have any family nearby," Robbie says solemnly.

"We're her family." Maya glances at me and firmly nods.

"Okay, then. Just to confirm, one of you will be with her at all times?"

Maya and Robbie nod.

"Good. Are there any further questions?" He tucks the folder under his arm.

I have a lot of questions. Number one, who am I? But I don't ask any of them. Sure, they could tell me all my demographics, but that's not who I am. Instead, I just tell the doctor I have no questions. I'll figure it out later, I guess.

"All right, get some rest and take it easy, Peyton. You're in good hands." Dr. Hersh leaves the room.

We sit in silence for a few beats, exchanging glances and letting it all sink in.

"Well, what do you think?" Robbie asks.

"I don't know. How can I just not remember who I am? How can I have no memories of the life I've lived?" Tears well up in my eyes again.

Maya pulls a tissue from her bag and hands it to me. I dab the wetness away. "They're not gone, Peyton," she says. "They're just buried somewhere in that big brain of yours, but we'll find them."

"What if they never come back?" I feel my bottom lip tremble, so I pull it in.

The two of them exchange a worried look, but then I see it contort. They put on a brave face for me.

"Then we'll make new memories," Maya says.

An alarm sounds. It's loud, and it's coming from Robbie. He shoves his hand into his pocket and retrieves his phone, shutting it off. His brows knit together, and he groans. "I'm so sorry. I have to go into work for a meeting. It's terrible timing, but I'm presenting so I can't miss it." He squeezes my hand. "I'll be back before you're discharged, Peyton."

I smile. It's a small one, and I think it probably looks sadder than anything.

He pulls his hand from mine and stands, retrieving his stuff.

I want to tell Robbie, *No, please stay*. But I don't know him, and I don't think I have the right to ask him to stay. Judging from the dark circles under his eyes, it's pretty clear he's been here for days, waiting for me to wake up.

"Okay." The word comes out just above a whisper, like I really don't mean it at all.

"Don't worry about it, Robbie," Maya says. "I got it covered. You go take care of your business stuff or whatever it is you do for work." She waves him off. "I don't even have amnesia, and I can never remember what your job is."

He chuckles. "I'll be back soon," he says, turning on his heel.

"Hey, Robbie," I call out.

He glances back. "Yeah?"

"What do you do for work?"

That smile of his returns. "I'm an actuary, so measuring and managing the financial costs of risk and uncertainty with the use of mathematics and statistics."

Maya pretends to snore and then jolts awake. "That's why I never remember. Puts me right to sleep like a lullaby."

Robbie leaves the room with a laugh. The door closes behind him, and it's just me and Maya. My friend. No, my best friend. Or was Robbie my best friend? I don't remember.

"His work seems kind of interesting," I say, looking to her.

"That's only because this is the first time you remember hearing about it."

"Wait, what about my job? Do I have one? Do I still have it? Do they know I was in an accident?" I try to sit up a little taller in the bed.

"Yes, you still have it. I've been keeping them updated. They're being extra supportive and flexible, so you don't have to worry about it at all." She points to the vases of flowers. "Several of those are from your coworkers and boss."

I nod. "What do I do for work?"

"You're a scientist."

"Really?" I pull my chin in and try to think of science-y things. There's the periodic table, but I can't really recall any of the elements, except for silver and gold. Oh, and hydrogen. And potassium. And iodine. I know more than I thought I did. But it doesn't seem like I know enough to be a scientist.

"Are you sure? I don't really think that's my career. It doesn't feel like me."

"Yes. You work on subatomic particles and neptunium chemical compound bonds," Maya says with a nod.

My eyes go wide, darting back and forth between Maya and the window behind her. I don't know what any of those words mean. How can I keep doing that job if I don't understand it? If my memories don't return, I'm going to have to get a new career or go back to school because there's no way I can fake knowing any of that.

Maya cracks a grin and tries to stifle a laugh, but it bursts out. "I'm just kidding. You're awful at science. You actually failed chemistry freshman year of college."

I frown but it doesn't last long, quickly morphing into a smile. I'm truly relieved that's not my job. But also, deep down in my gut, I knew it wasn't. That's gotta count for something.

"Okay." I squint. "What do I *actually* do?"

"You work in social media," she says through a snort.

"That sounds more like me. Or at least I think it does."

Maya pats my shoulder. "I had you going."

"Yeah, it's pretty easy to fool a person with a traumatic brain injury, *Maya*." I put emphasis on her name. "Now I'm even more confused." I pout.

Her face turns serious, and her laughter extinguishes. She leans in. "I'm sorry, Peyton. I shouldn't do that to you. You know how I am . . . well, I guess actually you don't. But I use humor to cope with anything and everything. I'm really sorry." She sighs heavily.

I stare back at her, holding my frown. But eventually it wavers. The corners of my mouth curve up. "I had you going too."

She rocks back in her chair, chuckling. "I should have known. Even without your memory, you'd still have your snark and wit."

I don't remember Maya, but it feels like she and I have one of those friendships where even if we hadn't seen each other in a long time, we could pick up like we never were apart. It makes me both sad and happy. Sad that I can't remember but happy that even though I don't have any memories of Maya, I can in a way feel a connection to her.

She jolts forward in her chair like she just thought of something important. "So, I know you don't remember this, but I was on the phone with you when you were hit by the car, and you were telling me—"

A double knock on the door interrupts Maya, and a woman dressed in casual yet professional clothes calls out, "Knock, knock," as she walks in. Is this another person I'm supposed to know? Her hair is pulled into a low ponytail, and her makeup is a bit heavy for a hospital setting— dark pink lipstick, false lashes, and a fully contoured face. She's not wearing scrubs, but I notice a name tag. Okay, she works here. I let out a sigh of relief that it isn't someone else I'm supposed to know but don't.

"I have some visitors for you, Ms. Sanders, but you're only allowed two at a time." The woman snaps her fingers, and three very nice-looking men file in, standing shoulder to shoulder before me in a line. No, not just nice looking . . . hot. I stop myself from having any more thoughts about them just in case we're related or something. I avert my eyes and look to Maya, trying to gauge if she recognizes them. Her mouth hangs open as her gaze skims over them. She's clearly just as surprised as I am.

"They're all claiming to be your boyfriend," the woman says with a smirk.

One holds a balloon that says GET WELL SOON. He's tall, dark, and handsome. The man lifts his hand. Another carries a stuffed teddy bear and a box of chocolates. He has a sleeve of tattoos and a clean, square jawline. He's just as handsome as the other one. The man nods and delivers a sympathetic look. The last one sports neatly trimmed facial hair and broad shoulders. His large hand clutches a vase full of roses, and his lips form a straight line, like he's unsure how to greet me. The woman scans over them as though she's appraising pieces of artwork. She clears her throat and directs her attention to me. "So, which one is your boyfriend?"

I inhale deeply and shake my head.

"I don't know," I say.

CHAPTER 3

No one has said a word for at least two minutes, which feels like a life-time given how uncomfortable and confusing the situation is. I have three boyfriends. How? *Was I a . . .* I don't finish that question. I look to Maya for help but realize she won't be of any because she's salivating over the men. I don't blame her, though. They're hot with a capital *H*, and my body is physically reacting to them. Perspired skin, flushed cheeks, even my heart rate is speeding up. And that damn beeping monitor is giving it away. The guys stare back at me and exchange glances with one another like they're sizing each other up.

The woman with the name tag clears her throat and squints. "What do you mean you don't know?" she asks, clearly unfamiliar with my medical file.

Maya takes a step forward. "Peyton has amnesia and can't really remember most things, like her name or who she is or who I am or who any of you are."

The woman's mouth falls open with surprise, but she quickly snaps it closed. Her lips curve into a coy smile. "Oh. Well, this is quite the predicament then. It's like two of my favorite shows combined, *Grey's Anatomy* and *The Bachelor*." She lets out a laugh but stops herself, regaining her professional composure. "You know, the two-visitor policy is pretty arbitrary anyway, so I can give you a little time to figure all this out." The woman gestures to the men and starts to back out of the room. "I'll be back in ten to find out who's accepted your roses." She stifles another laugh as she leaves. Her heels click down the hallway, growing quieter.

My gaze returns to the six men standing before me. Oh, wait. Three men. There's three of them. One, two, three. My vision doubled for a second there. I don't know who any of them are, but I do know that I have very good taste.

"Hi," I say awkwardly.

They greet me with a "Hey," "Hi," and "Hello."

"What do I do?" I whisper to Maya.

"This is what I was trying to tell you," she whispers back. "I was on the phone with you before the accident, and you were going on about how you were done with serial dating because you knew who you loved, who you wanted to spend the rest of your life with, and you were going to tell him. But then you got hit by that car."

I glance over at them and then back at Maya. "Did I tell you which one?"

She shakes her head.

Shit! Of course I'd lose my memory right after figuring out who I loved. *Perfect timing.* And why was I dating so many guys? Did I have issues with commitment or something? Do I like playing the field? Do they know about each other? Oh God, I hope so.

"What do I do?" I whisper to Maya.

"You could just wait until you remember."

"But what if my memory never comes back?"

"Right." She taps her finger against her chin, contemplating. "You could date them . . . again?" Maya grins. "Could be fun." She waggles her eyebrows.

"How can I date them if I don't even know who I am?"

I don't think Maya realizes how little I know or how confused I am. And I mean without this new knowledge of having three boyfriends.

Maya leans down and speaks soft and fast. "I know practically everything about you, except who you love. But everything else, I know it. I'll help you navigate, and we'll tag team this whole re-dating thing. I'll be like your talent manager, but I'll set up dates rather than gigs." She grins excitedly.

I let out a sigh. This doesn't seem like a good idea, but if I was running to one of them before the accident to express my love, I feel like I owe it to myself to figure out who it is. Maya's eyes are pleading. I remember what the doctor said. He said memories tend to come back faster when you surround yourself with the people you love. So maybe this isn't such a bad idea.

"Fine," I say.

She nearly squeals but keeps her cool composure. "All right, suitors," Maya says, pulling a notebook and pen from her bag. She stands and addresses the room. "I'm Peyton's best friend, Maya. Like I said, she can't remember anything, so I'm going to need each of you to reintroduce yourselves. Name, occupation, how long you've been seeing Peyton, and bank account balance."

"Maya!"

"What?" She looks to me.

"I don't need to know their bank account balance."

The guys chuckle.

"Fine, no bank account info." She holds her pen up, ready to write, and points it at the man standing closest to us, the one holding a vase of red roses.

He takes a step forward and sets them down on the table next to my bed. "These are for you," he says, flashing his teeth.

I thank him.

He's tall with broad shoulders and thick biceps. He sports long brown hair wrapped up in a messy bun. Surprisingly, he pulls it off well. Most men can't. I think it's the strong jaw paired with a neat beard and those intense green eyes that brings the whole look together. The man standing before me has a rustic look to him too, donning ripped blue jeans (not intentionally, like they were torn from hard labor), work boots, and a flannel button-up.

"I'm Tyler Davis," he says with a nod.

I feel my cheeks warm, so I know I'm blushing. But I hope he doesn't notice. I'll blame it on the head injury. "Nice to re-meet you, Tyler."

Tyler continues his introduction. "So, we've been dating for about six weeks. I recently asked if we could be exclusive, but you said you wanted to take it slow, which I respect and understand, given some of the things you confided in me. We get along really well, and I think we're great together." He rocks back on his heels and slips his hands into the front pockets of his jeans.

I really like him. Maybe this is the guy I love. He said I was vulnerable with him. I'm not sure what I divulged, but it sounds deep, so we must have a strong connection. I'm not sure why pre-amnesia me said no to being his girlfriend. My eyes scan the other men. *Yum.* That's probably why. Clearly, I was conflicted.

"Occupation?" Maya pauses her note-taking and glances up at Tyler.

"Oh yeah." He clears his throat. "I'm a contractor."

"Construction?" Maya asks.

I knew he worked with his hands.

Tyler nods. "Yeah. I'm also working on starting my own construction business."

"No need to sell yourself yet. This is early stages, but I'm marking you down as a dark-haired, less buff Chris Hemsworth with Thor hair, just so I can keep you all straight."

"Thanks, I guess," he says.

"You can step back in line." She dismisses him. "Next."

I give Maya a stern look. "Can you stop treating them like they're in a police lineup?"

She playfully narrows her eyes. "Fine, will the next suitor please step forward?"

The second man moves up one step. Clutched in his hand is a string attached to a balloon that says GET WELL SOON. He places the weight tied at the end on the floor beside my bed and smiles wide. It's contagious because I grin right back. My stomach turns over, like that feeling you get on a roller coaster when it dips fast and sudden.

"I'm Shawn Morris," he says, never letting his smile falter. He's tall with a dark complexion, dressed in a white button-down and tailored blue slacks. It looks like he just came from the office. The shirt is tight around his biceps and chest. He clearly works out. I bet he could bench me and Maya. His hair is freshly cut, and his face is free of any facial stubble. He's nearly the complete opposite of Tyler.

"Hi, Shawn." My voice comes out soft and flirty. I think I love him. It must be Shawn. I look over to Guy #1. Or do I love Tyler?

He nods and licks his lips before he speaks. "We've been dating for two months, but I do travel a lot for work, and sometimes we've gone a week or two between dates. Actually, I also asked you to be my girlfriend recently, but you told me you wanted to get to know me better and spend more time together, which I understood, given what my work life is like."

"And what do you do?" Maya asks.

"I'm a consultant."

"Not sure what that means. But it sounds important," she notes.

"It's nice to meet you again, Shawn," I say.

"Hey, and I'm glad you're okay, Peyton."

"Oh yeah, me too," Tyler adds. "I forgot to mention that."

"No talking out of turn, Hemsworth," Maya says, holding a finger up. He drops his chin slightly.

"All right, Shawn, you may fall back in line. I'll mark you down as young Denzel," she says.

"Thanks," he gushes. His grin grows a little wider and brighter.

"Next," Maya calls out.

I groan.

"I mean Man Number Three, you may approach the beautiful lady."

The third guy holds a box of chocolates in one hand and a stuffed teddy bear in the other. He steps forward and smiles sheepishly as he hands each of them over.

"Hi," he says with a quick wave.

He seems shy but also confident. It's a quiet confidence. His hazel eyes bounce around for a moment before they finally land on me, like he was working up the courage to make direct eye contact. I notice there are flecks of yellow in his irises. His light-brown hair is cut short in a low-maintenance way. He's dressed casually, wearing a white tee and blue jeans. His left arm is covered in a sleeve of colorful tattoos. It's quite beautiful the way each design blends seamlessly into another. He has more of a slim build, but he's just as tall as Shawn and Tyler.

"I'm Nash Doherty," he says. "The chocolates are homemade, by the way." He shuffles his feet. "We've been dating for around five weeks. I almost feel like I've entered the friend zone because most of our dates have been during the day or on Monday or Tuesday nights due to my work schedule. I also told you I wanted to be exclusive, and you said you needed a little more time. But you did assure me that you have feelings for me beyond friendship. I hope that's still true." Nash laughs nervously. "Umm, I'm a chef at Gretel in Logan Square. We actually had our most recent date there on a night it was closed." The corner of his lip perks up, and he trails off.

"You're the chef at Gretel?" Tyler pats him on the shoulder. "That place is awesome! Y'all have, like, the best burger in the city."

"And that chicken liver mousse with grilled sourdough bread," Shawn chimes in. "I could eat that every day."

Nash nods. They high-five one another and exchange firm pats on the back.

"Boys! Focus. The snack is over here in the hospital bed. Worry about dinner later," Maya snaps.

"Sorry," they say in unison, and return back to their spots in line, standing shoulder to shoulder with one another.

I glance at the box of chocolates and then to Nash. I can't believe he made me candy. If my heart was made of chocolate, it would be melting right now. I think I love him too.

"Very good," Maya says, finishing up her notes. "Nash, I'm marking you down as Adam Levine, looks-wise not personality-wise, hopefully." She raises a brow.

He nervously laughs again. "I'm nothing like him."

"We'll be the judge of that," she quips.

I smack her thigh lightly and give her a half-serious look.

"I mean, that's good to know, Nash. Thank you," Maya adds.

"Now what?" I whisper to her.

"Speed-dating round?" She smirks.

"I'm really not up for that. This is . . . a lot." I swivel my head to look at them. "I really appreciate you all coming here to check on me and for the gifts, but I have to ask, did each of you know I was dating other people?" *Please say yes. Please say yes.* I don't know who I am, but I hope I'm not a liar or a cheater.

They all nod. *Whew!* It gives me a little reprieve that I was honest and transparent with them. But this whole serial-dating thing mixed with amnesia has left me in a tricky situation.

Shawn clears his throat. "I was dating multiple women up until a week ago, but you were the only one I looked forward to seeing when I came back from my work trips, and that's why I ended it with the others."

My heart flutters. *I love Shawn.*

Nash stands a little taller. "Same with me. You're the only girl I'm seeing. I broke it off with another woman last week when I decided that

I only wanted to spend my free time with someone I could see a future with, and that's you, Peyton."

There goes my heart again. Pitter. Patter. His smile isn't as wide and bright as Shawn's. It's more subdued but equally cute and inviting. *I love Nash.*

"Not to jump on what Shawn and Nash said, but the same goes for me. About a week ago, I deleted my dating apps. I know you said you weren't ready to be exclusive, but I am, and I wanted to make sure you knew I was one hundred percent committed to you, whenever you happened to be ready for that next step," Tyler says. He runs a hand over his head, smoothing a few flyaway hairs. He delivers a serious look, smoldering, actually.

My heart is doing full-on somersaults now. *I love Tyler too.*

All right, I totally get why I've been dating all three of these men and haven't been able to narrow it down. They're kind of perfect, each in their own way. Tyler is strong, funny, and down-to-earth. Shawn is intelligent, confident, and charming. Nash is creative and quirky and passionate. I don't know how I decided that one of them was my person. How was I so sure, like, five days ago, and now I have no idea?

"I don't know what to say." I fiddle with my nails. The clip that's attached to my pointer finger falls off. The slow beep turns to an annoying long and loud one. "Whoops, that's supposed to stay on." I reclip it and the beep returns, steady and slow. "Listen," I say. "I know this is an unusual situation, and I don't want to waste anyone's time, but I have to be honest. I don't know when my memories are going to come back. It could be days, weeks, even months, and in the rarest case, they may never come back." I swallow hard and look away.

"If I may interrupt," Maya chimes in, clapping her hands together. "Just before the accident, Peyton told me that she loved one of you, like that real soulmate type of love. The love that makes the world go round and gets you out of bed in the morning."

Each of the men grin. Shawn stands a little taller, puffing out his chest. Tyler shuffles his feet, removes his hands from his pockets, but then slips them back in. It's like he doesn't know what to do with them. Nash scratches his forearm, which is covered in tattoos.

"The problem, as you know, is she doesn't remember any of you. Double problem is she didn't tell me who it was before the car hit her." Maya briefly squints at me. "So, because we don't know when or big 'if' her memories will come back, she's going to have to date you all again. Any objections?"

Shawn speaks first. "If that's what you need, Peyton, then I'm on board."

"Same here." Nash nods.

"I'm not bowing out," Tyler says with a firm nod. "We had a good thing going, and I'm not gonna let something like you not remembering who I am get in the way." A little bit of a country accent slips out as he chuckles.

"Perfect," Maya says. "Peyton is getting discharged today." She looks to me. "I assume you're not interested in a date tonight?"

"Sorry, no." I shake my head.

"Tomorrow night?"

"I'd like to get settled at home first." It's weird saying *home* and not knowing where that is.

"What about a cocktail party or a group date like they do on *The Bachelor*?" Her brows bounce twice in quick succession.

"Maya, no. Normal dating, please. This isn't a reality show."

"Fine. Fine. Fine. I'll keep it standard." She turns back to the guys and flips the page in her notebook. "All right, the soonest date would be Wednesday. Any takers?"

Nash's hand shoots up. "I could do Wednesday afternoon."

"Perfect, I got Nash down for Wednesday afternoon." She jots it down and looks back at the guys. "What about Thursday?"

Tyler raises his hand. "I'm free Thursday night."

35

"Noted." Maya scribbles it down. "And what about you, Shawn?"

"Friday works for me. Anytime after 6:00 p.m."

"I got Shawn down for Friday night."

Hearing all this seems like a lot. I have to get my memories back, date three guys, and figure out which one I love. Plus, I literally don't know anything about myself. I don't even know what I look like. I must be somewhat appealing to have these three guys vying for me. Or maybe I have one of those captivating personalities that's impossible to resist. Either way, this feels like a bad idea, but I also feel like I don't have another choice. I mean I do. I could just call it off with all three of them and potentially give up that opportunity to be with the man I love. That doesn't feel right either, especially since they're all willing to try whatever this is with me. If they're ready to go through with this, then I should be too.

Maya closes her notebook and places it on the empty chair. She reaches into her purse and pulls out several small pieces of paper. "These are my business cards," she says, handing one to each of them. "You may call or text the number at the bottom to coordinate your date. If you need Peyton to meet you somewhere, I will bring her. You can also visit the website to see when my upcoming comedy shows are."

"Maya, what does that have to do with dating me?"

"A.B.M., Peyton. Always be marketing."

Maya redirects her attention back to the men. "Now, let me get a picture of each of you." She slips her phone from her pocket.

"What's the picture for?" Tyler asks.

"Personal collection and to help Peyton jog her memory," Maya says it so quickly, they don't even register the first part. I snicker while she takes several photos of each of them, directing them to pose so she can get close-ups and full body shots from all angles. When she's done, Maya scrolls through her phone, saying, "Nice," several times. "These are really going to help us. I mean, Peyton." She stows her phone away and looks at the guys. "Any questions?"

They glance at one another and then back at Maya, shaking their heads.

"Great, then we'll be in touch. Thank you all for stopping by, but Peyton needs her rest now," she says, corralling them out of the room. Shawn tells me he'll text me. Nash says he'll see me on Wednesday. Tyler tells me to feel better. I wave goodbye, but before I can get a word out, Maya closes the door behind them.

With her back pressed against the door, she looks to me with wide eyes and a huge smile. She is way more excited about this than I am. I'm actually a little scared and nervous, and I don't have a clue as to what I'm doing.

"You know I think you're great, but how in the hell did you bag those three men?" She clutches at her heart dramatically. "They're all so gorgeous. I think I'm in love with them too. Don't tell Anthony," Maya says with a laugh.

"Who's Anthony?"

"My boyfriend. But less about him and more about them. How were you dating all three of those guys?"

"I have no idea," I say, shaking my head. "But the real question is, how am I going to decide who I love if I don't even know who I am? And they're all so perfect . . . and I'm"—I gesture to myself, looking down at my legs wrapped in a hospital sheet and my hands that are scuffed and scratched up—"not."

"You clearly are to them, and you owe it to yourself to figure out what your heart wants. It's not your fault you got hit by a car." She pauses and squints. "Well, technically it is because you ran out into an intersection when you didn't have a WALK signal, but that's neither here nor there. You were so excited to tell one of them how you really feel that you got yourself hit by a car. If that's not romance, then I don't know what is." Maya takes a seat beside the bed and reaches for my hand, holding it. "For as long as I've known you, you have never let anyone truly love you. This is your chance."

"Really?"

"Yes, you're like a clam in that way. You got a tough shell to crack."

I frown. I've never loved anyone. And no one's loved me. That's kind of sad. Maybe Maya's right. This is my chance. I was finally open to it right before the accident, and I shouldn't let amnesia get in the way of that. They clearly like me because they all showed up.

"Wait, how did they even know I was here?"

"I posted about your accident on your Instagram yesterday. Thank God I knew your password. It's actually your most liked photo. You're welcome," she says with a pleased look.

"What did you post?"

Maya slides her phone from her pocket and clicks around. She rotates the screen to me. "Cute, right?"

I squint, looking at it closely. In the photo, I'm lying in the hospital bed, eyes closed and mouth partially open. "You posted that? There's drool dribbling out of my mouth."

"Is there?" She quickly glances at the picture and shrugs. "It's pretty hard to get a cute shot when you're all comatose. Filters can only do so much."

"And what's with the caption?"

"What's wrong with it?"

"You wrote that people could show their support by attending your comedy show."

Maya smirks. "A.B.M., baby."

I laugh while she pockets her phone.

"I just don't know if I can go through with this, and I don't want to string them along," I say, looking to Maya.

She rests her hand on mine again. "You can do this, and you're not stringing them along. They all know what they're getting into. They clearly care about you, and they're willing to take that risk. So should you."

Maya's right. She made it clear to them how this was going to work, so they know what to expect from me and whatever this dating-with-amnesia experiment or journey is. If I was really running to tell one of them I loved them right before the accident, it must have meant a lot to me. It must have been the most important thing because I put myself in danger just to tell someone how I feel.

I let out a sigh. "Okay."

"Yes!" Maya jumps to her feet and does a little shimmy dance complete with finger guns. "This is going to be so much fun."

I furrow my brow. "Wait, do you just want me to date these guys again for your own personal entertainment?"

She stops dancing. "Mine and others. This is going to be fantastic set material." Maya laughs but quickly stifles it, getting serious again. "But really, Peyton, I want to see you happy. Your brain has always gotten in the way of that. You're cautious to a fault, and you keep people at arm's length. It's like you've tried to protect yourself before you were ever in danger of being hurt. Aside from the accident, of course. But I think it's kind of a blessing that your brain isn't functioning properly, because it'll give you a chance to open up and allow yourself to be truly happy for once."

I wipe at my eyes because they're filled with tears. It makes me sad hearing that I've lived my life that way, closed off and unwilling to let anyone in. Why did I do that? What made me so scared of love and loss? And why was I all of a sudden ready for it?

The door swings open and Robbie pops his head in.

"Sorry I took so long. What'd I miss?"

"The season premiere of the new *Bachelorette*," Maya says with a snort.

CHAPTER 4

"You're just going to date them all again when you're suffering from amnesia and a traumatic head injury?" Robbie jumps from his seat and paces the room. He shakes his head like he's trying to wake himself from a bad dream. "This is a terrible idea. I should have never gone to my meeting. I could have stopped this rather than encouraged it." He tightens his eyes at Maya, but his face softens when he looks to me. "Peyton, this is a lot of stress to put on yourself when you're supposed to be recovering. You shouldn't do this."

Maya places her hands on her hips. "She loves one of them. What is she supposed to do, just throw that away because she can't remember?"

"Yes," he says with a firm nod. "If any of them really loved her, they would wait until she was better and of sound mind."

I'm not sure where these strong reactions are coming from. Robbie has a point. Dating is stressful. It's emotional. It's time-consuming. And it rarely ends well. Especially in my experience, or so I've learned.

But Maya has a point too. This was obviously so important to me that I risked my own safety and ended up here. And from how Maya talks about me before the accident, I never took risks. I never opened up. I never let anyone in. But for the first time, I was going to. That has to count for something.

"What if her memory never comes back?" Maya asks.

"It's going to."

"You're an apiary, not a doctor."

Robbie rolls his eyes. "I'm an actuary. An apiary handles bees."

"Whatever." Maya crosses her arms in front of her chest.

"Was I the only one listening to Dr. Hersh? He said it was extremely rare that her memories would never return."

"They just say that to make the patient feel better," Maya huffs.

I flick my hands and glare at each of them. "Will you guys stop talking about me like I'm not in the room?"

Robbie lowers his head and takes a seat in the chair beside me. "I'm sorry."

Maya sits down. "I'm sorry too."

He lifts his chin, staring back at me. "I'm just worried about you, that's all. I don't think it's a good idea, and I want you to get better."

Maya leans forward in her seat. "Well, it's Peyton's decision. Not yours, Robbie."

I look to Robbie. I could wait, hope that my memories return, and hope that the man I do love is still waiting for me. My gaze flips to Maya. Or I could see how this plays out and trust that my heart can steer me in the right direction even though my mind can't remember what direction that is.

"So, what do you want to do?" Robbie asks.

They both want the best for me, even though they want different things. Robbie seems more analytical, which makes sense considering his job. He thinks of risk and uncertainty first. Maya is more go with the flow, see where life takes you, live in the moment. They're like yin and yang, complete opposites. I see the excitement in Maya's big brown eyes. She wants me to find happiness and love and believes that I need to do this now. I see concern in Robbie's, making his blue eyes a little dimmer. It's like he's pleading with me to take it easy, rest, heal, and then worry about finding love later. The accident may have stolen all my memories, but it did teach me one thing: nothing in life is guaranteed . . . not even *later*.

"I want to date them again," I say firmly, so they know there's no changing my mind. "I think I owe it to myself to find out who I was running to the night of the accident."

Robbie sighs and sinks back into his chair. Maya lets out a tiny squeal.

"If that's what you want," he says.

I fold my hands in my lap and nod. "It is what I want."

Robbie shoots me a disappointed look. "But I don't support it."

I give the smallest shrug in return.

The nurse from earlier enters the room. "Hi, Peyton. Are you ready to go home?"

I don't say yes because I don't know what home is or where it is. *Do I live alone? In an apartment? A house? Will it feel like home to me?* I force my head to go up and down.

She grabs the clipboard from the end of the bed and reads through a couple of pages, going over each medication, listing side effects, when I should take them, and with food or not. Thankfully, Robbie and Maya are listening intently because, for me, it's going in one ear and out the other. All I can think about is whether my memories will come back and what will happen if they never do.

Robbie parallel parks his car on a tree-lined street. It's a beautiful neighborhood, quiet, but not one I recognize.

He shuts the engine off and turns to me, saying, "We're home."

"Yeah. *Home*," I say with zero confidence.

I feel like a baby bird that jumped out of the nest too soon, trying to navigate a world I'm unfamiliar with. I glance at the townhomes that sit tightly next to one another, lining both sides of the street. Some are modern, recently built, while others maintain their old structure of brick and concrete, a mix of the past and present. Nearly all the homes have fenced-in courtyards. If you asked me to tell you which one was mine, I couldn't point it out.

"Do I live alone?"

Robbie's eyes widen with disbelief as though he's realizing how little I actually know about myself. He quickly relaxes, trying to maintain his calm composure, and nods.

"Yes, you live on the top level of that duplex right there." He points to a house just in front of our vehicle off to the left. It's cute and charming, with a large porch and a set of steps leading up to it. Unlike the newer homes on the street, it retains its old facade of tan brick and black-trimmed windows. Two doors stand side by side, each painted a bright red. There's a small grassy area in front. It's fenced in with a black iron gate. Green vines wrap up and around the spires, a melding of nature's creation and man's.

"Who lives in the bottom unit?" I ask.

"Debbie. She rents the top one to you. But we haven't been able to get ahold of her. I think she's out of town."

I don't know who that is, so I don't ask. I'm still trying to keep my three boyfriends straight in my head. Nash the cook. He has tattoos and looks like some singer that Maya said was a dog. Shawn the consultant, or as Maya called him, a *young Denzel*. Tyler the construction worker. I think she said he looked like Shore or Roar. I don't remember. She made me flash cards and told me to review them, but I think they're making me more confused.

I open the car door and step outside, holding it to steady myself. It all feels a little wobbly. The world, that is.

Robbie peers over the top of the car. "Are you okay?"

"Yeah."

He grabs my purse and a bag from the trunk and joins me on the other side. I stare up at the building, taking it all in. There's a balcony above the porch. I like to think I've spent a lot of time out there, but I don't know for sure. Maybe I'm just feeling that way because I spent the last four days lying in a hospital bed. A squirrel scampers across the courtyard carrying a cracked walnut in its mouth.

"How long have I lived here?"

"At least five years," he says, leading me up the sidewalk. He unlatches the iron gate and gestures for me to go first.

It's a weird feeling not knowing your home. A strong breeze passes through, rustling the fall leaves and pulling more of them from the trees. I draw my knit cardigan a little tighter around me. At the door, Robbie pulls a set of keys from my purse. I only know the purse is mine because he told me it was mine. Inside, I hold the wooden railing tightly as I make my way up a flight of carpeted stairs.

"Home sweet home," he says with a friendly expression as he sets my stuff down on the small kitchen table.

The place is larger than it looks on the outside. The stairwell opens up to the kitchen, dining room, and living room. The ceilings are high, and large-arched windows let in plenty of natural light. Although the design style is a mix of rustic meets modern, there are pops of dark green and royal blue, which makes the home cozy. I must love plants because there are a number of them spread throughout. Succulents line the windowsill above the sink. Two large snake plants sit in white pots on either side of the door leading out to the balcony. A fig leaf tree is situated in the corner. Its leaves and branches loom over a large area of the living room. In the kitchen, there's an air fryer and a coffeepot on the counter. I must like coffee, and I must also enjoy cooking quickly. It's all so tidy and clean, and it seems I take great pride in it.

"Maya texted. She wanted to know how you're doing," Robbie says.

"Tell her I'm fine."

Robbie quickly types out a message and sends it. "She'll be here tomorrow morning to take over while I'm at work."

I nod and walk toward the hallway, exploring more of my home. My fingers skim along the beige-colored wall. The first door on the left is a bathroom. It's small with just a toilet, sink, and walk-in shower. The next door opens to a closet with a stacked dryer and washing machine. The door on the right opens to a small room that looks like a makeshift office. There's a desk, chair, treadmill, and recliner. A tall bookshelf sits against the far wall. I walk to it and pull several books out. They're nearly all romance novels. I must have wanted love but found it only in books up until last week. There's also a handful of self-help books on various topics from self-love to healthy habits. I wonder what she . . . I mean, I wonder what *I* was trying to improve about myself.

At the end of the hallway is a master bedroom. The queen-size bed is decorated with pillows of all sizes in various shades of white and beige. A throw blanket is spread over the bottom corner with a wooden serving tray placed on it. The tray contains a tissue box, remote controls, a room spray, and a candle. I'm very organized and everything out in the open has a purpose, like I was intentional with my space. On the opposite side of the bed, a large flat-screen television hangs on the wall. I wonder what I enjoy watching. Below the TV sits a long wooden dresser painted emerald green. I suppose I can safely assume my favorite color is green, emerald to be exact. My fingers graze over the top of it. It's adorned with a jewelry box, several bottles of perfume positioned neatly in a gold tray, and two framed photos. One is a picture of me, Robbie, and Maya. We're bundled in cold-weather gear, smiling up at the camera, which Robbie holds out at arm's length. In the other photo, I'm standing between two people—an older man and an older woman. I pick the frame up and bring it closer to my line of sight. I look like both of them. I have the button nose, high cheekbones, and blonde hair like the woman. My green eyes and arched brows come from the man.

"Hey," Robbie says.

I turn to find him standing in the doorway.

"Are these my parents?" I ask, holding up the framed photo.

"Yeah." He glances down at his feet and then back at me. There's a sheen to his blue eyes, and his lips form a straight line.

"Where are they?"

45

I think I already know the answer. Regardless of whether I have my memories or not, some things you can just feel. Like their memories exist in my heart too. There's a pain there, a dull ache. I think it's been there this whole time, but I'm just noticing it now. It's as though I've learned to live with it.

"I'm sorry, Peyton." He rubs his forehead and lets out a sigh like he doesn't want to be the one to tell me. "They passed away."

The words are a punch to the gut, fast and sudden. Without the memories, it's just pain. I look at the photo again, taking in their smiling faces, committing them to my memory, my new one, that is. I place the frame back on the dresser and stand there for a moment, waiting for the gut-punch pain to subside. But it doesn't. It's just there. It's been there for a long time. Not always so agonizing, more like a twinge.

"How long ago?" I ask.

"When you were eighteen."

My lip quivers. I blink several times, trying to fight back the tears. "How did they die?"

"In a car accident." Robbie takes a step toward me, just close enough for me to feel his presence but far enough away to give me space. It's like he knows what I need. "Are you okay?" he asks.

"I don't know." I wipe at my eyes with the sleeve of my cardigan.

"There's a bathroom through there," he says, pointing to a closed door off to the side of the television.

"Thanks. I just need a moment." I walk to the bathroom and close the door behind me. It's large, with a stand-up shower and a Jacuzzi tub. Candles sit in a corner along with a jar of bath bombs. Another door leads to a large walk-in closet, but I don't venture in. At the sink, I splash water on my face and dry it off with a hand towel. I stare back at the girl looking at me in the mirror and let out a heavy sigh.

"Who are you?" I whisper to the reflection.

My long blonde hair is tied up in a high ponytail. But I can't even be sure it's mine. The same goes for the green eyes speckled with yellow looking back at me. I pull my hair loose and feather out a couple of short strands and baby hair to cover the bruising and cuts at the crown of my head. I wonder if they'll heal. I wonder if I will too.

To the side of the sink is a clear acrylic container full of makeup and skin-care products. I slather a moisturizer on my face, followed by some flawless filter product, hoping it'll erase the dullness in my skin. But I think that's coming from within. I brush mascara over my lashes, blot a bright pink blush on the apples of my cheeks, and apply a warm berry balm to my lips.

I don't feel any different, but at least I have some color now and I don't look like I just rose from the dead. I turn my face side to side, taking in every inch, trying to familiarize myself with it. I caught a few brief reflections of myself in the side mirror on the ride over. It was jarring seeing a face I wasn't familiar with. It felt like I was wearing a mask. But no, it's me, whoever that is. I smile so wide it crinkles the corners of my eyes, revealing two rows of straight white teeth. My tongue swipes over the front of the top row. I wonder if I had braces. I frown, make an angry face, and then I return it to a neutral expression. Lips parted slightly, muscles relaxed. I'm Peyton, but without knowing who that is, it has no meaning. They're just words without context.

I consider walking into the closet, looking over each article of clothing to get a sense of my style. But what I wore won't tell me who I am.

In the kitchen, I find Robbie, pulling food from the fridge and cabinets. This place seems more like it's his than mine.

"Are you okay?" he asks.

"Was I okay before the accident?"

I know it's a weird question, and I hope he understands why I'm asking it.

"Yeah, you were."

He does. I nod and deliver a tight smile. "Then I think I'm okay now."

I take a seat at one of the barstools lined up against the island counter and watch Robbie make his way around the kitchen. I can tell it's not his first time cooking in it because he knows where everything is. He tosses a hunk of butter and a couple of pieces of bread into a frying pan. They sizzle in the burning butter. Robbie slices half an avocado and several pieces of cheese off a block of cheddar.

"What are you making?"

He pauses and looks to me. "Sandwiches."

"Sandwiches?"

"Not just any sandwich. These are gourmet. Toasted sourdough slathered with sofrito aioli and layered with roasted turkey, two-year aged cheddar, pickled onions and Fresno chilies, avocado, and pea sprouts." He tosses a dish towel over his shoulder and plops a handful of the sprouts into a strainer. I'm not sure where he got the ingredients from. He must have had them in his bag, ready and prepared to make me something comforting to eat.

My mouth is already watering, and I don't even know why. Well, actually, I do. I've been tube-fed for the last four days, so anything solid that I can munch on sounds amazing to me. I prop my elbows on the counter and my hands under my chin. "Have I had this *gourmet* sandwich before?"

"Many times. You say it's your favorite." Robbie rinses the sprouts under the faucet and quickly flips the pieces of bread in the pan.

"I guess I'll tell you if it still is," I tease.

He lets out a laugh. "I guess you will."

Robbie plucks the bread from the pan, slathers aioli onto each slice, and piles up all the ingredients. He tops it with another piece of toasty bread, cuts it in half, and serves it on a plate to me. "Let's see if I still got it."

My stomach rumbles as I pick up half the sandwich and bite into it. A multitude of flavors pop out: spicy, sweet, sour, and herbaceous—all melding together perfectly.

"So?" he says.

I wipe the corners of my mouth with a napkin and nod. "Still a fave."

He claps his hands together in delight.

"This was exactly what I needed. Thank you," I say, biting into it again.

"Anytime," he says, while assembling his own sandwich. "Want to eat out on the balcony?"

I look over at the glass door leading to the outdoor area. There's a couch, a chair, and a small table, as well as several planters. I was right. I must spend a lot of time outside.

"Yeah, I'd like that."

"Good. Let me clean up a bit, and I'll meet you out there."

I take a seat on the outdoor couch and continue eating. The pots are full of wilted plants and flowers. With the seasons changing, they'll die and come back in the spring, vibrant once again. I wonder, do they remember their past lives, the seasons they spent in bloom before withering away and going dormant? Or are they like me, waking up without a past, only a future?

Overlooking the balcony, I spot several people out walking their dogs or pushing strollers. Some text on their phones, others take in the neighborhood, appreciating the changing fall colors.

The door squeaks open, and Robbie walks out with a throw blanket over his shoulder, a plate of food in one hand, and two bottles of water clenched between his forearm and his chest. He leans down, and I retrieve the waters from him. Robbie takes a seat and splays the blanket over both of us.

"It's nice out here," I say.

"It's why you wanted it. The private outdoor space."

"I feel like I knew that." I bite into my sandwich, chewing slowly and savoring the taste. His eyes linger on me for a moment before he starts eating. We sit in silence while we eat and sip our water, listening to a mix of sounds from both the city and nature. There's the traffic from the main road at the end of the street. The cars whoosh. There's a bird chirping and a breeze rustling branches and fallen leaves. Car horns honk intermittently. A dog barks in the distance. Somehow, it all blends together seamlessly.

"How are you feeling?" he asks.

I think he'll keep asking until I give him a real answer. Something with more substance than "Fine" or "Okay." I sip my water, trying to form a response.

"Confused. Sad. Curious. Frustrated. Angry. Worried. Anxious. I think those are some of the things I'm feeling." I shrug and set my plate down on the table. There's a couple of bites left, but for some reason I don't want them. Maybe it's too hard to swallow anything right now.

"That's understandable," he says. "But I think you'll be back to normal in no time."

I turn my head toward Robbie, studying his face. Does he really believe that, or is he just being hopeful? "Why do you think that?" I ask.

His brows shove together as he stares back at me. "Because you're Peyton. You're the strongest person I know."

"I don't feel very strong."

"You are, though."

"Are you trying to make me feel better?"

"No, I mean it." Robbie pops the last bite of his sandwich in his mouth and chews happily.

"You can have the rest of mine too." I gesture to my plate.

The corner of his lip perks up. "You haven't changed a bit."

"What do you mean?"

"You always leave two bites of food on your plate, so I always finish them." Robbie picks up my leftover hunk of sandwich and tosses it in his mouth.

I furrow my brow. "Really?"

"Yep," he says, dusting his hands off.

Knowing that pieces of me are still here is comforting, like I'm still me even though I don't remember who me is. I lean back into the cushion and watch the sun slide past the horizon. The sky begins to darken, and a set of tiny string lights wrapped around the length of the balcony railing flicker on. Robbie picks up both our plates and stands.

"What would you like to do now?"

I look up at Robbie and crack a smile. "Want to watch that movie Maya was talking about, the one she said she'd give up all her memories to see for the first time again?"

"*The Sixth Sense?*" He nods and laughs. "Yeah, let's do it."

"What?" I jump from my seat, nearly spilling the bowl half-full of popcorn. "He was dead the whole time!" Robbie pauses the television. Bruce Willis's stunned face fills the screen. Pacing the living room, I put my hands on either side of my head, holding it. Robbie grabs the bowl and tosses kernels of popcorn into his mouth, chuckling.

"This is more shocking than when I realized I had no memories earlier today." I laugh.

"I don't know about that." Robbie grins.

"Were you this surprised the first time you saw it?"

"Oh yeah. Most everyone was."

"Incredible. I wish I could watch it for the first time again."

"Well, you technically got two first-time watches. Pretty lucky if you ask me." He picks a piece of fallen popcorn from his shirt and pops it into his mouth.

I plop down on the couch next to him, putting my feet up on the coffee table.

"Thanks for watching it with me."

Robbie angles the bowl toward me, and I snag a few kernels.

"Anytime." He leans forward and sets it down on the table. "Ready to call it a night?"

I toss the popcorn in my mouth and dust my hands off. "Yeah. I suppose I should rest from my four days of coma rest," I tease.

He laughs as he gets to his feet. "By the way, I ordered you a new phone because yours wouldn't turn back on. It'll be here tomorrow."

"Thanks. Do you need any extra blankets or pillows?" I don't know where they are except for what's on my bed, but I offer them anyway.

"Yeah, I'll grab them." He brings the bowl to the kitchen, emptying the remaining kernels in the trash and then slipping it into the dishwasher.

It's nearly midnight, but I'm not tired at all. Regardless, I should try to get some rest. And maybe, just maybe, I'll wake up with my memories tomorrow. Robbie sets out a glass of water and a couple of pills on the counter.

"Don't forget about these," he says.

I meet him in the kitchen. "I don't know what I would do without you," I say, tossing them into my mouth and drinking several gulps of water. When I finish, I make a refreshing sound. "Yummy."

Robbie gives a tight-lipped smile. I take in his appearance, noticing his bloodshot eyes and dull skin. I wonder if he slept at all while I was lying in the hospital bed this week. Did he stay up, waiting for me to wake? I don't know Robbie, or at least I don't remember that I know Robbie, but he seems like the type of person who would do that.

"Need anything else?" he asks.

I almost say *my memories*. But instead, I just tell him good night.

CHAPTER 5

My eyes burst open, and it takes me a moment to ground myself, to realize I'm lying in my own bed, to remind myself I was in an accident, and to remember that I don't remember anything. I'm Peyton Sanders. I have two best friends, Robbie and Maya. And I have three boyfriends. There, I'm all caught up.

I turn my head, glancing at the alarm clock on my nightstand. The numbers glow a red hue, reading 6:15 a.m. I consider lying in bed for another hour, but before I can even really consider it, my feet land firmly on the white shag rug. I keep myself steady for a moment, gripping the side of the bed to ensure I won't topple over. My head feels fine one minute, and the next it feels too heavy, like there's a bowling ball stacked on top of my shoulders.

In the bathroom, I splash water on my face and stare at my reflection. I move my lips side to side and wiggle my nose, trying to get used to the girl looking back at me. She's getting a little more familiar. I swipe on several makeup products, brush my teeth, and comb out my long hair—all the while deciding that I'm going to have a positive attitude about this. I can't change what happened. I can't force the memories to come back. All I can do is embrace it, a clean slate, a fresh start. Yeah, that's what I'll call it. A fresh start. I smile at my reflection and nod.

"You're Peyton Sanders. You are . . ." I squint. "Blonde and . . ." I deflate for a moment and take a deep breath. Lifting my shoulders and looking back in the mirror, I continue. "You are Peyton Sanders. That is your name. The rest, well, we'll figure it out. This is the first day of the rest of your life."

Okay, that's enough pep talk for me. I clap my hands together.

In the closet, I pick out a plaid shacket, a white top, and a pair of slightly distressed blue skinny jeans. After getting dressed, I slip on a pair of sneakers and pluck a crumpled twenty-dollar bill from the drawer in my bedside table. Tiptoeing down the hallway, I try not to make any noise. The home is quiet and mostly dark aside from the rays of sunshine peeking through the living room windows. Robbie is asleep on the couch. His hair goes in all directions and his lips sit partially open. One of his legs is bent while the other extends a foot past the arm. I immediately feel bad for the sleeping arrangements. He's clearly too tall for the couch. I consider waking him, but I remember how tired he looked last night. Instead, I cover him, pulling the blanket up to his shoulders.

In the kitchen, I find a note from Robbie with a glass of water and a few pills laid out. The note reads, *In case you're up before me. —Robbie.* It's like he knew I would be.

I swallow the pills and take a gulp of water. Okay, what now? What should I do with myself? I scan the kitchen and the living room in search of something to occupy my time. When nothing jumps out at me, I decide to go for a walk. Fresh air will do me good. I creep down the stairs and carefully open and close the front door.

Outside, I breathe in the cool, crisp air before heading down the porch steps, through the courtyard, and out the gate. I look left and then right. It appears the same both ways, townhomes like mine and a tree-lined street. I'm not sure where I'm going but I turn left, and at the end of the street, I turn right. The city is quiet, like it hasn't fully woken up yet. Birds chirp and sing. A squirrel scampers across the sidewalk in front of me.

This is my neighborhood. It's where I chose to live. I clearly enjoy the city, but it seems I like to be close enough to feel it but far enough away that I get pops of greenery and nature. I turn on a four-lane road called Division. Small boutiques, bars, restaurants, and coffee shops fill both sides of the street. Several people pass by—some walk their dogs, others have their heads buried in their phones. A few smile at me, and I return each one. I wonder if they're just being polite or if they recognize me. Do I usually go for walks? Have I seen them before?

A sign propped up outside a place called Foxtrot catches my eye. Written in colorful chalk are the words WARM UP WITH A CARAMEL MAC-CHIATO. That's perfect. Inside, I'm greeted by a woman a little younger than me with red hair and a face full of freckles.

"Morning, Peyton," she says. "The usual?"

I stare back at her, forcing the corners of my lips up. She doesn't know that I don't know who she is, and I think I like that. It's in the way she looks at me. "Actually, I'm going to try something different today. Can I have a cold brew and . . ." I pause and skim over the large menu above her. "One of those blueberry muffins."

The woman offers a confused look, but then she lets out a laugh.

"What?" I ask.

"You're pulling my chain, aren't you, Peyton? That is your usual order."

I force a chuckle and cover it up by telling her I was just messing around. She takes the crumpled twenty-dollar bill from me and counts out my change.

"It'll be just a minute," she says, turning around to pour the cold brew.

The shop is cute and quaint with racks of wine, shelves full of snacks, and a wall of coolers filled with drinks and freshly prepared meals and appetizers. I can't believe I stumbled into the place I frequent, and not only that, but I also ordered my usual. It's like deep down I know who I am, I just can't remember her. But she's there. And I think

I have to trust myself, even though I don't know who that is. Somehow, I found this café. It was the first one I walked into, and I ordered what I would have anyway. That's gotta count for something. At the very least, it's progress.

She hands me my coffee and a blueberry muffin and tells me to have a good one. I say the same to her as I leave the shop. There's no breeze today. The sun shines bright without a cloud in the sky to block out its rays. I take a seat at one of the dozen small tables set up outside and unwrap my blueberry muffin. Tearing off a piece, I toss it in my mouth.

"Hey, Peyton," a woman's voice calls out. It's warm and friendly. I look up to find an older woman dressed in a colorful knit sweater and a pair of relaxed jeans. Her gray curly hair is clipped on top of her head, with loose, shorter strands hanging freely to frame her face. She has bright, kind eyes—ones that look as though they've seen a lifetime of ups and downs. Her neck and ears are adorned with colorful costume jewelry. She pushes her glasses up the bridge of her nose and smiles. "I've been trying to get ahold of you."

I chew longer than I need to, turning the hunk of muffin into mush. I don't know what to say, so I just utter, "Sorry. My phone's not working." Again, I like the way she's looking at me, just like the girl in the coffee shop did, but more affectionate, like she knows more about me than my usual coffee order.

"Ahhh, okay. Well, as you know, I was out of town for a funeral this past week. I got in late last night." She twists up her lips.

"I'm so sorry," I say, because I know that's what people say in these situations regardless of how well you know one another.

"Eh." She flicks her wrist. "You know I wasn't fond of her. She was a distant relative but an up-close B-I-T-C-H." She laughs.

I give a tight-lipped smile.

"But I got to see my grandbabies. Ever since Jason moved his family to Florida, I don't get to see them as much as I like to. You staying long?"

"For a bit, yeah."

"Great. I'll join you. Just going to get myself a coffee and a snack first." Before she opens the door, she's already waving to the cashier through the window. Obviously, she's a regular here too. But I don't know who she is. Maybe we met here.

Do I tell her about the accident and the amnesia? Maya said she posted on my Instagram about it, but maybe this woman doesn't use social media. If she doesn't know, do I pretend that I'm the same Peyton she knew last week? It's nice having someone look at me like there's nothing wrong with me. Robbie, Maya, and even the guys all deliver the same sympathetic glances. They don't mean to, but they do. I don't want sympathy. I just want people to talk to me and look at me and treat me like they would have before the accident. The older woman pushes the door open with her hip and walks out carrying a drink and a brown paper bag.

She takes a seat across from me and pulls a blueberry muffin from the bag. "I got the last one," she says with a pleased look.

I tear off another piece. "Good choice."

"So, I haven't gotten an update in a while. Have anything new to share?" She raises her thick brows and takes a cautious sip of her hot coffee.

An update? An update on what? Where do I know her from, and what's her name? Do I work with her? Is she my boss? No, my boss knows about the accident, according to Maya. So that can't be it. I could just tell her what happened to me, but I really like that she's looking at me like I'm a whole person, not some broken thing that needs fixing.

"What was the last update I gave you?" I ask, tapping my finger against my chin.

"Last week. You said you were breaking it off with one of the boys you were dating because he turned out to be not who you thought he was. So, did you?" She pulls a fork from her bag and stabs it into the muffin, scooping off a large piece.

Okay, so she and I are close. I share personal stuff with her like who I'm dating. But wait? I was going to end it with one of the guys. For what? And which one? Oh God! This is getting more and more complicated. Dating is supposed to be easy. Boy meets girl. Boy and girl fall in love. Boy and girl get married. End of story. But no, not my story. Mine contains amnesia, a hidden bad boy, more than one guy, and a soulmate. What if I pick the one I was going to break it off with? And then my memories come back? But by that time, we're engaged or married? I need to know more.

"Oh yeah. That. Did I mention what he did?" I seal my question with a small smile, hoping she won't notice my confusion or lack of memory.

She gives me a peculiar look but smiles back anyway. "I guess you caught him in a few lies. Small ones, but it was a red flag, as the kids say these days. And I told you, if someone lies about the little things, they'll have no problem lying about the big things."

So, there's a liar in the midst. I wonder who it is. They all seemed so nice. Tyler the construction worker was funny and down-to-earth. Shawn the consultant was smart and charming. Nash the chef was thoughtful and kind. They're the cream of the crop, but now, not only do I have to figure out which one I love, I also have to weed out a liar. I sip my iced coffee, mulling over how I'll accomplish both without making a mistake.

"That's very true," I say. "Once a liar, always a liar."

She nods. "Exactly. My first husband was a liar. The only time he wasn't lying was when he was asleep, and even then I swear he was dreaming up lies to tell me." A smirk creeps across her face.

I laugh, and she does too. There's a warmness to her I really like, and I wonder how she entered my life. Talking to her feels like I'm getting a hug even though we're sitting across a table from one another. She's important to me. I can feel it. I see it in her vibrant eyes, in her infectious smile, and in the way she looks at me.

"Still worried about that marriage pact?" she asks.

I furrow my brow and quickly relax it, busying myself by eating a large bite of my muffin.

"Yeah," I say, but there's apprehension in my voice because I have no idea what she's talking about. I had a marriage pact. Who even does that? What am I, a character in a Hallmark movie? It has to be a joke. Or maybe she's talking about a movie or a romance novel she's reading?

She glances down at her watch. "Well, you have less than two weeks before you've gotta go through with it."

I swallow hard, and it feels like a hunk of muffin is lodged in my throat. I slurp my iced coffee, trying to force it down, but whatever it is, it's stuck there. Less than two weeks before I have to go through with what? This can't be happening. Amnesia. Dating multiple guys. A marriage pact. What is this? Every romance trope shoved into my life? What's next? Fake dating or sharing one bed? I let out a sigh and close my eyes briefly, wishing my memories would blast back into my head.

"What's wrong?" she asks.

"It's just a lot."

"That's life. If it wasn't a lot, it wouldn't be worth living."

"Yeah," I say.

"I think it's fun that you and Robbie made that pact when you were what, nineteen, was it? I remember you telling me about it, and at first, I thought you'd gone mad. But I saw what it did for you. It helped. You'd been so worried about ending up alone because you kept dating bad guy after bad guy. But then you and Robbie agreed if you weren't married, engaged, or in a very serious relationship by thirty-two, you'd be together. And those what-ifs melted away. You weren't anxious or scared anymore." She gives me a tender look.

A marriage pact in less than two weeks with Robbie? No, that can't be right. He's my friend, and he never once mentioned it to me. But I guess it'd be a lot to tell a girl with amnesia that she agreed to be with you if you didn't date someone seriously in the next two weeks.

Then again, he was the one saying it wasn't a good idea for me to date right now. He told me I should wait until I'm better. Perhaps he was just trying to run the clock out on our pact. Is Robbie a saboteur? No, he wouldn't do that. He makes me sandwiches. Saboteurs don't make sandwiches.

"But we're not actually going to do that," I say, squinting. And I'm dead serious. There is no way I'd go through with something that silly.

"Why not? You two agreed to it, and a person is only as good as their word."

"Yeah, but that's ridiculous. We're not just going to be together because we said we would over a decade ago when we were practically kids. And thirty-two isn't even old." I lean back in my chair and sip my coffee.

"I never said it was. I told you it was too young back then. But nineteen-year-olds look at thirty-two-year-olds like they're crypt keepers. The brain's not fully developed at that age, so I get it. What does Robbie say about your little pact?" She tilts her head and smirks.

"I . . . I haven't talked to him about it."

Because he didn't tell me about it, but I don't say that part out loud.

"PEYTON! PEYTON!" a voice yells in the distance. I instantly recognize it. Robbie. His ears must have been ringing.

We glance in the direction of Robbie's hollering. He comes into view dressed in a white T-shirt and plaid pajama pants, running full speed toward us. His hair loops and swoops in all directions, and his face is beet red. He stops yelling my name when he spots me and slows to a jog, then a brisk walk. A look of relief washes over him. Once he reaches the table, Robbie practically keels over, panting and trying to catch his breath.

"Oh, hey, Robbie. Is the house on fire?" the woman across from me asks. Her question is laced with sarcasm.

Robbie gives her a puzzled look. "What? No, I was just looking for Peyton. Sorry, Debbie."

Debbie. Finally, her name. I say it several times in my head in an attempt to commit it to my memory—my new one, that is.

"Pretty dramatic way to look for someone, if you ask me." Debbie laughs. "And you're still in your pajamas too?" She looks him up and down. "And where are your shoes?" she scolds, her lips forming a straight line.

Embarrassed, Robbie puts one foot over the other in an attempt to cover up his bare feet. I probably should have left a note or something, because him waking up with me missing clearly sent him into a panic. Then again, he's the one withholding secrets from me. Big secrets that involve marriage or a relationship or whatever pact he and I made. I squint at him, and he gives me a perplexed look, clearly confused as to why I'm doing that.

"Peyton was gone when I woke up, so I was worried," Robbie says, glancing at Debbie and then me.

"Oh, you two are settling that pact early, I see?" she says in a flirty voice.

"What?" he asks. He gestures to me. "No, it's because of the . . ."

A phone rings, interrupting Robbie. Debbie picks up her bag and fishes it out. "I've gotta take this. I signed up for one of those callbacks with some robot, so I didn't have to wait on hold forever." She gets up from her seat and gestures for Robbie to take it. "It's gonna be a while, so I'll see you at home. You can have the rest of my muffin." She holds the phone to her ear and waves as she walks away.

At home. Oh, Debbie's the woman that lives in the duplex below me. She's my landlord. The pieces of the puzzle are finally falling into place . . . well, sort of, if I jammed them in there and was still missing most of them.

Robbie takes a seat across from me. His tightened eyes tell me he's mad, and I hope he notices the same look on my face. He eats a bite of Debbie's muffin and stares back.

"Why didn't you wake me?" he asks.

I fold my arms across my chest. "I was being nice by letting you get some rest."

"Why didn't you leave a note?"

"I didn't realize I had to."

"You didn't have to, necessarily." Robbie furrows his brow. "It just would have been nice. I was really worried about you, especially with everything that—"

I cut him off. "Well, I'm fine," I say, sipping the rest of my coffee.

There's silence. He eats his muffin while I stare at him, waiting for him to tell me about the pact before I have to ask about it.

I cock my head. "So, you're just not going to tell me about the pact?"

He shoves another piece of muffin in his mouth. "Pact?"

"Our marriage or relationship or whatever it is pact."

Robbie chews quickly, swallows, and then lets out a laugh. "That's what all this attitude is for?"

I nod.

"Wait, that's what Debbie was talking about? A pact?" He says the word *pact* like it's make-believe, a unicorn of some sort.

"Yep. Apparently, I brought it up to her a week ago because it's almost time for us to settle it."

He stifles another laugh. "Why'd you bring it up?"

"I don't know, Robbie. I don't remember anything."

He blows out a big breath. "I know that. Sorry. I meant, like, why is this a big deal? It was just some silly pact we made in college. We're not following through on it."

"That's exactly what I thought until you told me not to date any of those guys that showed up in my hospital room. You told me to wait until my memories come back. You told me I should focus on healing? Why?"

"Because I want you to get better."

I raise a brow of suspicion. "Or you want to run out the clock on our pact, saboteur." I grab my empty cup and stand from my seat. Turning on my foot, I storm off down the sidewalk.

"Peyton, wait. It's not like that," he calls out.

I glance over my shoulder and watch him pop the last two bites of my muffin into his mouth. He just can't help himself. Robbie starts off toward me, throwing the trash into a garbage can on the way. I quicken my pace. I know I'm probably overreacting, but he didn't tell me about the pact, and he should have since I don't have any memories. Something like, *Hey, Peyton, you know how you have three boyfriends? Well, you and I agreed to be together if we weren't in a serious relationship by thirty-two, which is in two weeks, so you better get to dating.* That would have sufficed. I would have been like, *Cool, let me add that to the list.* BUT HE DIDN'T.

"Peyton!"

I ignore him and keep marching forward. At the intersection, I turn right.

"Where are you going?" he yells.

"Home."

"That's the wrong way."

I stop abruptly and stomp my foot. I can't even make a quick dramatic exit. Exhaling an angry breath, I turn back and walk toward him begrudgingly.

"Please, can we talk?" he pleads.

"Sure. Talk." I stop right in front of him and throw a hand on my hip. I'm giving a lot of attitude for a person with no memories, and I have no idea where it's coming from.

"I forgot about the pact," he says, lowering his chin.

My eyes go wide. "What? How could you forget about a promise you made to me?" I think I'm more hurt than I am mad now. And I know I'm the one with amnesia who can't remember anything, but what's his excuse? He's got a fully functioning brain.

"I didn't think it was serious back then, and I sure as heck don't think it's serious now. Actually, I'm surprised you even remembered. And by that I mean before you lost all your memories." He stares back at me almost as though he's searching for the reason as to why I brought it up to Debbie in the first place. But the answer's not there, and I don't know it either.

The WALK signal changes, so I cross the street. Robbie trails behind but quickly catches up, walking in step with me.

"I don't understand why you're mad," he says.

Me neither. But I don't say that. I just keep walking while trying to get my thoughts and feelings straightened out. I was mad when I thought he remembered the pact and didn't tell me. Now he says he didn't remember the pact and . . . my feelings are hurt. That must be it. How did I remember and he didn't? Being told everything about my life is overwhelming, but not being told things is worse. I need to be able to trust the judgment of those closest to me because I can't depend on myself right now. When I nearly pass the street my house is on, he grabs my hand and leads me in the direction of home. His hand slips away and his arms swing side to side as he keeps pace beside me, waiting for a response.

"Why are you mad?" he asks.

"Because you lied to me and you forgot about the pact, and I also think you're lying about forgetting about the pact," I say, pushing open the gate to the courtyard.

"What? None of that makes any sense."

I stomp up the porch steps, through the door and up the set of carpeted stairs. He might be right. It might not make any sense, but I feel like it does. In the kitchen, I pour myself a glass of water. Robbie appears at the top of the stairs a moment later.

"It makes perfect sense," I say. "You don't want me to date those guys because you want to carry out the pact." I glare at him over the rim of my water glass.

He runs his hands through his bedhead (well, couch head) hair and groans.

"That's not true at all, Peyton. I forgot about the stupid pact. Even if I remembered it, I wouldn't bring it up or carry it out. You and I would never be good together, trust me."

My mouth falls open. *What's wrong with me? Or us?* I snap it closed and pull my chin in. I'm kinda hurt. How does he know we wouldn't be good together? And why is he so sure of that? Have we been together before? Was it explosive? Did it almost ruin our friendship? Or am I just not his type? I bite my lower lip before it starts to tremble. I'm not even sure where these emotions are coming from.

"What do you mean?" I ask.

"We wouldn't work as a couple. We're friends. We're good friends, and I wouldn't want to jeopardize that for a pact we made when we were nineteen." He leans against the counter.

I narrow my eyes. "I don't believe you just forgot." Mostly because I don't want to believe him.

"Why would I lie?"

"To cover up your sabotage plan, obviously."

"Peyton, I'm telling the truth."

"Sorry, Robbie. I don't believe it." I shake my head. He had to have remembered because I did. But wait. Debbie did say the pact helped me. It calmed my anxiety and my worry of never having someone to love and to love me back. It obviously meant more to me than it did to him.

He scoffs and throws his hands up.

"I'll tell you what," he says, staring directly at me. "I wasn't on board with the whole dating-these-guys thing because I wanted you to get better first, but I'm fully on board now. Heck, I'll help set up your dates. I'll vet these guys. I'll do all that gossipy crap you do with Maya about boys and dating. I'll weigh out the pros and cons. And I'll make sure you know which one of them you love by your birthday, so you don't feel any pressure to go through with our silly pact." Robbie exhales deeply, never dropping eye contact. "I only want you to be happy, and

I know you won't be if you fall back on a promise we made when we were practically kids."

I lift my chin and stare back at him, studying his face, looking for a tell. "You really mean all of that?"

"Yes, I mean it."

Either he's not lying or he doesn't have a tell. But I don't know what's true and what's not. Without my memories, all I have are feelings with nothing behind them.

"Okay," I say quietly, because I don't know what else to say.

Maybe he really did forget about the pact, and maybe he was looking out for my best interests. Maybe it mattered so much to me because the pact was almost like a safety net, a fallback plan. I don't know. It's all just so confusing. There's so little I do know, and it's tangled up in the unknown. Robbie extends his hand for a shake. I glance at it and furrow my brow.

"What?" I ask, looking to him.

"Let's shake on it. Let's make a new pact."

"What's the new pact?"

"I will help you figure out which of these guys you love before your birthday."

I squint. "And what's in it for you?"

"I don't have to go through with the old pact."

We stare at one another for a moment, like we're in some sort of a showdown.

"Are you sure that's what you want?"

He nods and says, "I'm sure."

Finally, I extend my unsteady hand toward him. "Good," I say.

And we shake on it.

CHAPTER 6

Robbie and I are seated on opposite ends of the couch while a rerun of *Friends* plays on the television. For me it's a first-time viewing, but he said it was one of my faves. His nose is buried in his laptop, and he takes notes on a pad of paper, flipping his attention back and forth. I thought he was working. But he's not. He's doing *research*, as he put it—going through social media profiles, searching Google, and even pulling background reports on each of the guys in an effort to help me pick the right one. Robbie's already taking the new pact too seriously. But I find it kind of cute . . . in a Robbie way.

The front door opens and closes.

"Hello," Maya calls out in a singsong voice as she climbs the stairs.

"Hey," I say.

Robbie's too focused and doesn't say anything. Maya sets down her backpack and several shopping bags. She's dressed much differently from when I saw her at the hospital. Instead of sweats, she's in ripped skinny jeans, an off-the-shoulder sweater, and high-heeled boots. I like her style. It matches her sassy, outgoing personality. She pulls a box from one bag and tosses it to me.

"This was on the front porch."

It's from Verizon, so I know it must be my replacement phone Robbie mentioned. I quickly rip it open while Maya sorts through items from her shopping bags, a mix of groceries and stationery. Robbie hasn't even looked up from his laptop yet. He's in a whole other world full of new pacts.

"I ran into Debbie on my way in." Maya looks to me. "She doesn't know about the accident, does she?"

"I don't think so."

"What? Why wouldn't you tell her?" Robbie asks, finally pulling himself from his *research*. I figured he already knew that based on how Debbie was acting toward him this morning, but I think the whole pact thing distracted him.

"Well, I didn't know who she was at first. By the time I realized we clearly knew each other, it felt too late." I busy myself, looking at my new shiny iPhone.

"You should tell her," Maya says.

My eyes flit between them. "Why didn't you guys tell her when I was in the coma?"

"Because neither of us had her number. Apparently, she recently changed it because of some online-dating fiasco, and we never got the new one. Plus, your phone was broken, and she wasn't home. Trust me, we tried. If she had Instagram, she would have known. The only reason I was able to find you was because I was on the phone with you when it happened. I called all the hospitals in the area over and over until you were admitted into one of them." Maya puts her hands on her hips. "You have to tell her."

"Maya's right," Robbie says. "She's going to lose it if she finds out you didn't tell her."

"I don't want to," I say defiantly. The phone screen lights up with a welcome greeting.

"Why?" Robbie and Maya ask in unison.

"Because I like the way she looks at me."

"What do you mean?" Robbie asks.

"She looks at me like I'm not broken. If she knew, she'd look at me the way you two do." I point at both of them.

Maya's mouth drops open. "That's not true. We look at you how we've always looked at you."

"No, you don't."

"Yes, we do. You don't even remember how we looked at you before," she argues.

"First of all, rude. And second of all, no, you don't. You both look at me like you feel sorry for me." I glance down at the phone and swipe through the various setup instructions, including the forgot password process, for obvious reasons. Robbie gave me a handwritten note earlier with my Apple ID and answers to any potential security questions, so I could hopefully get back into my account without having to call Verizon. He didn't know my password, but it seems he knew everything else—my mother's maiden name, where I attended elementary school, my childhood best friend's name, the street I grew up on, and the make and model of my first car.

"Well, I do feel bad," Maya says.

"Me too," Robbie adds.

"I know you do, but I don't want anyone's sympathy. That's why I don't want to tell Debbie."

"But it's Debbie," Maya says.

"So? She's just my downstairs neighbor." I huff.

They exchange a worried look. Maya takes a seat in the chair kitty-corner to the couch. Robbie sets his laptop on the end table and repositions himself so he's partially facing me. It feels like this is going to be a serious conversation, and I don't think I'm ready for that. I let out a heavy sigh and give them my attention anyway.

"Debbie isn't just your downstairs neighbor," Maya says, leaning forward in her seat.

"Who is she then?"

Robbie clears his throat. "You know when you asked me about that photo in your bedroom, and I told you that they were your parents and they had passed away?"

I nod. Tears pool in the rims of my eyes. I knew I wasn't ready for a serious conversation.

"Your parents died in a car accident in December of 2009," Maya says.

My heart rate quickens so much, I can feel it in every part of my body. It's that same punch-in-the-gut feeling I got yesterday when I looked at the photo of my parents. "What does that have to do with Debbie?"

"Peyton, you were in the accident too," Maya explains. "There was a freak snowstorm that came out of nowhere, and it caused a pileup on the highway. Debbie was there, but she was able to stop her vehicle and pull it off to the side, avoiding the crash. She's a medical doctor, retired now, and she went searching for people to help while waiting for the ambulances to arrive. It was impossible for them to get there quickly given the weather and the size of the accident. She came across your parents' vehicle and tried to help them, but they were already gone. Then she found you in the back. She saved your life. When the ambulance finally got to you, Debbie came with. She stayed with you until you were better, and she's been there for you ever since. You spent all your holidays with her after that, and when you moved to the city, she rented this duplex out to you for far below what she could get for it. It's practically a steal. So Debbie isn't just your downstairs neighbor. She's your family, and she's basically your guardian angel." Maya's voice cracks. It's the first time I've seen her serious and emotional.

Tears fall all at once, and my lip trembles. Robbie pats my leg and hands me a tissue, telling me it's okay. But I don't know if it is. Maybe the reason I can't remember anything is because it's all so awful. How did I survive that? And I don't mean physically. I mean emotionally and mentally. Maya pulls a tissue from the box and wipes at her own eyes. I can't believe what Debbie has done for me. She's saved me . . . more than once.

"I'm sorry. I didn't know," I say, looking down at my lap.

"There's nothing to be sorry about," Robbie says.

"Can I tell her tomorrow?"

They both nod.

"Yeah, of course," he says.

Maya asks, "Are you all right?"

"Yeah, it's just a lot. I didn't realize how much I had been through before losing my memory, and now, I'm not so sure I want to remember."

"Don't say that," Robbie says.

Maya clears her throat and pulls her chin in. "The bad things that happened to you weren't your whole life, even though at times they felt like it. You have so many good memories, Peyton. Trust me, they're worth remembering, I promise."

I glance down at my phone, hoping what they're saying is true.

The phone setup process finishes and several missed text messages pop up on the screen. I start to read through them. They're from the guys.

Tyler's text reads, Good morning, beautiful. I just got to work but wanted to let you know I was thinking about you, and I can't wait for our date on Thursday night ☺

The next one is from Nash. Hey, Peyton. Hope you had a good morning. How are the chocolates?

Shawn's text reads, Hey, babe. Flight's about to take off. Thinking of you. Rest up.

Robbie peers over my shoulder, peering at my phone. I lean away and give him a look that I hope conveys *What do you think you're doing?*

Maya squints. "What's with all the phone action?"

"They're texts from Nash, Shawn, and Tyler."

Robbie leans farther into me. He smells nice, like a combination of trees and citrus. "Let me see them, so I can mark it down," he says. I hold the phone against my chest and smile at him.

Maya crosses one leg over the other and bounces her foot. "Mark what down?"

"Robbie thinks he's helping me figure out which of the guys I love."

He cocks his head. "I don't think. I am. That was the pact."

Maya's brows shove together. "I thought I was the one managing all of this."

"We can comanage. Peyton and I already shook on it."

"You said she shouldn't be dating until she's healed."

Robbie grins. "I changed my mind."

Maya cocks her head. "Why the change of heart?"

"Because he wants to cancel out the first pact we made when we were nineteen." I roll my eyes.

"What pact did you two make?"

"That he and I would be together if neither of us were married, engaged, or in a serious relationship by thirty-two, which is in less than two weeks for me," I say, scanning through the texts.

Maya bursts out laughing. "You both know you don't have to follow through on a pact you made."

"I know," Robbie says. He points to me. "She's the one that's adamant about it."

"A person is only as good as their word," I say with a shrug.

"That's Debbie talking." Maya shakes her head, still in the middle of a fit of laughter.

"She may have said something similar to me today." I flash them the phone screen. "Now, help me respond to these texts. I don't know what to say."

Robbie holds out his hand, palm face up. "Let me see it."

I pause, tightening my eyes, but slowly set the phone in his hand.

"Oh, gross," Robbie says.

"What?" Maya leans over to try to get a better look.

"Shawn called you *babe*."

"What's wrong with that?" I ask. "It's a term of endearment."

"No, Robbie's right. *Babe* is something you call a girlfriend, not someone you're not even exclusive with." Maya makes a disgusted face.

"I think it's kind of cute."

"This is exactly why you need us," she says firmly.

Robbie takes notes and then types out a text and sends it.

"Hey, wait. What did you say?" I ask, leaning into him.

"I wrote back, *Have a good trip.*"

I push out my bottom lip. "Seems a bit casual."

"Exactly. It's called playing hard to get. Now, let's see what Tyler said. He called you *beautiful*—"

"Is that too forward?" Maya interjects.

"No, that's fine," Robbie says. "He also tells you he's at work and that he's thinking of you and can't wait for Thursday."

Maya looks to me. "How would you respond, Peyton?"

"Maybe I'd tell him I can't wait too."

"How about, *I'm looking forward to Thursday night too. Have a good day at work?*" Robbie says.

Maya nods. "Perfect."

Robbie types it out and hits "Send."

"All right, on to Chef Nash. He called you by your name. Nice. Especially with your memory loss. That's a good reminder for you. Then he wished you a good morning and asked how the chocolates are." Before anyone says anything, Robbie types out another message and hits "Send."

"What did you say?" I look to him.

"I wrote, *I loved them and hope you're having a good day.*"

I cross my arms across my chest. "But I didn't even try them."

"I did, and they are delicious," he says with a smirk. "Oh, shoot." Robbie hands me my phone, closes his computer, and stands from the couch. "I'm gonna be late for work. But we'll go over this later," he says, patting his laptop.

"Yeah, Robbie. Get out of here. I have a girls' day planned." Maya redirects her attention to me. "We're going over the boys. Then I have some spa stuff. Your skin is in need of some serious hydration. The coma really dried you out. Then I've got a bag of junk food because we're gonna kick back and watch *The Sixth Sense.*" She puts her feet up on the coffee table and laces the palms of her hands behind her head.

I glance over at Robbie, and we exchange a knowing look. Neither of us tells Maya that I already watched it. It'll be fun to "guess" the ending halfway through to mess with her. Robbie slips on his jacket.

"I'll see you tonight," he says with a wave as he jogs down the steps.

"Bye, Robbie," Maya and I call out.

She's already riffling through the bags she carried in when the front door opens and closes, signaling that Robbie's gone.

Maya turns to me. "What is up with him?"

I reposition myself in my seat, crossing and uncrossing my legs. "What do you mean?" Personally, I wouldn't know what is up or down with Robbie because I don't really know him.

"His change of heart, helping with the whole date-these-guys-again fiasco." Maya raises a brow. "He went from *No, not a good idea* to *Let's do a deep dive on each guy.*"

"I told you why. He's trying to prove that he wasn't attempting to sabotage my dating life to run out the clock on the pact we made." I get up from my seat and mosey into the kitchen, filling a cup with water. I take a long sip.

Maya pulls groceries from a bag and sets them out on the counter. "Why would he have to prove that?"

"Because I accused him of it," I say with a shrug.

"You what? How did you even remember that you two made a pact?" She pauses and squints. "Wait, are you getting your memories back?" Maya gives me a hopeful look.

"No."

She instantly frowns.

"And Debbie told me about the pact. Apparently, I brought it up a week or so ago. I guess I was worried if I didn't figure out which of these guys I loved, then I'd have to be with Robbie."

Maya snorts. "Seriously, you do know you don't have to go through with it. It's not a binding contract. It's silly."

"I know that. Robbie claims he didn't remember the pact anyway." I drain the rest of my glass and refill it.

"Maybe he didn't. I mean, you never even told me about it." She purses her lips. "I'm pretty upset with Pre-amnesia Peyton for not telling me." Maya slides a box of Cheez-Its across the counter.

I catch it before the crackers fly onto the floor. "Well, Post-amnesia Peyton is sorry for that," I say, searching the cupboards. When I finally find a bowl, I empty half the box into it and push it toward Maya. She grabs a handful and tosses a few in her mouth.

I wait for her to finish chewing and then ask, "Did anything ever happen between Robbie and me?"

Robbie was adamant that we weren't good together, so I'm curious to know if the reason he knew that was because we tried already.

She pauses her chewing and stares at me. "What do you mean?"

"Like, did we ever date or hook up?"

Maya says, "No, absolutely not. You two have only ever been friends."

"Are you sure?"

"Positive."

"But I didn't tell you about the pact. Maybe I didn't tell you about that."

"There's no way. I would have known in a heartbeat. Wait, why are you asking about Robbie? Did he say something to you?"

"No. I was just curious." I shrug. "He said the same thing you did. We've always been just friends." I toss a few Cheez-Its in my mouth and dust my hands off.

Maya raises an eyebrow but then relaxes it. "All right, enough about Robbie," she says, throwing up her hands. "Let's focus on your three boyfriends. Grab your purse, phone, and MacBook."

"For what?"

"Because there's probably evidence as to what you thought about these guys prior to your accident." Maya picks up her backpack from her pile of belongings and heads to the living room with the bowl of Cheez-Its.

A few minutes later, I join Maya on the couch and open my laptop. The screen lights up, requesting a password. I squint, trying to remember what it could possibly be, but nothing pops into my brain.

"Do you know my password?" I ask.

She shakes her head and continues skimming through pages of handwritten notes.

I sigh and place my hands on the keyboard. *Think. Come on, Peyton. It's just one word . . . one little password. You can remember that.* No word pops into my brain, but my fingers tingle and crawl across the keys, pressing down on several of them. I hit "Enter."

"Oh my God."

Maya lifts her head. "What?"

"I remembered my password. Look." I swivel the screen toward her. "It let me in."

The screen background is a photo of Robbie, Maya, and me huddled together on a picnic blanket surrounded by snacks and drinks.

"How? Did it just pop in your head?" She partially stands and tucks a foot under her as she retakes her seat. "What else can you remember?"

"I don't know how." I turn the computer back toward me. "I just let my fingers type it out. I wasn't even thinking about what I was typing, I just did. I think it's muscle memory."

"Maybe we can use that muscle memory on the guys and have your lady bits decide who you love." Maya waggles her eyebrows.

"Absolutely not." I laugh. "And I don't even know if I had sex with any of them before the accident. Do you know if I did?"

"You never told me. But I've been so busy lately, so maybe."

My eyes widen. "What if I did? Am I supposed to just continue with that level of intimacy, even though I don't remember?"

"No, you're starting all over, and if any of them don't get that, then they're not the one for you." She pats my shoulder. "Unless . . . you want to just bang it out and figure it out that way."

"No," I say with a laugh.

"Always an option," she teases. "Now, pull up your iMessage history on your laptop. All of your texts should be saved in the cloud. Let's see how you talked to these boys."

I nod and click around on the screen until I find iMessages. Then I open up a thread between Shawn and me. It goes back two months, like he said.

"All right, I have Shawn's messages up."

Maya thumbs through her notebook and puts pen to paper. "Young Denzel. Give me the gist. Frequency of texts, tone, and anything else that stands out."

"He texts me daily, always starting with a good-morning text."

She jots it down. "Very nice. So, he's thoughtful."

"He's had to cancel or reschedule a couple of dates due to work."

"Not sure I like that," Maya says, tapping the end of her pen against her chin.

"I mean, it's his job, so that's understandable."

I glance over and watch her write down *flaky* and *Peyton is not a top priority*. I roll my eyes.

"What else?" Maya asks.

"There's a long message in here from a week ago that says he understands why I'm not ready to be exclusive but that he's willing to wait. He said he's had a similar experience with not being ready to commit. Then he shares all the things he likes about me."

"That's sweet. And his story at the hospital checks out." She writes *honest* and *complimentary*. "Anything else?"

"He says he can't wait to kiss me again." I raise my brows. "And he mentions in another text that he won't be able to sleep because he's so hot and bothered from me."

"You dirty dog," she says.

"It sounds like a make-out sesh."

"With some heavy petting. I'll write down between second and third base for intimacy level with Shawn. Who's next?"

I click around and find another thread of messages. "Tyler."

"Less buff Chris Hemsworth with Thor hair, and go."

"Texts go back six weeks, so that time line checks out. He also texts me every morning, and he sends texts asking what I'm doing or saying he thought of me because of something he's seen or heard." I look to Maya. "That's sweet, right?"

"Kind of. Could also be clingy." She writes *clingy sweet.*

I continue reading through my texts. "We definitely kissed, and he's slept over."

Maya leans over to get a look at the screen. "Wait, how do you know?"

"Because, right here," I say, pointing to a message. "He writes: *Didn't want to wake you this morning, but I had to go to work. I had a great time, and I can't wait to see you again. There's a blueberry muffin and a cold brew in the fridge for you. I picked them up and came back, but you were still asleep. Love you.*"

"Holy shit," Maya says. "That's a bombshell right there. Case closed. It's Tyler the construction man."

"But wait! Look how I replied. I thanked him and told him I had a great time too. I didn't say *I love you* back."

"You put a heart emoji."

"That's not the same thing, is it?"

"Well, it's a red heart," Maya says.

"What does that matter?"

"Red means love. If it was a different color heart, it'd mean something else. Yellow heart emoji is friendship. Purple means hot physical attraction. Green is like love you'd use for a family member. But you used red. That's true love," Maya says with a nod.

"Can't it just be an emoji?"

She pulls her chin in. "It's never just an emoji."

"But I didn't say the word *love*."

"Maybe you did when you two were banging?" She smirks.

"Maya!"

"I mean making love."

"Just finish your notes on him," I say with a laugh. She scribbles down *maybe banged* and *love emoji*.

"All right, on to Nash. He and I have been talking for five weeks. He doesn't text me every morning."

"Minus one point," Maya says.

"He texts me every afternoon, probably because of his work schedule." I look to her. "He's a chef, so he must work a lot of late nights."

She moves her mouth side to side like she's deciding her point-system rules. "Plus one point back. What else?"

"There's no mention of kisses or sleepovers, but he's very sweet, just seems a bit busy and not all that good with texting."

"Not a lot to go on there. So I'll put a question mark in the texting category and *still batting* for intimacy level."

"That's all of it," I say, closing up the laptop. "Now what?" I place the Mac on the coffee table and grab a handful of Cheez-Its, popping them into my mouth one at a time.

"What about your planner?" she asks. "It's in your bag. You're very type A, and you write down everything, so there's gotta be something in there."

"I do?"

Maya nods. I toss the rest of the cheesy crackers in my mouth and fish out my planner. It's thick and heavy. Every page is filled with colorful handwriting, documenting appointments, dates, to-do lists, and work meetings. I really do write everything down.

"Oh, look what was on my to-do list the week before my accident." I point to the planner.

Maya leans over. "Find out who I love." She laughs. "Should have added: *and don't lose my memory after I do.*"

"Next time," I say with a chuckle.

"All right, go back two months, when you would have started dating Shawn."

I turn the page to the middle of August. "Looks like we had our first date at Gilt Bar."

"Oh, nice choice. He has good taste. I'll add *willing to spend a buck.*"

"I wrote down *oysters?* with a question mark after it. What does that mean? Do I like oysters?"

Maya looks to me. "Yes."

"So, that's a good thing?" I squint.

"Could be. But then again, maybe you thought it was weird you had oysters on the first date. It is an aphrodisiac. You may have thought he was looking for a one-night stand or something like that." Maya shrugs and writes down a dollar sign with a smiley face next to it.

I'm not sure her notes are helping, but at least she's having fun with it. Plus, I am learning more about the guys in a very cryptic way.

"Write down *oysters* too," I say. "Just in case I remember something later on."

She nods and gestures for me to turn the page.

"We had our second date a week later at Loyalist."

"I am impressed with his restaurant picks." The corner of her mouth perks up. "Their burger is to die for."

I point to the page and look to Maya. "I wrote down *oysters* again."

"What is wrong with you?"

"I don't know. It must have meant something."

Turning the page again, I see my third date with him was supposed to be at Gretel but it's crossed out, so that was a canceled or rescheduled date. But the day after, *coffee date with Nash* is written down.

"See this?" I ask, turning the planner to Maya so she can get a glimpse.

"That's interesting. I wonder if you went to Gretel and got stood up, and then you met Nash there since that's where he works, and boom, another date." She looks to me.

"Or maybe after the canceled date, I accepted another on one of the dating apps and thought it was meant to be since my date was supposed to be at Gretel and Nash works there."

"Actually, that sounds like you. I'll write down *forced kismet* in Nash's column."

I continue leafing through my planner, relaying information to Maya. On average, Shawn and I had one date a week, with two cancellations and one reschedule. So, altogether we've been on six very nice dinner dates, and we've definitely made out or maybe more. Nash and I typically went on two daytime dates a week, usually over coffee or lunch. So we've been on ten dates, but I can't tell if he and I have ever even kissed. I'm not sure if I should be concerned about that or not, so I shrug it off.

"What about Tyler?" Maya asks.

"We went on our first date six weeks ago. He took me axe throwing, and then we had dinner at Tuman's Tap and Grill."

"How manly. I can see why you got down and dirty with him. I wonder if he wore flannel on your date. That would have got me going," Maya says, fanning herself.

"What? Why?"

"It's those damn thirst traps on TikTok of men chopping wood. I never knew I was into that until it popped up on my For You page." She shakes her head. "That dang algorithm knows me better than I know myself. Anthony will hear the same sound on loop over and over and be like, 'What are you watching?' I always say it's a makeup tutorial, but it's shirtless men chopping wood." She laughs.

"Wait. Who's Anthony again?" I ask.

"My boyfriend of nearly a year. We met at the comedy club when he was working security. It was actually the night I had Robbie heckle me."

"Wait, why *did* you have Robbie heckle you?"

"I needed a heckler for my set material. Plus, I figured it'd be good for word-of-mouth marketing. People would be like, 'She's great at crowd work.'"

I give her a confused look.

She waves her hand. "It's an industry thing. Anyway, Anthony was the one that threw him out. Love at first sight. After the show, he asked me on a date. Kismet." She beams.

Her face practically lights up, and I realize how badly I want that. I want to glow just talking about the man I love. But first I gotta figure out who that is.

"That's really sweet. Not the part about Robbie getting thrown out," I say with a laugh.

"He was a good sport about it, and him and Anthony are great friends now."

"I can't wait to meet him . . . I mean again," I say.

"Oh my God. We have to double-date. That way I can help you and get a feel for these guys."

"I'd love that, but I should probably do solo dates with each of them first."

"Good thinking," she says. "Anything else about Tyler?"

"Obviously he slept over, but that doesn't mean we slept together. And he said he loved me, but I did not technically say it back. All of our dates are always dinner and some activity, so he seems fun and adventurous. I've had fewer dates with him than Nash, but more than Shawn." I close up the planner and place it on the laptop while Maya finishes jotting down the rest of her notes.

"You've got some solid contenders here. It's no wonder why you were dating all three of them. I'd have a hard time choosing too."

"There is one issue, though. Debbie told me that I was going to break up with one of them because I apparently caught them in a couple of lies."

"Okay, which one? I'll cross him off right now and cancel the date." Her hand clutches the pen. It stands at attention, ready to strike one of them out.

"I don't know. I guess I didn't tell her."

Maya squints. "The plot thickens."

I toss a few more Cheez-Its in my mouth and sink back into the cushions.

"Going forward, I'm going to either need you to keep a fully detailed diary or disclose way more information to myself, Robbie, or Debbie. But mostly me." She places her notebook on the table and eats a handful of crackers.

"Noted."

There's a knock at the front door, and I'm the first to get up to answer it. I don't know who it could be because I also don't know who I know. Hopefully, it's someone I've already been introduced to post-amnesia.

Standing on the porch, I find Nash. His hazel eyes appear brighter in the sunlight. Dressed in a beanie, scarf, and a navy-blue jacket, he cracks a shy smile.

"Hey, Peyton," he says.

I give him a quizzical look, not because I'm not happy to see Nash but because I'm confused as to why he's here. "Is our date today?" I ask. "I thought it was tomorrow."

"It is tomorrow, but I just wanted to drop this off." He extends a round to-go container toward me. It's warm in my hands and looks like some sort of food, but the Tupperware is cloudy. "It's homemade chicken noodle soup to help you feel better." Nash shuffles his feet, then looks down and back at me like he's embarrassed by his gesture. "I know you're not sick . . . but you know what they say, it's good for the soul."

I glance at the container of soup and back at Nash. I can't believe he made me soup. I want to kiss him but I remember the research Maya and I put together. I don't think Nash and I have kissed.

"That's really sweet of you, Nash. Thanks."

He rocks back on his heels. "It's nothing. I'd stay and chat, but I've gotta go do some prep work for a special we have on the menu tonight."

"No, it is something." I quickly lean forward and give him a peck on the cheek.

His cheeks flush, and he tries to hide his growing smile. "All right, I'll see you tomorrow then." Nash stumbles back a step, waves awkwardly, and jogs down the porch steps. "Hope you feel better." He pauses. "I mean, enjoy the soup."

I laugh and call out, "See you tomorrow." He turns back again and waves before half jogging, half walking away. The door next to mine opens, stealing my attention.

"Hello," Debbie says.

"It's just me," I say, peeking my head around the corner.

"Oh, what's that?" She gestures to the container in my hands.

"Homemade chicken soup."

"Are you sick or something?" She lets the door close behind her and places the back of her hand against my head. "You don't have a fever."

"No, I'm not sick, but . . . umm, do you wanna come up for some soup? There's something I need to tell you." I press my lips together.

She delivers a warm smile. "Of course, sweetheart. Let me just grab my cardigan."

After what Maya and Robbie told me about Debbie, I know I owe it to her to tell her what happened. I can't look her in the eyes again without her knowing. She deserves the truth.

CHAPTER 7

I finish telling Debbie everything. She's seated in the chair next to the couch with her legs crossed at the knee, staring intently at me. She hasn't taken her eyes off me since I started talking.

"I knew it," she says.

"You knew I had amnesia?"

"No, not necessarily. But I knew something was off. This morning, you didn't look at me like you usually do. At first, I thought you were mad at me for something, but then we got to talking and I realized it wasn't that. Then I thought you were pregnant."

"What? Why would you think that?"

She shrugs. "Everything else that crossed my mind, I figured you'd just come out and tell me." Debbie picks up her bowl of soup and spoons a heavy helping into her mouth.

"Amnesia would have been my second guess," she adds with a snicker.

Maya and I exchange a look.

"Now, which one of these guys brought you this soup?" Debbie asks.

"Nash," Maya says. "He's a chef at Gretel."

"If you don't pick him, think he'd be into me?" Debbie simpers, spooning another bite into her mouth.

Maya and I laugh.

I pick up my soup from the coffee table and take my first spoonful. "Oh my God. It's so good!"

"See? That's what I'm saying," Debbie says. "But from what I've heard, it sounds like your connections are deeper with Shawn and Tyler."

Maya nods. "Yeah, I agree with that."

"But one of them is a liar." Debbie raises an eyebrow over her bowl of soup. She brings it to her mouth and slurps.

"We gotta weed out a liar and weed in a lover," Maya says, looking down at her notebook. She picks up a Twizzler from the bag resting on the end table and bites off a chunk, then twirls the rest of it.

"This is exactly why you shouldn't procrastinate, Peyton. If you would have dumped the liar, you'd only have two to pick from." Debbie nods.

"I'll remember that for the next time I get amnesia," I say sarcastically.

"Good," Debbie says, ignoring my sarcasm. She must be used to it. She stands from her chair and extends her hand. "All done?"

I drink the rest of my broth and hand my bowl to her. "Yeah, thanks."

"Of course, sweetie." Debbie leaves the living room. The kitchen faucet turns on and dishes clink together.

"I'm giving Nash a bonus point for the soup," Maya says.

"What do the points even mean?" I lean over, trying to steal a glance at the sheet of paper. There are three columns with each of their names written at the top and tally marks beneath them. Shawn has seven. Tyler has nine. And Nash just got his sixth for the soup.

"When I think something about them is appealing, I give them a tally mark." Maya delivers a pleased look.

"But what does each mark mean?"

"Something is appealing to me."

I cock my head. "That doesn't seem helpful for me, the one dating them."

"I think it is. We like the same things."

Debbie returns with a wineglass filled to the brim. She settles back into her chair and takes a long sip, making a refreshing sound when she's done.

"Debbie, it's two in the afternoon," Maya says.

"I'm retired, Maya. Time means nothing to me." She drinks again and places the glass on the end table beside her. "So, have we narrowed it down yet?"

"No, I don't think I can until I actually have a date with each of them."

"That's true," Maya says. "We're just going off initial impressions and text messages."

"But I don't know how I'm going to date them when I don't even know who I am. How do I talk to them about my likes, dislikes, beliefs, values—any of it?" I deliver a worried look to both Maya and Debbie.

They glance at one another and nod. "Time for a crash course on you," Maya says.

"We got thirty-two years to cover, so buckle up," Debbie adds.

This will be interesting. Being able to learn about myself from the viewpoint of those who know me. I wonder what kind of person I am or what makes me happy. Hopefully, it's all good stuff. I re-situate myself and fold my legs into a pretzel, getting comfortable. "Okay, what do I like to do for fun?"

Maya and Debbie start listing off things rapid fire. I pick up a fair amount and try to commit it all to my memory. Long walks, but Maya called them *hot girl walks*. I'm not entirely sure what that is. Reading. Mostly romance novels. I gathered that from the bookshelf in my office. Going out for dinner and drinks. My favorites are fried chicken sandwiches, Caesar salads (but not the healthy kind), and lemon drop martinis. I can't do spicy. Apparently, sometimes I find

McChicken sandwiches too spicy if there's too much black pepper on them. Comedy shows. I'm not sure if that's true or if Maya is plugging her own show again. Watching movies. I love rom-coms and horror films. Attending Broadway shows. I guess I've seen *Waitress* three times. Travel. Hiking. Hanging out with friends. Maya said hanging out with her. Debbie added Robbie. Cooking. I didn't know I was a good cook. My eyes wander toward the kitchen. Perhaps I'll have to try to whip something up. Okay, that all seems pretty typical and should be easy to remember.

"Where have I traveled?" I ask.

"You've been to Florida, New York City, San Fran, and you did a two-week trip to Europe after graduation with Robbie and me. We visited London, Amsterdam, Paris, Barcelona, Vienna, and Budapest," Maya says.

I try to commit them all to memory, but I know I've already forgotten some of the cities. "That sounds fun. I wish I remembered it."

"It was a blast . . . and you will remember it."

"The Europe trip was my graduation present to you," Debbie says.

My eyes go wide. "You paid for a trip to Europe for me?"

"Of course. I did it for my two boys too, when they graduated college." She says it like the gift was never a question in her mind.

Debbie really has treated me like her own. She's been so good to me, and I feel like I owe her the world. Technically, I do, since she saved my life. I don't know what I could ever do to repay her for what she's done for me. I smile at her, and she returns it.

"I know I probably said it before, but I don't remember, so thank you."

"You have many, many times, Peyton. You are an extremely grateful person. That's something you should know about yourself. You expect nothing, but you appreciate everything."

Maya's head bobs up and down as Debbie speaks. "That's true, and you're very generous. For my first comedy set, I was so nervous that I was going to bomb, and I was freaking out over what I should wear and how I should start. On the day of my set, you gave me a red leather jacket. It's literally the nicest thing I own. You told me to channel Eddie Murphy from his *Delirious* special. He's an idol of mine. It didn't help because I still bombed, but I looked good while doing it," she says with a snicker.

Debbie and I laugh too.

"You were really bad," Debbie adds. "But you're killing it now. Everyone starts somewhere."

"Exactly. Some of us have to restart, though." Maya glances over at me.

I toss a pillow at her teasingly. "Anything else I should know?"

Debbie leans forward in her seat, and her face turns serious. "You're a good person, Peyton. You haven't had an easy life, but somehow you came out kind, and that isn't always the case for people that have gone through hard times. I know you don't remember who you are or the experiences you had, but know you deserve the best. You deserve someone that cherishes you, respects you, and loves you deeply. So remember that when you're dating these men again. If it doesn't feel right, it's probably not." She places her hand on mine, patting it.

Maya hands Debbie and me each a tissue. We dab at our eyes and exchange looks of understanding. I don't know much about myself, but knowing I'm a good person feels like everything I need to know. But if I'm so good and deserving, why haven't I found love yet? I consider asking but I'm not sure I want to know the answer.

"I cosign everything Debbie just said," Maya says, biting into her Twizzler.

A knock at the door interrupts us. Maya jumps up, declaring that she'll get it. She disappears down the set of stairs. The front door opens, and I hear her tell someone to come in. A set of footsteps pounds slowly up the stairs. Tyler appears at the top of them. I can still hear

Maya talking, so either someone else is at the door or she's practicing a comedy bit.

"Hey," he says with a small wave. "Sorry for just dropping in, but I was in the area and thought I'd dip over on my lunch break to see how you're doing."

"Wowzer!" Debbie says, looking him up and down. It seems Tyler has that effect on all women. His dark hair sits on top of his head in a bun, and his facial hair is a bit scruffier today. He's dressed in a black-and-red flannel shirt, and I imagine that was the one he was wearing on our first date. Tall, burly, and rugged, like a sexy lumberjack.

He glances at her and closes the distance, extending a hand. "I'm Tyler. Nice to meet you."

"Debbie," she says. "I'm Peyton's single-and-available fairy godmother."

Tyler gives her a peculiar look and then cracks a grin. He takes a step back and slides his hands into the front pockets of his jeans.

Maya appears at the top of the stairs, carrying in an oversized vase filled with at least three dozen red roses and a sprinkling of baby's breath. She sets them on the kitchen counter and exhales sharply, shaking out her arms.

"Wow, thank you, Tyler," I say.

"Oh, uhhh."

Maya pulls out a small card that was tucked between the flowers. "They're not from him. They're from Shawn."

Tyler scratches the back of his neck. "Yeah, that's what I was trying to say."

"Since you showed up empty-handed, you mind helping me with a leaky faucet?" Debbie stands from her seat. It's less of a question and more of a suggestion.

"Debbie!" I give her a stern look.

"What? You said he worked construction, and he can talk to you while he's fixing it. And I'll make you a nice BLT sandwich for your work."

Tyler nods. "You got a deal."

"You really don't have to do that," I say.

"It's no problem at all." He smiles. "Plus, win-win for me. I get to chat with you, and I get a BLT."

"See? It's a fantastic offer," Debbie says. She redirects her attention to Tyler, beckoning with her hand. "Follow me."

"I'll be right down," I call out before turning back toward Maya. "You coming?" I ask.

She takes a seat on the couch and pulls out a notepad and a pen. "I'll let you have some alone time with the lumberjack Thor." Her eyebrows bounce up and down. "Besides, I gotta work on my new set."

I slip on a pair of tennis shoes and head down the stairs, yelling to Maya, "Be back soon."

Debbie's home is extra cozy. It's filled with a hodgepodge of furniture and decorations that appear to have been collected throughout her life. Even though I don't remember it, it feels like home. The drapes are thick and velvet, and the couch is adorned with pillows in all colors. It matches her style—eclectic and colorful.

I holler, "Hello."

"In here," Debbie answers from the other side of the house.

I follow her voice through a long hallway. Antique sconces adorn the walls on either side, lighting the way. Several open doors lead to three bedrooms and a bathroom. Framed family photos are hung up in a collage. I notice I'm in many of them, at Christmases, Thanksgivings, and other special events and life moments. There's a picture of Debbie and me at my college graduation. There's another of me holding a cardboard box in my home upstairs. It looks like I was just moving in. I smile at the photos that hold memories I can't recall but can somehow feel.

In the kitchen, Tyler is lying on his back with half his body tucked under the sink. A sliver of his abdomen is exposed, revealing a chiseled

V line. The very sight of it causes my heart to race and my skin to perspire.

"I know, right?" Debbie waggles her brows as she hands me a glass of water. "It'll help you cool off," she whispers.

My cheeks warm, and I let out a muffled laugh. At the stove, Debbie throws a half slab of thick bacon into a frying pan.

"Anything I can help with?"

Tyler jerks up, hitting his head on a pipe. "Ouch," he says, crawling out from beneath the sink, holding his head.

"Are you okay? Let me get you some ice." I scurry to the fridge and pull a bag of frozen peas from the freezer.

"I'm okay," he says, but I'm already bending down and locking eyes with him. He gives me one of those half smirks, the flirtatious kind, and I can't help but return it. I bring the frozen bag of peas to the corner of his forehead where a red mark has already begun to blossom. He winces slightly when I press it against his skin.

"Is that better?" The question comes out flirty in a low, raspy voice.

"Yeah," Tyler says, still grinning.

Bacon sizzles in the pan and a meaty, intoxicating smell permeates throughout the kitchen. I glance up at Debbie. She lifts a brow before turning away to slice up a tomato and slather the toasted bread with mayo. My eyes go back to Tyler, who hasn't taken his off me. The color of his cheeks match the red bump on his head.

"How's that feel?"

"Amazing." Tyler clears his throat. "I mean, much better. I think I'm good to keep working on this."

"Are you sure?"

"Yeah," he says, briefly glancing over at Debbie. "Otherwise, I don't get my BLT and my time with you."

"That's right," Debbie says.

I chuckle and pull the bag of frozen peas from his head and get to my feet. Tyler leans back, careful not to hit his head again, and shimmies under the sink. I put the peas in the freezer and stand next to Debbie. She playfully bumps her shoulder into me.

"I think I'm in love with him," Debbie whispers, letting out a tiny snicker.

"So, you want Nash *and* Tyler?" I whisper back.

"Just for the cooking and the fixing."

I let out a laugh. "Can I help with anything?"

"Yeah, grab the lettuce from the crisper and four plates from the cupboard next to the fridge."

She tells me exactly where everything is, remembering I don't remember. It's thoughtful, and I can tell that's just who she is.

"You got it."

I retrieve the items for Debbie, and she immediately begins assembling a sandwich on each plate. Tyler climbs out from under the sink and turns the faucet on, then off, then on again, double-checking that it's in proper working order. The water gushes out and then stops abruptly. No leaks.

"All fixed," he says, dusting off his hands. He places the cleaning supplies back under the sink and closes the cabinet.

"Thank you, Tyler," Debbie says, extending two thick BLT sandwiches, each set out on a plate. "Here's my end of the deal. Why don't you go on out to the back courtyard?" She winks at me. "I'll eat in here and bring one up to Maya."

"Thanks, Debbie," Tyler says.

She nods and shoos us away. I lead Tyler out to the courtyard. I didn't even realize it was back here. Well, I guess I did before. A large privacy fence surrounds the grassy area. It's beautiful, with strung-up lights, a round table, and six chairs. There's a gas grill, an outdoor fire-pit, and a heat lamp. Like the front courtyard, the plants and flowers are starting to wither and die, but they're alive enough to appreciate.

Tyler and I take a seat at the table and immediately sink our teeth into our sandwiches. They're delicious, comforting, and familiar—at least to me. The BLTs are tangy, meaty, salty, and refreshing. I know I've had them before. They taste like something I would eat when I was going through a hard time. I don't know how to describe it, but they taste like home feels, in a way.

Tyler wipes his mouth with a napkin and looks to me with those mossy green eyes. I feel like I could lose my way in them, and maybe I have.

"How are you feeling?" he asks.

I move my mouth side to side, deciding on the right word. I land on, "Confused. But just taking it one moment at a time. I figure that's how I navigated life before I lost my memories, so that's how I'll find my way again." I bite into my sandwich and chew slowly, savoring it.

"Have any of your . . . ?" He pauses, swallowing so hard his Adam's apple rocks up and down. "Memories come back?"

"No."

His lips press firmly together, like he's disappointed or worried. I feel the same way but there's nothing I can do about it. They'll come back when they're ready to come back, I guess.

"Why? Is there anything you'd like to refresh my memory on?" My question comes out a little flirtatious, which I didn't mean for it to. Perhaps like finding the coffee shop this morning and ordering my usual and typing in my password, it too is like muscle memory.

"Maybe." The corner of his lip perks up, and he runs a hand over his head, taming flyaways. I think he might be flirting back.

I lift my chin, delivering a small smile. "Can you remind me of the best date we've had?"

Tyler lowers his head briefly as though he's thinking it over. When he lifts it, his cheeks are ruddy, and a grin has settled on his face. "It would have to be the date we had about a week or so ago. We went for a long walk stopping at stores, bars, and restaurants in the various surrounding neighborhoods. We drank, ate, and shopped our way through Wicker Park, West Town, Fulton Market, and the West Loop.

Total, I think we walked well over five miles. It was great, just complete spontaneity. We ended up back at your place with two bottles of wine and leftover food." His grin grows a little bigger. "Then I left the next morning." Tyler takes a large bite out of his sandwich.

I raise my brow. "It seems like you skipped over some of that date."

"I'd rather you remember than for me to tell you."

I frown slightly. "That might not be an option."

What if I never remember? I need him to know that's a possibility, a rare one, but still one. I also want to get an idea of how far I went with him. Has my relationship with Tyler progressed on an intimate level further than the others? It doesn't necessarily mean that he and I have a deeper connection, but I guess it'll tell me more about us.

"Well." He pauses for a moment. "We slept together," he says with a serious yet smoldering look.

"Oh," I say. I skim over his large hands, imagining them on me, pressing into my skin, maybe even tugging on my hair if that's what I'm into. The top of my head tingles, so I assume I must be. "Did you enjoy me—I mean, it?" I stammer.

"Would you hold it against me if I said yes?"

I smile faintly. "Is that a line?"

"Not at all. I don't even know any cheesy pickup lines." He studies my face. "Are you feeling tired?"

"No? Why?" I pull my head back.

"Because you've been running through my mind all day." He lets out a husky laugh.

I giggle and pat the side of his arm. It's like a rock, sculpted and hard. Did he pick me up with those muscular arms? I imagine he did. Maybe he threw me on the bed, or perhaps he set me down gently. His eyes tell me it was gentle and tender. But his long dark hair that's tied in a bun tells me he pulled it loose and then tossed me. I take another bite of my sandwich to distract my mind from playing out every possible scenario I can conjure up. It's a blank canvas inside my head currently, so I could sit here daydreaming up a plethora of sexual possibilities.

"So, what do we have in common?" I ask with a smile. *Aside from sexual attraction . . .* but I don't say that part out loud.

He finishes chewing the last of his food and wipes his mouth with a napkin. "Let's see. We both are adventurous, which I love. You're always down for anything, like axe throwing, wandering the neighborhoods, a haunted house, an escape room, and an afternoon trip to the Indiana Dunes."

"We've done all of those?"

He nods. "Oh yes, and we had a blast every time."

"I wish I remembered." I let out a quiet sigh.

Tyler leans in and places his hand on mine. "Me too," he whispers. His forehead puckers as though he's picturing our dates in his head. "We also love wine, which you introduced me to. I was more of a beer drinker before you came into my life. But I'm digging the Paso Robles reds. And you love my dog, so we both love my dog." He grins.

I smile back. "Aww, you have a dog? What kind and what's its name?"

"A golden retriever, and his name is Toby."

"I'd love to meet him—I mean, see him again." I shake my head. "Sorry."

"No need to be sorry. He adores you, and of course we'll swing by my place before or after our date this week." His fingers graze against mine.

"I'd like that."

Our eyes lock and neither of us utters a word. It's time for our bodies to take over and speak the language they know best. His mouth parts as he leans forward. My stomach somersaults with anticipation and nervousness. But I remind myself I probably wasn't nervous before I lost my memory. Our lips lock, and somehow, I can feel his hands all over me, even though they're not. Muscle memory, I think. Or maybe it's just my imagination. The kiss is sweet and warm and tender. His lips are soft, moist, and patient. I don't want it to end. I bring my hands to his face, pulling him even closer. My fingers graze his surprisingly soft facial hair. He must condition it or something. I kiss him a little harder.

The sound of someone clearing their throat stops us instantly. We pull away from one another, and I glance over at the back deck. Robbie stands there dressed in casual business attire, a white collared shirt, a pair of navy-blue dress pants, and camel-colored oxford shoes. A messenger bag hangs from one shoulder. He watches both of us as we wipe at our mouths and try to appear nonchalant.

"Oh, hey, Robbie," I say casually, but it doesn't come off that way. It comes off as someone that was just caught doing something wrong. But it's not wrong, and I don't know why I feel that way or why I'm responding the way I am.

"Don't tell me there's a fourth guy," Tyler says with a laugh.

Robbie jogs down the steps and approaches the table. "Nope, just a good friend. I'm Robbie," he says, extending his hand.

"Nice to meet you. I'm Tyler."

Robbie firmly shakes his. "I didn't realize you had a date today, Peyton." His blue eyes swing to me.

"Me neither."

"I just dropped by. Debbie had me fix her sink, and then she made us some sandwiches," Tyler explains.

Robbie spots the last two bites I left behind on my plate. "All done?" he asks.

I nod and push it toward him. He pops it in his mouth and makes a slight moaning sound while he chews. "Debbie's sandwiches are divine."

"They really are. I feel like I got the better end of our deal. Ha ha," Tyler says.

"You definitely did." I give him a small smile.

Robbie finishes chewing and turns his attention to Tyler. "So, I hear you work construction."

"That's right."

"I built a desk one time." Robbie lifts his chin.

"The one in my home office?" I ask.

He nods.

"That's from IKEA," I say with a laugh.

Robbie looks to me. "Still counts."

Tyler leans farther back in his chair and crosses his arms over his chest. "I build much bigger things, like buildings and houses."

It's like they're having a pissing contest, and I'm not sure why.

A loud alarm startles us. Tyler pulls his phone from his pocket and silences it. "Whelp. Lunch break is over," he says, standing from his chair and stretching his arms over his head. His shirt lifts just enough to reveal the deep *V* line. I can't help but stare. I glance at Robbie. He raises a judgy brow and squints. I roll my eyes and shrug.

"It was good meeting you," Tyler says to Robbie.

He nods in return. "Likewise."

"I'll walk you out," I offer as I get up from my chair.

Tyler throws me a smile and says, "I'd like that."

I lead him through the house and out onto the porch. Debbie isn't inside, so I assume she's upstairs with Maya. Tyler lingers, turning toward me.

"I had a great lunch with you."

"Me too."

"Thanks for letting me drop by unexpectedly," he says. "Don't worry. It won't happen again."

I bite at my lower lip. "That'd be a shame."

He doesn't hesitate this time and just goes for it, leaning down and planting his lips on mine. It warms me from the inside out. When he pulls away, I'm disappointed and already want his mouth back on mine.

"I'll text you," he says, jogging down the stairs of the porch.

I tell him bye as he waves and disappears down the street. I don't leave the porch until I can't see him anymore.

On my way to the back courtyard, I grab two cans of Coke from the fridge. That kiss has left me thirsty. Outside, Robbie is seated with his feet up on another chair and the palms of his hands resting on the back of his head. It feels like I've been called into a boss's office for insubordination.

"Well, well, well," he says with a smirk.

"What?" I feel myself blush.

Robbie raises his brows. "Things are progressing quite quickly with Bob the Builder."

I set a can of Coke in front of him and push his feet off the chair, taking the seat. He dramatically flings forward and chuckles.

"His name is Tyler," I say, cracking open my soda.

Robbie opens his can and brings it to his lips. "I like him," he says, slurping it. He doesn't take his eyes off me as he drinks.

"Really?" I tilt my head.

He makes a refreshing sound and places the can on the table. "Yup. Why? Are you surprised?"

"Kind of." I sip the sugary soda.

"Why's that?"

"I thought you wouldn't like any of them."

His brow creases. "How am I supposed to figure out which one you love if I just dislike them all?"

I shrug but there's a little ache in my heart, and I'm not sure what's causing it. Maybe I want Robbie to be overprotective or put up a stink over these guys. He did for a little bit with Tyler, but now he's so nonchalant about it all. I'm starting to think Robbie really did forget about our pact—and not only that, he never believed it was a good thing for us to be together in the first place. But then why did he agree to it all those years ago? Well, probably because he thought it was silly to begin with. It's easy to agree to silly things you never plan on following through with.

"I guess you're right," I admit.

He leans forward, placing his hand beneath my chin and lifting it. His eyes lock with mine. They're so blue and inviting. I feel like I could swim in them. "Do you not want me to like them?" he asks.

"No, it's not that."

"Then what is it? You seem disappointed."

He's right. I am. But I'm not sure why that it is. My eyes trace the outline of his sharp jaw. "I don't know. I guess I just thought you'd be a little protective of me."

Robbie leans back and lets out a laugh. "You want me to rough one of them up? Probably not Shawn or Tyler. They're my size or bigger. Maybe Nash?" he teases.

I giggle. "No, just question them and make sure their intentions are right. One of the guys is apparently a liar, and I'd hate to pick the wrong one."

"I'd hate that too," he says.

CHAPTER 8

Robbie opens his laptop and places it on the kitchen counter. A large easel stands beside him with an oversized notepad propped up on it. On the first page are the words *Dude Deep Dive* written in Sharpie. Maya is seated next to me on the couch munching on popcorn. Debbie sits in the sofa chair. A notebook is in her lap, a pen is in one hand, and a glass of red wine is clutched in the other.

"Do we really have to do this?" I groan. "Can't I just go on the dates and decide from there?"

Robbie dramatically extends a metal pointer stick. It clicks as it grows in length to nearly three feet. "No," he says. "We have all gathered to ensure you make the right decision, and the only way to do that is by having all of the information. This will lessen the risk of heartbreak and potentially picking the wrong guy. Assessing risk is my specialty."

"That's right," Debbie says. "This is more fun than my soaps." She sips wine.

"And I'm in the funny business, so I'll be a pro at making sure none of your wooers are up to any funny business." Maya gives a firm nod but is barely able to contain her growing grin. She slides a pad of paper from her bag and finds her page. It's the same one she's been using to take notes in since I woke up in the hospital. "All right, Robbie. What do ya got?"

He exhales and paces in front of his easel. "I've conducted a digital deep dive on each of Peyton's suitors, and I found some interesting and less than interesting things during my research. Let's begin with Tyler Davis."

Robbie flips the piece of paper over the easel, revealing a page with a drawing of Bob the Builder and a list of bullet points off to the side. He gestures to each one as he goes over them. "Tyler works construction, lives alone in an apartment over in Fulton Market, and has a dog named Toby. He has two brothers and is the middle child, which tells me he craves attention."

"What? Why?"

"Classic middle-child syndrome," Maya says. "Trust me. I'm one of them." She delivers a coy look.

Robbie nods. "Maya's right. I've never met a person that needs more attention than her."

"Robbie," I chide.

"It's true, Peyton," she says.

"All right, back to Tyler." Robbie points at the easel. "His last serious relationship ended nearly two years ago."

"How did it end?" Debbie perks her head up.

"Mutually, according to social media posts from both him and the girlfriend. He wanted kids. She didn't."

"Do you want kids, Peyton?" Maya asks.

"Yeah, I think so. Someday."

Robbie continues. "Tyler's background check came back pretty clean. A couple of traffic violations for speeding, which tells me he moves fast . . . probably in relationships too." He raises an eyebrow and taps his pointer stick at the easel.

"Speeding tickets equates to moving fast in relationships? Did you stretch before you made that reach, Robbie?" Maya asks, cocking her head.

"No, I did not, Maya," he mocks.

I raise my brow. "You seriously pulled background checks, Robbie?"

"Of course. That's what a deep dive is."

"Tyler seems perfect." Debbie beams. "And he fixed my sink. Double points for that."

Robbie motions to her. "*Seems* is the right word. He has one fatal flaw."

I lean forward in my seat. What could possibly be wrong with Tyler? I really like him, and it's clear we have a strong connection. I hope he's not the liar because I think he's my strongest connection so far.

"What? What is it?" I ask.

Robbie turns over the page on the easel, revealing a new sheet. Written in large, bold letters is the word *Nickelback*.

"Noooo!" Maya yells.

"What's a nickelback?" Debbie asks, squinting.

"It's something we don't talk about. Very taboo, Debbie." He looks to me. "But I'm sorry to break the news to you, Peyton. He's a fan of Nickelback." Robbie lowers his head.

Confusion comes over me because I also don't know what or who Nickelback is. Or at least I don't remember.

Maya picks up on it and explains. "Nickelback is a Canadian rock band. Very commercial and all their songs sound the same. So people disliked them because they're bland and popular."

"That's it?" I ask.

"They're not true rock. They're corporate rock," Robbie says, shaking a fist to punctuate his words.

My brows scrunch together. "I'm not breaking it off with him because he's a fan of a band called Nickelback." I lean back, sinking into the cushion.

"I thought you'd say that." Robbie lifts his chin, and a look of determination comes over him. "There's more." He glances at the easel

103

and sighs, lifting the sheet of paper. A large blown-up picture is taped to it. Robbie taps the end of his pointer stick against the paper. "Look at this photograph," he says in a husky, singsong voice. It's a photo of Tyler standing shoulder to shoulder with four guys. NICKELBACK MEET AND GREET is written on a banner hung above them. "He's a superfan!"

I roll my eyes.

"Well, that is damning," Maya says. "Should I cross him off the list?"

"No." I glance back at the photo, taking in every detail. Tyler doesn't even have long hair in it. It's cut short. "And that's a really old picture, Robbie. He has to be, like, twenty-one in it."

"Once a Nickelback fan, always a Nickelback fan," he says.

"How did you even get that photo?"

"It's called a deep dive for a reason." Debbie hiccups and takes another sip of wine.

"Doesn't matter." Robbie smirks, tapping the metal pointer against the picture. "So, this isn't a deal-breaker for you?"

"No."

"Wow, I thought you had higher standards than that," he jokes. "All right, moving on."

Robbie flips the piece of paper, revealing a drawing of a rat in a chef hat. Written at the top is *Nash Doherty*. Just like with Tyler, there's a bulleted list beneath it.

"Why is he a rat?" I ask.

"Like in *Ratatouille*," Robbie says. "He's a Disney character that helps an inexperienced chef cook."

"Are you saying he's inexperienced as a chef?" I squint.

"No, that's why he's Remy the rat from *Ratatouille*." He points to the picture again. "Never mind."

"I could really go for another bowl of that chicken noodle soup right about now." Debbie smiles fondly.

Robbie slides the pointer stick down. "Anyway, Nash is thirty-five, originally from Wisconsin. He enjoys reading, mostly literary novels.

He recently announced a book deal for his very first cookbook, so he's been spending much of his time working on that. He has two sisters, and he's the youngest in his family. He lives alone in Logan Square. As far as a background check, he has an underage drinking ticket from when he was nineteen."

"Sounds like he likes to party," Debbie says, raising her glass of wine.

"Yeah, sixteen years ago," Maya teases. "That all seems fine," she says to Robbie and gestures for him to continue.

"Yep. Sounds good to me too," I say with a nod.

"But wait, there's more," Robbie adds dramatically in an infomercial-like voice. He slowly turns the page, revealing the word *RELATIONSHIP* written in all caps. A red circle is drawn around it with a line slashed through the middle.

"What does that mean?" Debbie asks.

"It means he has never been in a serious relationship," Robbie explains.

"Red flag." Maya puts her hand up.

"Maybe he hasn't found the right person," I argue. "Or maybe he just didn't post about his relationships?"

"Nope, I cross-checked with his family and close friends. His mother has commented on a number of his Facebook posts asking when he's going to bring a girl home for them to meet," Robbie explains.

"That's kind of embarrassing. I'd block my mom if she did that to me," Maya says.

I toss a few kernels of popcorn in my mouth and chew slowly. It's definitely something I should ask Nash about. Maybe he doesn't do serious relationships, or maybe there is something wrong with him.

"Wait, have I had any serious relationships?"

Robbie, Maya, and Debbie each deliver a sympathetic look.

"Not super serious," Maya says.

Debbie taps her finger against her chin, pondering. "I think all of yours have ended under the eight-month mark."

My eyes widen. "Why?"

"They just weren't right for you." Robbie pulls his brows together.

I lean back into the cushion and put a pillow in my lap, folding my arms over it. "It sounds like I'm a red flag too."

"No, sweetie." Debbie gives me an endearing look. "You're like a walnut, tough to crack."

I let out a huff. "Sounds more like tough to love."

Maya turns her body toward me and grabs my hand. "That's not true. We all love you," she says.

"But you're like family. I'm talking a romantic relationship." I press my lips together, forming a straight line, and let my shoulders slump. If that were true, I wouldn't be in this situation. I would have woken up in that hospital with the love of my life sitting beside me, waiting for me to come back to him. I would have known instantly even without my memories that he was my other half. But instead, it was three guys I've been serial dating for less than two months, and my heart has no clue which one I truly love.

"You have three guys vying for you, and any one of them would be lucky to be with you," Robbie says. His face has turned serious. "Trust me, Peyton, you're not hard to love."

"He's right." Debbie smiles warmly.

Maya pats my hand and leans back in her seat. "And if I didn't love you, I'd have pretended I didn't know you when I realized you had amnesia. Like the husband in *Overboard*, I would have been like, 'Peace out, stranger.'"

I let out a laugh. They're right. I may not know which of these men I love, but I know I love Maya, Robbie, and Debbie, and they love me back. That's been enough for me all this time.

"All right, are you good to continue?" Robbie asks.

I nod.

He returns to his oversized notepad, flipping the page. "Moving on to Shawn Morris." There's a drawing of an airplane with money falling from it. His name is written at the top, and there's a bullet point list beneath it. "Shawn is originally from Chicago. He's thirty-four and one of three children. He's more of a homebody, probably because he travels so much for work. It appears he either enjoys interior design or hires someone to do it for him. His apartment is remarkable. I'm talking sleek and modern with a rustic feel. Very bachelor pad style in a classy, upscale way."

"Can you stop talking about his apartment? And tell us about him?" Maya says.

"Fine. I was just very impressed. He lives in a high-rise in the Gold Coast. He's neat and organized, and also a gym rat. I'm talking daily Instagram Stories of him hitting the weights," Robbie says. "I've actually started doing some of his routines." He flexes his bicep.

"You've been watching his daily Insta Stories?" Maya asks.

"Yeah, for research, obviously."

"You know he can see who watches them?"

"I did not know that." Robbie lowers his head. "So that is going to be awkward if it's brought up. Anyway, he works in consulting, as you all know, hence the airplane with all the monies. He's also a foodie and enjoys fine dining. Background check was clean as a whistle."

"What's the catch then?" I ask.

Robbie turns the page and flicks his pointer at the paper. Written eight times in all caps is the word *RELATIONSHIPS*.

"What does that mean?" Debbie asks.

"He's had a lot of serious relationships."

I squint. "Do any of them overlap?"

"Not that I could find. It seems on average his relationships last one to two years. And he was engaged once."

"Why did the engagement end?"

"I don't know. It was very unclear. Neither of them released one of those lame statements you write up in the Notes app and screenshot.

But they're both still friends on Instagram, so it seems like it was at least amicable."

"So, he moves on quickly?" Maya asks.

Robbie nods. "There's usually only a month or two between each of his relationships."

"Maybe he doesn't like being alone," I say.

"That could definitely be it." Debbie creases her brow. "My first husband had a new wife three months after our divorce. For him, though, probably couldn't stand not having someone to lie to." She shakes her head like she's trying to shake the memory of him away.

"So." I lift my chin. "I've got a Nickelback fan, Mr. No Relationships, and Mr. Lots of Relationships."

"Nickelback superfan," Robbie corrects.

"And one of them is a liar," Maya adds.

"And if you don't pick one before the twenty-eighth, you've got to marry Robbie," Debbie says with a wink.

"That's not true," he argues. "Peyton and I have already agreed there is no pact."

"I didn't," I say with a small smile just to egg him on.

He rolls his eyes. "And that's exactly why I'm helping you figure this out. I won't be your fall guy."

"I think you two would be cute together," Maya taunts, lifting a brow.

Debbie glances at him and then at me. "Oh yeah. I see it too."

Robbie groans and closes his notepad. "Peyton loves one of these men. She may not remember, but she does, and I'm going to make sure she picks the right one." He eyeballs Maya and Debbie and then turns to start disassembling his research easel and supplies.

"You're like a knight in aluminum foil, Robbie." Maya laughs.

I get up from my seat and help him. "They're just messing with you," I whisper. He bends down, trying to get the easel to fit in the carrying case. "Are you okay?"

Robbie pauses, clenching his jaw for a moment before relaxing it. "I just want you to be happy."

"I am happy."

"Good." He nods. "Because that's all I care about."

I pull my chin in and really stare into those blue eyes of his, searching them. "Are you happy, Robbie?"

He hesitates. "I am if you are."

It's an odd answer, but I don't push for another response or a clearer one because I don't want to upset him. One minute, he's cool with the whole dating-with-amnesia thing, and the next it seems like he has an issue with it. I know he wants the best for me. And I want the same for him. We exchange tight-lipped smiles and finish packing the easel away before taking our seats on the couch.

"Do you feel a little better about going on these dates?" Maya asks.

"A little. At least I know more about the guys and myself."

"Good, and it should help you weed out the liar too," she adds.

"Just bring them all here. I'll sniff him out," Debbie says confidently.

Maya stands from her seat and starts to collect her belongings. "We know you would, Debbie."

Debbie could identify the liar, but I think that's something I need to figure out on my own. I did it before, and I know I can do it again. I just have to trust my heart.

Maya swings her bag over her shoulder and slips on her shoes. "I've gotta get to work. The jokes aren't going to tell themselves."

"Have a good set," I say.

Robbie and Debbie say their goodbyes. Maya waves and trots down the stairs. The front door opens and closes. We all exchange glances while Debbie slowly gets out of her chair.

"My shows are starting soon, so I better get going."

"What shows?" I glance up at her. She straightens the chair, fluffs the pillows, and refolds a throw blanket, draping it over the back.

Debbie turns to face me. "Mostly reality TV. Tonight, it's *Bachelor in Paradise* and *Below Deck*."

"I thought you'd watch something more serious, like a drama or a legal series."

Debbie flicks her wrists. "Nah. I spent my whole life being serious. Now I just want to be entertained with a glass of wine in one hand and a carb in my other."

Robbie and I chuckle.

"You two holler if you need anything," Debbie calls out as she takes it slow down the set of steps.

It's a couple of hours later when Robbie and I are getting ready to go to bed.

"What are you doing?" he asks. He's dressed in a white T-shirt and a pair of plaid pajama pants. The handle of a brown ditty bag hangs from his pointer finger.

I tuck part of a fresh sheet under the couch cushions and set out a blanket and pillows. "Making my bed," I say.

Robbie delivers a stern look and walks over to his duffel bag, dropping his stuff into it. "You're not sleeping on the couch, Peyton."

"Yes, I am." I throw my hands on my hips so he knows I'm serious and won't be backing down. "You're too tall for this couch. I saw you this morning. Your legs extended, like, a foot past the armrest."

"Yeah, so?"

"It's not comfortable for you. I fit fine, so you can have my bed."

It's the least I can do. He's done so much for me, and I want him to be comfortable not sleeping like a folded-up pretzel every night.

"I am not taking your bed and having you sleep on the couch." He raises his chin. "You are supposed to be healing."

"And I'm not having you sleep on the couch." I raise my chin to match his.

He sighs and blows out his cheeks, running a hand through his dark brown hair. "Guess I'm not sleeping then."

"Don't be dumb, Robbie." I point toward the hallway. "You're sleeping in my bed."

"Nope. Not gonna happen."

I stare back at him but he doesn't budge. Grabbing the pillows from the couch, I let out a groan and stomp down the hallway.

"What are you doing, Peyton?" Robbie calls out as he follows me.

I turn on the bedroom light, toss the pillows on the bed, and start assembling a wall of them right in the center, from the headboard all the way to the foot of the bed.

"Really?" he asks.

"Really," I say, briefly glancing over at him with squinty eyes. I finish assembling our new sleeping arrangements and turn to face Robbie. "I've constructed a Great Wall of pillows," I say, gesturing to my creation.

"I can see that." He chuckles.

"You'll sleep on one side, and I'll sleep on the other. That way, we'll both be comfortable and well rested."

"This is unnecessary," he says, folding his arms across his chest.

"It's necessary, and it'll make me feel better knowing you're sleeping comfortably. So, go ahead and get snug as a bug."

Robbie laughs but stands there, assessing the situation. His gaze bounces from me to the bed and back again. This is a no-brainer. I won't have Robbie sleeping on the couch when I have this perfectly nice bed with more than enough space for the both of us and a pillow wall. I tell him I'm going to change quickly and disappear into the bathroom. When I return, I expect to have to storm into the living room and drag him back to my bed, but he's there, lying on the right side with the comforter pulled up to his chest.

"I'm snug as a bug," he says, wiggling his body under the covers.

I can't help but smile back at him. "Good," I say, turning off the bedroom light. I crawl into bed and pull the blankets up to my chest. Robbie and I lie on either side of the pillow wall in silence. After a few minutes, his breathing deepens, and I think he may have fallen asleep.

"Robbie," I whisper in the dark.

"Peyton," he whispers back.

"Do you think my memories are going to come back?"

"Yeah, I do."

I pull the covers up a little farther so they're practically nestled under my chin.

"Thanks."

"What are you thanking me for?" he asks.

"For being here."

"You don't have to thank me for that. That's what friends are for." I can't see him, but I feel like he's smiling, just a small one.

I stretch out and roll over, my foot accidentally slipping under the pillow wall. It touches his. His skin is warm and soft.

"Sorry," I say, pulling it back to my side.

"Jesus." Robbie flicks the comforter off him.

"What?" I jolt up.

It's dark but I can see the outline of his body. He jumps out of bed and walks to my dresser. A drawer slides open and closes.

Robbie shuffles toward me and flips the comforter up at the end of the bed.

"What are you doing?"

"Your feet are freezing." His hands find them. I giggle at his ticklish touch. He slides a thick sock onto each foot, making sure they're positioned correctly, the seams at the tips of my toes. He tucks the comforter and pats the top of it, right where my newly clothed feet are positioned. "Better?" he asks.

"Yes," I say with a laugh as he slides back into bed.

I wait a few minutes and whisper his name again. His breathing slows and deepens. When he doesn't respond, I know it's because he's fallen asleep. I close my eyes and smile, feeling safe and warm and knowing I'll sleep much better tonight.

CHAPTER 9

Nash leans his back against a vintage red Corvette parked in front of my townhome. He holds up his hand and delivers a small smile. He texted me earlier today, telling me to dress casual for our date. Well, specifically he said to wear *something I could get dirty*. I opted for a pair of blue jeans, Keds sneakers, and a graphic tee that says something like MICHAEL SCOTT'S DUNDER SCRANTON MEREDITH MEMORIAL CELEBRITY RABIES AWARENESS FUN RUN RACE FOR THE CURE. I know Debbie said I was a good person, but I had no idea I was into rabies charities. Must be a passion of mine. It's a bit chilly today, so I threw a jean jacket over the tee. I jog down the steps of the porch toward him.

When I reach Nash, he asks, "Ready?"

I nod. "Yeah. Ready to get dirty."

His cheeks flush as he pulls the passenger door open for me and gestures for me to step in.

"Nice ride," I say.

"Thanks. It was my dad's."

Nash closes the door and scrambles to the other side at a hurried yet casual pace. It's like he's trying not to appear anxious, and I find it cute that he's just as nervous as I am. He hops into the driver's seat, and we click our seat belts into place. The car revs to life.

"What's the plan?" I ask.

"It's a surprise," he says, tossing a smile at me. Nash puts the car in drive and pulls out onto the street.

"You said this car *was* your dad's." I give him a sympathetic look. I know what it's like to lose a parent—well, I don't remember. But I can feel it.

He nods. I want to ask him more, but I don't know what to say. There's never a right thing to say when it comes to grief and loss. I fiddle with my fingernails, busying myself.

"He passed a few years ago." Nash swallows hard, keeping his attention on the road.

"I'm sorry. I lost both my parents when I was eighteen." I take a small, deep breath, closing my eyes for a moment to stop myself from crying. It's strange—ever since Robbie told me they passed, I've wanted to cry but I've also not let myself. It almost feels like a defense mechanism, my body telling my mind, *You've grieved. You don't need to do it again.*

"I'm really sorry for your loss too," Nash says, briefly looking over at me.

I nod slightly. There's silence for a few moments as he drives through Wicker Park. I recognize Division Street, the one I found myself on when I stumbled into that coffee shop. It's bustling with people enjoying the sunny fall afternoon.

"Want to listen to some music?" he asks.

I tell him yes because I think we need to change the subject. Not exactly a great start for a first date . . . er, first date for me. He turns up the volume and death metal music plays. I instantly don't like it but I smile politely.

"Do you like it?"

"Sure," I say with a laugh.

He bobs his head and lip-synchs as he drives. It's definitely an acquired taste. I wonder if Robbie would think this was worse than Tyler liking Nickelback.

Around fifteen minutes and at least three scream-o songs later, the car stops in front of a restaurant called Gretel. It's a decent-size brick building painted white with oversized oak wooden doors. I remember him mentioning it at the hospital. It's where he works and where we had our first date (according to my planner).

"Here we are." Nash shuts the car off, and we exit the vehicle.

"Is it open?" I ask, peering at the unlit windows.

"Nope. It's just me and you."

He fiddles with his set of keys and unlocks the front door. Inside, Nash switches on the lights, illuminating the bar-restaurant. It has a rustic feel with dark finishings and warm lighting. Behind the bar and against the wall are floor-to-ceiling shelves filled with liquor bottles. A black iron ladder is attached to a sliding bar. It's looks like it belongs in a bookstore . . . the shelves and ladder, not the alcohol. The restaurant is a mix of booths and high-top tables, and even though it's empty, it feels full.

"This is amazing," I say, taking it all in.

"Thanks. I don't have anything to do with the design, just the cooking."

"I'm sure that's incredible too."

"Do you want to find out?" He glances at me. "I was thinking you and I could make lunch together and eat it here."

"Sounds good to me. What are we making?"

He raises a brow. "How about our famous Gretel griddle burgers and fries?"

"I'm in."

Nash leads me through the swinging door off the bar. It opens up to a large commercial kitchen. The lights flicker a couple of times before fully turning on. It's pristine and sterile with every metal surface shining. He clearly takes great pride in his work. Nash walks to a metal tub and turns a valve. He waits a few seconds and then lights the pilot.

"What's that?" I ask.

"A restaurant fryer. Gotta turn it on so it has time for the oil to heat up." He pulls a bin from a top shelf and rummages through it. "Now you gotta look the part."

I watch him, waiting to see what he has up his sleeve. He turns toward me, holding two dark-blue aprons with brown leather straps. Nash puts his head through the strap and quickly ties it behind his back.

"These are nice," I say, running my fingers over the thick denim-like fabric.

"Can I help you put it on?" His voice is low, and his rosy cheeks give away the fact that he's clearly nervous. We've had dates before, but maybe he's always been nervous like this. After all, he's never been in a serious relationship.

I remove my jean jacket and toss it onto a stool. "Nice shirt," he says with a chuckle.

I glance at the string of text plastered along my graphic tee and back at him. "Why are you laughing?"

"Your shirt. It's from *The Office*, the TV show."

I glance at it again and laugh. "I thought I was into rabies charities or something."

Still chuckling, he loops the apron over my head. I turn so my back is facing him. Nash ties and adjusts the leather straps, making sure it's a snug fit. His fingers graze my lower back through the T-shirt, and a tingle runs up my spine.

"There you are."

I turn to face him. We lock eyes but he looks away first, clasping his hands together and scanning the kitchen. "All right, burgers. Come with me."

Nash gathers the ingredients from the walk-in cooler, calling out each one as he hands some over and collects the rest. Ground beef. White American cheese. Yellow American cheese. Brioche buns. Red onions. Pickles. Garlic. Mayo. Olive oil. Lemon juice. Potatoes.

"Now what?" I ask, placing my armful of supplies on the metal table. He plops his down too.

"First, the fries. They take the longest. I'll scrub and slice up the potatoes. Why don't you form four beef patties, each about half the size of the palm of your hand?"

I nod and pull ground beef from the container, forming each hunk into balls.

Nash prepares the french fries. "Did you like the soup?" He glances over at me while continuing to rock the knife back and forth. I'm nervous he'll cut himself, but he never comes close. He's good with his hands. My cheeks start to blaze imagining what else he can do with those hands.

"Yeah, very much. It was delicious. Thank you."

"Glad you enjoyed it," he says with a smile, dropping the fries into the fryer. They sizzle in the hot oil. "Six minutes on the fries." His voice is commanding and in control. It's like I'm getting a glimpse of Chef Nash cooking up a hot dish on a Friday night, and I like it a lot. The fries aren't the only things sizzling right now.

He joins me at the table, his body standing just a few inches behind me. I fight the urge to back up into him. "Doing great," he says as I finish up the last patty. I can feel his hot breath on my skin. Nash turns on the griddle and then peels an onion with ease. The outside shell just falls right off, and I imagine my clothes doing the same. "Can you cut two thin slices?" he asks.

"Yeah." I pull a knife from a block and carefully slice through the onion.

Nash moves like lightning, slicing cheese and rough-chopping garlic. I can't imagine how fast he moves during a dinner rush on a weekend or in other places . . . I shake the thought away, forcing myself to focus on the task at hand. Who would have thought watching a man cook could be so sexy? He pulls out a small mixing bowl and adds the garlic, mayo, fresh ground pepper, and lemon juice.

"All done," I say.

Nash slides the bowl to me. "Can you mix that?"

I nod, getting right to work, but my gaze keeps going back to him. He drops the four balls of ground beef onto the griddle. They sizzle as he smashes each ball with a spatula, thinning them out as much as he can. The way Nash commands the kitchen is incredibly hot. It's like he finds his confidence here. I could literally watch him all day.

"How's this?" I ask, tilting the bowl of pale-yellow sauce toward him.

He sticks his pinkie in it and brings it to his mouth, licking it. "It's perfect."

"What is it?"

"Garlic aioli for the burgers and fries. Here, taste it." He dips his pointer finger into it and holds it up. I stare at him and then bring his finger to my mouth, sucking the aioli.

"Yum," I say, looking up through my lashes at him.

His cheeks flush again, and I think he might kiss me, but he wipes his hand on his apron and gets back to work at the stove, flipping the patties and toasting the buns. There's a real shyness to Nash that I find both frustrating and sexy, and I wonder when/if he'll break out of that shell.

"Can you pull the fries?"

"Yeah," I say, although I'm not entirely sure what that means.

I eye the bubbling, hot oil and then glance over at Nash. His back is toward me as he alternates between plopping white and yellow cheese on each patty.

"Nash."

He looks over his shoulder at me. His brow is already furrowed, but he quickly relaxes it, rushing to me. "Here," he says as he snakes his arms around my waist and guides my hand to the handle of the basket. Together we lift it and hook it on the wall, letting the excess oil drip back into the basin. "You got it," he whispers. His hot breath grazes my ear, sending a shiver down my spine.

Before I can say anything back, he's in front of the stove again, tending to the burgers. "Can you grab two plates from the corner over there?" Nash points off to a shelf. "Then go ahead and drop the fries again."

I do as he says like I'm the sous to his chef. "How long this time?"

"Just two minutes. Double-fried french fries are the best. Gives them a nice crunch," he says as he assembles a burger on each plate. "These are smash-patty burgers." He gestures to them. "They're far superior to hockey-puck patties, and smashing them creates these lacy, charred edges."

"They look amazing."

"And they taste even better." Nash winks.

I throw a smile over my shoulder while I keep an eye on the french fries and the clock on the wall. I glance back every few seconds or so, watching him assemble the toppings. He's laser-focused on his task at hand, and perhaps that's why he hasn't been in a serious relationship. Career over romance. But then what's my excuse? What have I been so focused on?

A hand brushes against my waist as I pull the fries again. I turn to find Nash standing behind me.

"Sorry," he mumbles as he shuts off the fryer.

"No need to be sorry," I say with a coy smile. *Because I liked it.* I don't say that part out loud.

He smiles back at me. Up close, I notice how clean shaven he is. Not a stubble or even a nick on his angled jawline. He smells of baked goods, and I wonder if he was baking before he picked me up for our date. Nash grabs the basket of fries and tosses them into a shallow metal basin.

"If you want to grab a table for us, I'll finish plating and bring these out," he offers.

"You got it." I untie my apron and hand it over.

In the dining area, I take a seat at a corner booth in the front. A large window sits behind it, overlooking the sidewalk and street. A sprinkling of people pass by.

"Who's ready to eat?" Nash calls out. He crosses the restaurant carrying a plate in each hand and smiling all the way. I've noticed his grin growing throughout our date, like he's getting more confident in showing off his happiness. It makes me smile a little wider too.

"It looks great," I say as he sets down the food and pulls two bottles of water from his apron. The cheese and garlic aioli ooze out of the sides of the burgers. There's a heaping pile of crispy fries on each plate with a small ramekin of dipping sauce beside it. Nash takes a seat and tells me to dig in.

I pick up the burger and practically unhinge my jaw in order to get a full bite of it. It's the perfect balance of flavors, a mix of acidity, saltiness, meatiness, and tang. Plus, the char on the meat is a nice addition. Nash was right about that. All together it creates a sort of umami flavor. I nod several times while chewing and wipe my mouth and chin with a napkin.

"So, what do you think?" Nash waits to dive into his own until he hears my feedback. Such a gentleman and a chef.

"Incredible. You were right about the smash patties."

"That's exactly what you said last time." He smiles, picks up his burger, and bites into it.

"Really?"

Nash nods as he uncaps the bottle of water and takes a swig. "It's been like déjà vu for me today. Even without your memories, you did and said everything practically the same. Rather remarkable." He dips a couple of fries into the aioli and eats them.

I wonder if this date was boring for him since I did and said everything the same. I hope it wasn't. But at least I know I'm still Peyton. I eat a couple of fries, one with the aioli and one without. It's better with the sauce.

He glances over at me. "What's it like?"

"What's what like?"

"Not having memories." Nash sighs. "I know it's a strange question, so you don't have to answer it." He bites into his burger. Gooey cheese, aioli, and oil squeeze out the other side, dropping onto his plate.

He's the first one to ask me that question, and I like that he did. It shows he cares how I'm feeling and what I'm experiencing.

"It's strange. It's like there's nothing guiding me. You know? Most of what we do and say is dictated by our past experiences. But mine is a blank page. And sometimes I can sort of feel the memories, but I don't know what they are." I swirl a fry in the garlic aioli.

"What do you mean you can feel them?"

"Like I'll do something or taste something or smell something, and it'll be familiar and comforting. But I don't why it is," I say, eating the warm, crunchy french fry.

"You could write a book about it." He gives me a half smile.

"Yeah, maybe. Something like *Dating with Amnesia*." I laugh.

"I'd read it." He chuckles and clears his throat. There're a few beats of silence. Nash tilts his head. "Are you scared your memories won't come back?"

I pull my lips in and glance down for a moment, knowing it's something I've thought about a lot—even though I've tried not to. "Terrified," I say.

"I'm sorry it happened to you."

"Me too." I shrug. "But on the bright side, I got to cook with you twice." I bump my shoulder into his playfully and smile.

"Lucky me," he says.

We take a couple more bites of our burgers, exchanging glances and small smiles while we eat. I like this. I like the moments we're talking and engaged, and I even like the quiet ones. But then I remember there are two other guys I'm dating, and that I need to figure out which one I love. One thing I have to ask Nash about is his past relationships—or lack thereof. Maya said it was a red flag, but maybe it's not. Because if it is for him, it is for me too.

"I'm not sure what we've all talked about, so I'm sorry if this is repetitive. But can you tell me about your past relationships?" I briefly glance over at him. "I'd tell you about mine but I don't remember."

He cracks a grin and wipes his mouth with a napkin. "There's not much to tell. I haven't really had any serious relationships."

"Oh, why's that?" I stare into his hazel eyes.

His cheeks flush. "I'm not really good at dating."

I reach for his hand and place mine on his. The color on his cheeks deepens, but he doesn't pull away. I think he and I are more alike than I know. I'm not so much timid. But I do understand keeping people at arm's length—almost like a defense mechanism.

His fingers graze mine. "I have a hard time opening up," he says, pulling his chin in. "And I've put such a focus on my career that everything else has taken a back seat, but I also think I've used my career as an excuse for a long time because I am scared to let someone in."

"I understand," I say. "At least I think I do."

Nash delivers a small smile.

I study his face, taking in the smattering of freckles on the bridge of his nose, his clean-shaven skin, and his slender lips. My gaze lands on his armful of colorful tattoos.

"Did those hurt?"

His hand slips away from mine as he picks up his arm, twisting and turning it so I can see more. Nash pulls up his short sleeve, revealing his strong bicep and putting all his tattoos on full display. "Only some of them did. This one right here"—he points to a detailed angel with golden wings on the back of his upper arm, the words *RIP Dad* written in cursive below it—"hurt the most. Probably because it meant the most."

My fingers skim over the meticulously drawn tattoo. "It's beautiful," I say. His skin blossoms with goose bumps, and he smiles.

"Thanks." He slides his sleeve down as I pull my fingers away. "Do you have any tattoos?"

"Not that I know of," I say with a giggle.

"Do you want one?"

"I don't know. Maybe." I shrug. "What made you want them?"

"Initially, I wanted one to piss off my parents back when I was eighteen. But after that, I actually really liked them. It's fun going through the design process, ensuring they look good together, and they all have some sort of meaning to me. Some have more significance than others." He smirks. "This one was a dare." Nash points to a small tattoo on his wrist.

"Does that say *live, laugh, love*?"

He nods and stifles a chuckle. "It reminds me to live and to laugh and to love every day." He can barely finish his sentence due to his growing laughter.

"I could use that reminder given the amnesia," I joke.

"Do you want to get a matching one?" he says playfully.

I shake my head and laugh before biting into my burger once more. I set it back down on the plate, leaving two bites behind.

"Even with the live, laugh, love tattoo, I think it's a cool look." I smile at him and wipe my hands and face with the cloth napkin.

"Thanks." He pops the last bite of his burger in his mouth.

The lock on the front door clicks and the door swings open. A younger guy with a goatee and dark hair walks in. He jumps a little when he sees us.

"You startled me, boss." The man holds his hand to his chest and chuckles in relief.

"Sorry, Vince," Nash says. "This is Peyton." He gestures to me. "And this is my sous chef, Vince."

He waves and tells me it's a pleasure.

"I thought I was your sous chef," I say to Nash flirtatiously. He blushes as I look to the real sous chef. "Nice to meet you, Vince."

"He put you to work on your date, didn't he?" Vince cracks a smile. His gaze darts between Nash and me.

"He did," I banter. "Made me cook my own fries and everything."

"This is why you're perpetually single, Nash." Vince chuckles.

"All right, get to work," Nash says with a lighthearted tone.

Vince tells him he'll be in the back prepping. He waves us off and disappears through the swinging door into the kitchen.

"Do you have to work too now?" I ask. There's an air of disappointment in my voice.

"Unfortunately." Nash slides out of the booth and grabs our plates. "I'll just clean these up quick."

As he walks toward the kitchen, my phone buzzes with a text from Maya. Hey, I can swing by and pick you up from your date if you're ready. I'm in the area because I've gotta return a pair of pants to Nordstrom anyway. But no worries if not. Let me know.

I text back. Actually, now's perfect. I figure I may as well have Maya pick me up so I don't take up any more of Nash's time, especially since his sous chef is here.

"Ready to head out?" Nash dusts his hands off as he walks toward me. He's so much more confident in himself here. I wish I could see that side of him outside the restaurant, but perhaps all our dates will have to be here. I slide out of the booth and slip my jean jacket on.

"Actually, Maya is on her way to pick me up. She was in the area anyway. Is that okay?"

His brows pull together and disappointment washes over him. He almost seems to deflate, but he quickly unfurrows his brow and picks his shoulders back up. "Yeah, yeah, of course."

"When would you like our next date to be?" I ask.

His face brightens, and he closes the distance between us, standing only a couple of feet away. "How about Sunday night, say 7:00 p.m.? I'd like to take you on a date at a proper time."

I smile up at him. "That sounds great."

He stares at me and licks his lips like he's preparing to kiss me, but I'm not sure he will. So instead I make the first move. I stand on my tippy-toes and lean in. My lips find his, and he kisses me back gently. It's warm and tender. It only lasts a few seconds before we both pull away. When I open my eyes, he's smiling back at me.

"Was that our first kiss?" I look up at him.

"Yeah." He blushes. "How'd you know?"

"I could feel it."

CHAPTER 10

"So, how'd it go?" Maya asks as I slide into her Nissan Altima. She raises her brows twice and slightly lowers her oversized sunglasses, showing just the top of her light-brown eyes. Her lips are painted a bold red, making her teeth appear even whiter.

"Amazing. Nash is such an incredible guy." I close the door and buckle my seat belt.

"Did you kiss?" Her mouth twitches.

I can feel my cheeks warm. "Just a little."

Maya pats the steering wheel and snorts. "Look at you. Wakes up from a coma and kisses two guys in twenty-four hours. It's like the PG-13 version of *Sleeping Beauty*," she says, pulling the car out onto the street.

"But Sleeping Beauty needed the kiss to wake up. I'm just trying to get my memories back." *But right now, I'm okay with not having them.* I don't say that part out loud because I know it sounds odd, and I also don't know how to explain it. As much as I want my memories back, I'm starting to enjoy living without them. It's freeing in a way.

"Ooooh, maybe it'll be like a movie and when you finally realize which one you love, poof, all your memories will return." Maya glances over at me with a half grin.

"One can only hope." I pull the visor down and apply lip balm and check my teeth in the mirror. All good.

"Since you've kissed Tyler and Nash now, which one do you feel you have a stronger connection with?"

I close the visor and cap the lip balm, returning it to my purse. "Tyler, I think. But maybe that's because we've been intimate."

She turns left at an intersection. "Or maybe it's lust with Tyler." Maya raises her brows.

"Could be. But with Nash, it's sensual and cute at the same time. There's just something about him."

"Oh la la, tell me more," she says, pulling the car into a parking lot.

"It was . . ." It takes me a moment to land on the right word. "Sweet." *Sweet, yes, that's it.* "He showed me around the kitchen, and he *really* knows his way around a kitchen."

"I don't know why, but that sounds incredibly hot." Maya waggles her eyebrows.

"Right? We literally cooked fries and burgers, and somehow it was sexy. He's really shy, though, but this sort of quiet confidence came out while he was cooking."

"Quiet confidence? That sounds hot too."

"It is, and I loved seeing another side of him."

"Speaking of another side of him, did you find out more about the whole no-serious-relationships thing?" Maya parks and we get out of the car. She pops the trunk and grabs a shopping bag from it.

"He said he's been focused on his career, but really he just has a hard time letting people in," I say as we stroll side by side across the lot.

"And he's ready to let you in?" She pulls her sunglasses off and slips them into her bag, raising a brow.

"I guess so. I mean, he's going along with this whole dating-again situation."

"True." Maya nods. "And he kissed you."

"No, I kissed him."

"Look at you being all forward."

We reach the store, and she holds the door open for me.

I push out my bottom lip. "Am I usually not like that?"

The department store is huge and brightly lit with tall ceilings. Racks of clothing are spaced out nicely, and customers and employees roam the floor.

"Not usually," she says, strolling to the customer service desk like she's on a mission, or trying to avoid all the flashy sale signs.

A middle-aged woman with a dark bob haircut helps Maya with her return. When she's done, Maya turns to me.

"Do you want to shop or go?"

I glance around the store again. It's all so overwhelming, and I don't even know what I would like or if I need anything. Or if I have money? Like, how am I financially? I remind myself to dig into that.

"Up to you," I say.

"My mind is telling me to shop, but my credit card balance is telling me to get my ass outa here." She looks fondly at the clothing and then back at me. "I better listen to my credit card balance."

Maya nods and makes a beeline for the exit before she changes her mind. Back in the car, she shoves her keys into the ignition, but before starting up the engine, she turns to me with a serious look. "Are you sure this all isn't too much on you? The dating multiple guys, I mean?"

"I don't think so—at least not yet."

"I just want to make sure since Robbie changed his stance on the whole thing. He's usually the voice of reason for us, so I guess I have to be, or at least try to be." She chuckles.

I smile at the thought of Robbie keeping us out of trouble over the years.

"I'm good right now. But . . . when I have to start making decisions, I don't know how I'll feel or if I'll be able to handle it." I fiddle with my nails. They're painted a light pink, but most of the polish has peeled off. The scrapes on my fingers are nearly healed. Soon the only evidence of the accident will be the memories I no longer have.

"You will. Anything life has thrown your way, you've always handled. And it's thrown a lot at you. Plus, you have me and Robbie and Debbie all by your side." She reaches over and squeezes my hand.

"Thanks."

"Now let's get you a manicure," she says, inspecting my nails. "Because this is not cute."

"In my defense, I was hit by a car and in a coma for several days." I pull my hand away and examine them up close. They're chipped and broken.

"No excuse," she says, turning on the engine and putting the car in reverse. "I actually tried to do your nails when you were in the coma, but one of the nurses yelled at me for removing that little device you had clipped to your finger."

"You mean the device that measures how much oxygen is in my blood and helps determine whether I need to be ventilated or intubated?"

"Yep. That's the one," Maya says as she points the car toward the city skyline and drives.

It's a few hours later. Our nails are freshly painted and up to Maya's standards. She opted for a bright red, and I picked the same color I had before the accident, a shade called Ballet Slippers. I was going to go bold, but I figured the version of me with my memories liked a more muted color, so I chose the same.

Maya and I exit the elevator of a high-rise building. I've been here before many times, but I don't remember it.

"This way," Maya says, directing me down a long hallway. Numbered doors are spaced out evenly on either side.

She knocks on one of them but then immediately opens it, not waiting for an answer. The apartment is minimalist, with large floor-to-ceiling windows overlooking the Chicago skyline. The kitchen and living room are open concept like mine but with a more spacious floor plan. The camel-colored leather couch, matching recliner, and big-screen TV give the whole place a real bachelor-pad appearance. A desk is tucked away in the far corner, complete with dual monitors and several stacks of paperwork. Robbie spins his chair around and pulls off a pair of reading glasses, blinking several times as though his vision is taxed from staring at his computer screen.

"Don't you knock, Maya?" He narrows his strained eyes, then stands from his desk and stretches his arms over his head, revealing a sliver of his abdomen.

"I did, and then I immediately opened the door," she says, placing her hands on her hips.

He rubs a hand over his face. "What are you two up to?"

Robbie moseys around the living room randomly, tidying up like he's trying to make it more presentable for us. He picks up an empty bowl, fluffs a couple of pillows, and folds a throw blanket.

"I'm working a server shift at Gilt Bar before my set tonight, so I've gotta go in early," Maya explains. "I figured since we were already in the area getting our nails done"—she splays her hands out and wiggles her fingers—"I'd just drop Peyton off, and you could bring her back when you're done with work." She seals her plan with a smile.

Robbie scratches the back of his neck. "Works for me. I'm finishing up, so it'll be another thirty minutes or so before we can head out. Is that all right?"

"Yeah." I kick off my shoes and plop down on the couch, putting my feet up on the coffee table. I run a hand over the couch. "This is nice. Is this real leather?"

"It is." He grins. "You actually helped me pick it out."

"Really?" I smile back. "I have good taste then."

"In furniture, yes," Robbie says coyly. He walks around the island counter into the kitchen area and places his bowl in the dishwasher.

131

Only in furniture . . . I wonder what it is he thinks I don't have good taste in.

"All good?" Maya asks, giving me two thumbs-up.

"Yep, all good," I say.

Robbie nods.

"Great, you kids have fun," she says, backing out of the apartment and closing the door behind her.

Robbie picks up two remotes from a tray on the coffee table and hands them to me. "That's for the TV, and that's for the Fire Stick. I have basically every streaming service because I keep forgetting to cancel them, so feel free to put on whatever you'd like."

I glance at the remote in each hand and then up at Robbie. "What do I like?"

He takes a seat, extending a hand toward me. I place the remotes in the palm of it. Robbie turns on the TV and begins scrolling through various apps.

"This is your favorite rom-com," he says, pointing to the screen.

"*Never Been Kissed?*"

He nods. "You've watched it, like, fifty times."

"Jeez, you'd think I'd remember what it was about."

Robbie glances over at me and laughs.

"What's my favorite action movie?"

"*Die Hard,*" he says. "Whenever you're sick, you watch all the *Die Hard* movies, and you claim they make you feel better."

"Do I feel better after watching them?"

Robbie taps his finger against his chin as though pondering my question. "Actually, yes. But there are five in the series, and it takes you a couple of days to get through them, so it's more likely the illness just runs its course."

"From a scientific standpoint, my theory is sound."

He chuckles and browses through more apps.

"What about you? Favorite rom-com? Or are you one of those guys who claims to hate them?" I shift in my seat so I'm partially facing Robbie.

"I am, but you and Maya have made me watch an ungodly number of rom-coms, so I've basically been forced to have a favorite simply due to the sheer number of them I've seen." He simpers.

Pulling the throw blanket from the back of the couch, I drape it over our laps. "And which is your favorite?"

"*13 Going on 30*," he says without missing a beat.

"Why?"

"I don't know. The nostalgia, being able to get a different perspective on life by going back and doing things differently." Robbie shrugs. "It's just a cute movie with a good message."

"I'll have to watch it then . . . or better yet, rewatch it."

Robbie glances down at his watch, noting the time, and passes me the remotes. He shuffles the blanket off his lap and stands.

"All right, let me finish up my work real quick and then we can head out." He claps his hands together like he's giving himself a pep talk.

My gaze swings from the TV screen to him as he crosses the living room and takes a seat at his desk. I scroll through a selection of movies and shows, none of which are familiar to me. I'm sure I've seen most of them but nothing sticks out. I glance over at Robbie again. He types quickly like he's racing to be done. I notice his shoulders are tense.

My phone buzzes, stealing my attention. It's a text from Shawn. Hope you're having a good week. Looking forward to our date on Friday night.

I punch out several replies, deleting and retyping them. First I type out, I can't wait too!! But I figure it sounds too eager, especially considering I'm dating two other guys. I delete the exclamation points and replace them with a period. Now it sounds like I'm not excited at all. I delete the whole text and start over. I type, Hello, Shawn. I too am looking forward to our date on Friday evening. Nope, that's entirely too formal and sounds kind of creepy. What is wrong with me? Why can't I just type out a simple text to a guy I'm dating? I let out a groan.

"What's wrong?" Robbie asks, swiveling his head in my direction.

"Nothing," I say, pressing the delete button firmly until the whole text disappears from the screen.

He scrunches up his face. "It doesn't seem like nothing."

"It's dumb. I got a text from Shawn, and I don't know how to reply." I sigh. "This whole dating more than one guy is harder than I thought it'd be because I don't want it to seem like I'm more interested in one over the other, at least not at this point."

"What did he say to you?" Robbie spins his chair around and crosses his arms over his chest.

"Just that he hoped I was having a good week and that he couldn't wait for our date on Friday night."

"Well, say the same thing back."

Another text pops up on the screen from him. "He also just texted that I should wear something nice for our date. What does that mean?"

"I think it means not *The Office* rabies T-shirt and ripped jeans you're currently sporting." He stifles a laugh.

I stare at the screen and type out another text. Looking forward to Friday night too! And how nice? I hit "Send" and exhale.

Another text pops up. Dress to impress 😊

I eye Robbie, who's staring intently at me. He clears his throat and straightens up.

"Shawn told me to dress to impress. Do I have anything impressive to wear?"

"I'm sure you do. But if not, we'll figure something out."

A corner of my mouth lifts. "You're going to help me pick out a dress for my date?"

"Of course, that's what friends who don't want to honor silly marriage pacts do." He half smiles.

I press my lips into a thin line and force a smile back. Robbie spins around in his chair, refocusing on his work. Why is he so adamant about me dating one of these guys to avoid the dumb pact we made when we were in college? Is he not attracted to me? Have we tried dating before? I know Maya said we didn't, but maybe we did and she didn't know about it. Does he really only see me as a friend? Sometimes I get the feeling that he sees me as something more. It's in his pauses, the words he speaks and doesn't speak, the way his gaze lingers on me, and everything he's done since I've woken up from my coma. But if that's what Robbie wants, then I'll date the hell out of these guys. I pull my phone back out and send three texts. One to Tyler. One to Nash. And one to Shawn. They all say the exact same thing: Thinking of you.

I turn my attention to Robbie, staring at the back of his head. His dark hair is cut close and tapers at the nape of his neck. There are three small moles right below his hairline, stacked in a curved line like Orion's Belt. I wonder if I ever noticed them before.

My phone buzzes, a text from Shawn. I know. We were just texting.

Well, that's embarrassing.

Two more texts come through. One from Nash and one from Tyler. They both say, Thinking of you too.

My stomach rumbles, and Robbie snaps his head in my direction. "Was that your stomach?"

I slowly nod as my cheeks warm like I'm standing next to a fire.

"All right, let's go," he says, powering down his computer.

"Don't you have work to finish?"

"Yeah, but the work is never finished, so it can wait." He waves his hand dismissively at the computer. Robbie scoops a backpack from beside his desk and walks to the door, slipping on a coat and a pair of tennis shoes. "Besides, I can't work with all that loud rumbling, so let's get you something to eat." He cracks a smile, and I can't help but do the same. The heat dissipates from my cheeks. Somehow, Robbie makes me feel fearless.

We're seated across from one another in a booth at a restaurant just a couple of blocks away from my home. It's spacious with high ceilings and exposed wood beams. The place has an industrial style mixed with black finishings and pops of dark green. It feels both cozy and sprawling. A young server sporting a pixie haircut hands us two menus and says she'll be back with waters. She skips off into the busy restaurant, tending to other patrons.

"Whatcha thinking?" Robbie asks, flicking his menu.

I take my eyes off the hustle and bustle of the place and refocus them on the menu.

"The Wrightwood salad looks good," I say.

"It is." He grins at me. "And it's what you always order."

I'm not sure if I should groan or be happy about that. I keep doing the same things I would have done with my memories. Like ordering the same dish. Picking the same coffee shop. Saying the same things. Maybe I don't have to worry that I'll make the wrong choice when it comes to figuring out which man I love. Even without my memories, I'm still me. It's like my essence—my personality and soul—has remained intact. But should I really be trying to do and say the same things? Doing all that has led me down a path of fling-y relationships, serial dating, and the inability to love and be loved.

I shrug. "Guess I'll have to try something new then."

Robbie gives me a peculiar look but doesn't say anything.

The waitress sets two glasses of water in front of each of us. "Ready to order?" she asks in a high-pitched, cheery voice.

Robbie gestures to me.

I order the chicken dip sandwich. Time to switch it up. He orders a cheeseburger and a pilsner beer.

"Anything else?" she asks.

"Yeah, let's start with the cheese curds too," I say, handing over the menu.

She jots down our order and tells us she'll be right back with the drink.

Robbie peers over his glass as he sips his water. "So, you had a date today?"

"I did. With Nash."

"The chef?"

"That's the one."

"And?" Robbie raises his brows. "Is he a top contender?"

"He could be." My eyes jump around the restaurant before landing back on Robbie. "He's really sweet and thoughtful, but I don't know him all that well yet."

"Well, that's going to be true for all of them at this point, right?"

I nod and sip my water.

"Did you get the feeling you knew him well before the accident?"

The server returns, setting the beer in front of Robbie and a basket of cheese curds in the center of the table. She leaves us with a smile. Robbie plucks a cheese curd from the basket and dunks it into the aioli. I watch him as he waits for the excess sauce to drip off before popping it into his mouth. He moans quietly as he chews, savoring the flavor.

"Maybe," I say, eating a curd. "But then again, maybe not."

Robbie drinks his beer and surveys me over the rim of his glass like he's appraising my answer. "Who's your strongest connection?"

"I've only had a date with Nash so far and an impromptu lunch with Tyler. My date with Shawn is Friday night, and tomorrow night is my actual date with Tyler. At this point, I guess I'd have to say Tyler."

Robbie leans back in his seat. "Why's that?"

I eat another cheese curd and wash it down with water, mulling over my answer. Robbie's gaze is intense as he waits for me to speak. I don't want to tell him I was intimate with Tyler before the accident, and I'm not sure why I don't want him to know that. But then again, does intimacy even equal connection? And maybe I didn't even enjoy it. I'm going off things I don't even remember because I have so little to base any of my feelings on.

I finally land on, "It feels easy with Tyler—or no, natural. Yeah, it feels natural, comfortable." Does it really feel easy or natural? What even is easy or natural? I don't know anymore.

Robbie furrows his brow, and his gaze veers to the right of me.

"Speak of the devil," he says.

I turn my head, following his line of sight. Standing at the bar, dressed in blue jeans, workman boots, and a flannel shirt is Tyler. His long hair is hidden under a black beanie, and he's surrounded by a couple of large guys in similar attire. They must have all come from work.

"First round's on me," Tyler says, slapping two twenties against the bar. The bartender slides four pints of beer toward Tyler and his friends. The guys cheers one another. Someone must have said something funny because they crack up laughing before extinguishing their laughter with a gulp of their drinks.

"It's like it's meant to be," Robbie says in a monotone voice. When I turn to glance back at him, he's already chugged half of his beer. "Should we call him over?" he asks, wiping his mouth with the back of his hand.

"No," I say. "He's with his work friends, and you and I are having dinner."

Robbie shrugs and delivers a devilish grin. "Sorry, Peyton. I gotta stay true to the new pact."

"Robbie, don't," I warn.

"Hey, Tyler!" he yells across the bar, ignoring my request. "Tyler!"

"Robbie, stop it."

He continues to call his name and flail his hand until he gets Tyler's attention. After fifteen seconds of yelling, Tyler finally notices Robbie . . . and then me. A crooked smile settles on his face, and he waves back.

"I've gotta be your wingman," Robbie says with a can-do attitude.

"I don't want you to be my wingman." I clench my teeth. "I wanted to have dinner with you."

He studies me, and his face becomes serious for only a moment before he shrugs and says, "A pact's a pact."

I groan and glance across the restaurant. Tyler leans into one of his friends, whispers something, and pats him on the back before making his way toward our table.

"Here comes your man," Robbie whispers.

I shoot him a glare. "He's not my man. He's one of three."

"You said he was a top contender, your strongest connection."

"I said he could be, now will you shush? He's going to hear you," I whisper back.

Tyler stops right in front of our table with a grin plastered across his face. "Hey, what are you two doing here?"

"Just having dinner," I say, forcing a smile. I'm not sure if I should stand and give him a hug or kick Robbie in the shin.

Tyler puts his hand on my shoulder and lightly squeezes. "It's good to see you," he says in a low voice.

"You too," I say with a nod.

"Sit. Join us." Robbie beckons.

I narrow my eyes at him.

"Oh no, I don't want to intrude." Tyler politely tries to protest.

"And he's with his friends," I say, kicking Robbie in the shin under the table.

He makes a quiet *ouch* sound but puts on a small smile. "You're not intruding at all. Go ahead and take a seat next to Peyton."

"Are you sure?" Tyler asks.

Robbie nods. "Yes, she is."

I scooch over, giving him room to slide in. Tyler shuffles in his seat. He smells like sawdust with a hint of tobacco. I kind of like it, so I inhale the scent.

"Did you two order already?"

"Yeah," I say.

"I can flag the server down for you," Robbie offers, already raising his hand.

"That's all right. I ordered at the bar, so I'll just snag it when it's ready." Tyler gulps his beer.

"A man with a plan," Robbie says. "I like it."

Tyler nods and half smiles as though he doesn't know how to respond. His beard is dark and cut close, showing off his strong jaw and prominent chin. He looks like one of those Greek statues you'd see in a museum, perfectly carved and sculpted. He glances at me from the corner of his eye again.

"What other plans do you have?" Robbie asks, staring directly at Tyler.

Is Robbie going to grill him right in front of me? The intensity in his eyes tells me he is. I pop a cheese curd in my mouth, bracing myself for an awkward conversation and whatever else Robbie has up his sleeve.

"What do you mean? Like in business or life?" Tyler asks, sipping his beer again.

"No." He gestures to me. "With Peyton."

I push the cheese curds more toward Tyler, offering him one as a way to distract him from Robbie's imminent interrogation. He shakes his head slightly, declining my offer, and clears his throat. "Well, I'd like to be her boyfriend."

"So, that's your plan?" Robbie asks.

He nods.

"And what if Peyton chooses someone else?"

They're talking about me like I'm not sitting right here. "Robbie, stop."

"What?" One side of his mouth pulls up and back, and he shrugs. "It's just a question."

"I don't mind," Tyler says to me.

"See? He doesn't mind, and I'm just making sure his intentions are pure." Robbie leans back and gulps his beer. "Someone that really cares for Peyton will respect her decision and want her to be happy regardless."

"I agree. If she chose one of the other guys, I'd still want the best for her, even if it's not me."

"Good answer," he says.

I'm starting to think Robbie doesn't believe Tyler is the right guy for me. Why else would he ask a question like that? Would he ask the same of Nash or Shawn? I stare at Robbie, skimming over his face in an attempt to get a read on him.

"It's just an honest one." Tyler takes a drink, peering at Robbie over the rim of his glass. He motions to both of us with his finger. "How long have you two been friends?"

Robbie lifts his chin. "Since college."

"Too long," I tease.

"How would you know, Peyton? You have no memories," Robbie jokes.

"Probably a good thing because what I've experienced so far has been mediocre at best," I crack back.

"Ouch." Robbie grabs his chest dramatically as though I actually inflicted pain on him. His blue eyes find mine, and he narrows them.

I smile but he doesn't return it.

The server sets our food down in front of Robbie and me.

"Wanna put an order in?" She directs her question at Tyler.

"I ordered at the bar. Tab is under Tyler Davis."

She nods and tells him she'll bring it out when it's ready.

"Can I get two more beers?" Robbie asks, gesturing to Tyler's glass and his own.

"Oh, you don't have to do that." Tyler lifts his hand to protest. "Put them on my tab," he says to the server.

"Nope, I got it," Robbie insists. He sits up a little taller in his seat and puffs out his chest. I don't know if he even realized he did it.

"All right, fine. I've got the next one then," Tyler says.

I glance at my plate and then briefly at Tyler. Do I eat or wait for his food to arrive? My stomach rumbles again. Robbie's eyes land on me.

"Go ahead and eat." Tyler gestures to my food.

"Don't have to tell me twice." Robbie bites into his cheeseburger.

I dunk a fry in the ketchup and toss it in my mouth. It doesn't have the crunch like Nash's double-fried french fries.

"Robbie, what do you do for work?" Tyler asks.

He chews slowly before answering. "I'm an actuary."

He raises a brow. "Not sure what that is."

"I analyze financial costs based on risk and uncertainty. It's not super exciting but it pays well."

Tyler doesn't say anything and just nods instead.

I bite into the chicken dip. Mayo and au jus drip from the other end of the sandwich, landing on my plate. It's savory and juicy. The server returns, setting two beers on the table and a Wrightwood salad in front of Tyler. She collects the empty beer glasses, asks how everything is tasting, and walks away. Robbie holds up his glass.

"Cheers to finding love," he says.

Tyler clinks his against Robbie's, glances at me with a smile, and they both drink.

"I almost ordered that," I say, pointing at Tyler's salad.

He pushes his plate toward me. "Do you want some?"

I shake my head. "Oh no, I'm good."

"I hear you two have an official date tomorrow?" Robbie points a finger at each of us, and then grabs several french fries, tossing them in his mouth.

Tyler swivels his head toward me and grins. "That's right. I'm taking Peyton axe throwing."

"Sounds dangerous," Robbie says.

"That's exactly what I'd expect an actuary to say." Tyler laughs.

Robbie seems to almost force a chuckle. "Good one," he says, chugging the rest of his beer. He sets it down on the table with force, causing the empty glass to echo.

"Axe throwing with a head injury doesn't seem like a very smart date idea to me." Robbie cocks his head.

"We've done it before." Tyler looks to me for approval.

"I'm sure it'll be fine," I reassure him. "It's not like we're throwing them at each other, right?"

"That's right." He nods and shovels a forkful of salad into his mouth.

Robbie looks to Tyler and then me like he's thinking of what to say. "I'm gonna hit the bathroom." He slides out of his seat and makes his way toward the back of the restaurant.

"Sorry about all this," I say.

"It's fine. I can handle an overprotective friend." Tyler bumps his shoulder into mine and takes another bite of his salad.

"Good. Robbie just cares a lot, and he's worried that I'm rushing into all of this."

He delivers a concerned look and finishes chewing before he speaks. "Do you feel like you are?"

"No. I mean, I got hit by a car trying to tell the person I love that I want to be with them, so I think I owe it to myself to find out who it is."

"I think you do too." Tyler nods and drinks his beer. "Any update on your memories?"

"Nope, they're still MIA," I say with a shrug.

Robbie returns to the table carrying a shot glass in each hand. They're filled with an amber-colored liquid. I glance at the shots and then back at Robbie. What is he doing? I don't know Robbie—well, I do, I just don't remember that I know him—but this doesn't seem like Robbie behavior.

I shoot an accusatory look at him. "I thought you were going to use the restroom?"

"I did, and then I got me and my new friend, Tyler, here a shot." He places one in front of Tyler and holds his up.

"I really shouldn't," Tyler says.

"Oh, come on." Robbie gestures to the shot in front of him.

Tyler sighs. "Fine," he says, picking it up and clinking it against Robbie's. "Cheers." They toss the shots back.

Robbie's face twists up and his lips pucker like he was just sucking on a lemon. Tyler has no reaction to it. It's like he drank water instead of alcohol. Robbie immediately flags down the server.

"Two more," he says, holding up the shot glass and still trying to compose himself from the first one.

She smiles and nods.

"Robbie, do you think that's a good idea?" I ask.

"I'd argue it's a great idea," he says.

I roll my eyes and sigh, knowing full well he's wrong.

"Sorry about him," I say to Tyler. We're standing outside the restaurant just a couple of feet apart, ready to finally call it a night. I wanted to leave an hour ago, but Robbie kept insisting on one more, and now he's had five more too many.

"It's all right. Man, he sure knows how to party." Tyler chuckles and glances over at Robbie, who's leaned up against a pole a few yards from us. He's drawing a lot of attention from people passing by.

Robbie's hand slips off the pole. He jerks forward, banging his head against it. "Ow!" he says. He rubs his temple while trying to get himself in an upright position.

"He does not know how to party," I say with a laugh.

"You sure you don't need my help getting him home?" Tyler offers.

"Yeah, it's just a couple of blocks away, and you should get back to your friends."

He slips his hands into the front pockets of his jeans and rocks back on his heels. "Okay." We glance over at Robbie again. He's now found himself a bench and is seated on the edge of it, completely folded over, mumbling.

"I'm excited for our date tomorrow," he says, stealing my attention.

"Me too."

Tyler licks his top lip, while his gaze runs over my face. It's like he's deciding whether or not to kiss me. And then he just goes for it. He leans down, planting his warm lips on mine. It happens so fast that my eyes stay open, but I kiss him back for a split second before pulling away.

"Kissy, kissy," Robbie mumbles.

I glance over my shoulder. He's still in the same position, but he's lifted his head so he's staring right back at me.

"I should go," I say to Tyler.

He nods. "All right, well, get home safe. It was nice seeing you again, Robbie."

Robbie waves a hand dismissively. "Yeah, whatever, caveman." His words slur, and his head lolls to the side. I shoot him a disappointed look.

Tyler furrows his brow. "What did he say?"

"He said, *Yeah, you too man*," I lie. "See you tomorrow." I back away from Tyler with a tight smile. I need to get Robbie out of here before he does or says something stupid again.

"Looking forward to it." He flashes a wide grin.

I grab Robbie by his arm and hoist him up, wedging myself under the crux of his shoulder so I can use my whole body to get him to his feet. "Let's go, you saboteur."

"What?" Robbie squints in confusion. "I'm not a sabertooth."

I let out a small laugh and shake my head. Robbie leans into me as I guide him down the street toward home. He half stumbles, half walks.

"What got into you tonight?"

He drunkenly smiles. "Alcohol." He tries to make a serious face. "I think Tyler's a bad influence. Look how drunk he got me."

"You did that all on your own." I stare at him, my lips forming a straight line. The corner of his mouth curves up.

"No, I didn't. It was all Tyler. Probably should break it off with him."

A couple of guys in a car driving by stick their heads out of their windows and hoot and holler at us as we cross the intersection. Robbie eats it up, making a *whooo* sound. He nearly trips over his feet, but I hold him up.

"Fine, it was me," he admits. "But I was testing him, and he failed my test."

"Oh yeah?" I say. "How did Tyler fail?"

"Peer pressure. He gave in. He's too easily influenced. That's not the type of man you want."

I giggle at his drunk logic. Robbie cracks a grin.

Together, we stagger down the sidewalk. I'm careful not to let Robbie fall. We've had enough head injuries for a while.

"You're the one that got drunk. He wasn't even tipsy," I say as we turn onto my street.

"Yeah, well, I need to adjust some of my test parameters. But he still failed . . . mis . . . er . . . ab . . . ly."

"If you say so," I say, shaking my head.

Robbie stops abruptly and pulls away. He stumbles backward into a fence and stares at me through bloodshot, half-open eyes. "Do you *really* like him?"

I ignore his question and instead grab his hand, helping him regain his footing. There's no use in having any serious conversations tonight because it's unlikely he'll remember them, and he's not making much sense as it is.

His brows pinch together, and his face turns serious. "So, do you?"

"Yeah, Robbie. I do."

He pulls his chin in. "Okay . . ." His clouded blue eyes search mine like he's waiting for a different answer, but then he shakes his head and stumbles forward. "I was just checking."

All I want to do is get him home in one piece, safe and sound. I position myself underneath his shoulder again and steer him forward. We're almost there. I push open the courtyard gate and help Robbie up the porch steps. He trips on the top step and falls, clamoring against the wooden porch. Thankfully, he catches himself with his hands, landing practically on all fours.

"Ouch," he moans.

"Hello!" Debbie's voice comes from the other side of her door. The porch light flickers on and she pops her head out. "I'm locked and loaded," she declares.

"Debbie, it's just me and Robbie!" I say in a panic.

She takes a step onto the porch, dressed in a long nightgown and a robe.

I look to her. "Wait, you have a gun?"

"No, I just say that to scare away burglars. But I do have a cattle prod, and I'm not afraid to use it." She surveys Robbie and me. "What are you two doing?"

"*HeyDebbie,*" he says. His words slur together, forming one word.

Debbie flares her nostrils. "Robbie, are you drunk?"

"No," he lies.

I nod. "Yes, he is."

"Way to be a tattletale," he pouts.

"She didn't need to tattle. It's clear you're drunk as a skunk, Robbie."

Bending over, I grab his arm and force myself underneath his shoulder. Debbie takes his other arm and helps hoist him up, getting him back on his feet.

"This porch is uneven, Debbie," he says. "Probably wanna get Tyler over here to inspect it."

She narrows her eyes. "My porch is perfectly level."

Robbie leans into me.

"Let's get you to bed," I whisper.

"I'm not even tired," he slurs, backing away from both of us and standing upright on his own. His body sways side to side. My arms and hands are already braced, ready to catch him if he falls again.

Debbie takes one step back and surveys him. She folds her arms across her chest. "You're the one that's supposed to be taking care of Peyton. Not the other way around."

"I did by testing Tyler's ability to withstand peer pressure. He failed, by the way. He's no good."

I roll my eyes.

"Are you okay to get him upstairs?" Debbie asks.

"Yeah," I say, leading Robbie to my door. He walks a little better this time, still wobbly, but he's trying. I unlock it and push it open. "Good night."

"Night, you two. Holler if you need anything," she says.

I lock the door behind me and eyeball the staircase. It seems more like a mountain now with drunk Robbie by my side. "All right, one more flight of stairs. Think you can make it?"

He swivels his head toward me and leans it against mine. "You smell nice."

"I'll take that as a yes." I push more of my weight up and under his shoulder, and we sway side to side as we stumble up each carpeted step. Robbie holds on to the railing for balance but leans into me. At the top of the stairs, I blow out a deep breath. "Almost there," I say as I start guiding him down the hallway.

In the bedroom, I switch on the lights. Robbie closes his eyes and holds a hand to his face, shielding them. "It's too bright. Turn them off."

"I'll turn them off once I get you into bed," I say, helping him to the other side.

"I can't believe you thought I was trying to run the clock out on our pact."

I help him get his jacket off, unzipping, sliding it off his arms, and tossing it aside.

"Yeah, and I can't believe your forgot about our pact."

Robbie stumbles back a step but he keeps his eyes on me. They're intense right now. He unties the drawstring on his joggers and slides them down his legs. Underneath, he's wearing a pair of black boxer briefs. He steps out of his pants shakily, using the nightstand to keep himself standing upright, and kicks them aside.

We stare at one another for a moment, but it's one of those moments you can fill a lifetime in. "I didn't forget about it," he says under his breath.

"What?" I ask. Did he just say what I think he did?

"Nothing." He exhales noisily.

I squint at him, trying to get him to repeat what he said, but he's fallen quiet.

His fingers curl under the hem of his hoodie and, in one fell swoop, he pulls it up over his head, letting it drop to the floor. My breath hitches, and I swallow hard. I don't know what I was expecting but it wasn't what I'm seeing right now. Sculpted biceps, firm pecs, and carved abs. His skin is smooth and clean shaven. It makes me forget what he even just said. I'm not sure if he does it on purpose or not, but his biceps flex and his pecs bounce. Is he flirting with me? I look away and clear my throat, taking a step back.

Robbie lowers his chin. "Maybe you were right about the pact. Maybe it wasn't silly." That sounds a little flirty. Or perhaps he's finally seeing things my way. Promises between friends aren't silly. Well, this wasn't so much a promise. It was a full-on commitment pact.

"No, it was. No one makes a relationship pact when they're nineteen and follows through on it." I smile back at him, trying to make the conversation a little lighter. "Besides, you said we wouldn't work together."

He doesn't return the smile. He just stares back at me with those cloudy blue eyes and nods.

"I say a lot of things."

Wait, is he saying we would work? Or is he just saying he says a lot of things? I'm so confused. Drunk Robbie is like a blank crossword puzzle. The clues are there but the real words are missing. "What do you mean?" I ask.

His mouth forms a straight line, and I notice his Adam's apple rocks up and down like he just swallowed the true words he was going to say. "Nothing." He shrugs and slides into bed.

Okay, maybe he doesn't know what he's saying.

"All snug as a bug?" I ask, trying to get him to lighten up.

It doesn't work, though. He doesn't say anything and instead rolls over, turning his body away from me. I want him to say more things but I can tell he's already falling asleep. His muscles relax, and his breath becomes slow and controlled. I know he's going to wake up tomorrow feeling horrible, and I feel bad, so I want to take care of him like he's done for me. Quietly, I race around my apartment, gathering items for him. I grab Tylenol, a bottle of water, a packet of electrolytes, and a granola bar. I splay them out on the nightstand and leave a handwritten note that reads: *Morning, Robbie. Hope you feel better. Xo, your dame in shining armor, accompanied by amnesia.*

CHAPTER 11

The intoxicating smell and crackling sound of bacon wakes me from a deep sleep. Rolling over, I find the other half of the bed empty. Robbie's gone and his side of the pillow wall is made. The items I left out for him are gone too, so I assume he's in the kitchen, cooking breakfast to make up for his behavior last night—if he even remembers it. Looks like we both might have some memory loss. I really can't believe how drunk he got, but I hope he's feeling better. I follow the smell of bacon to the kitchen.

"Good morning," I say.

Debbie turns from the stove and smiles. She's dressed in a pair of pajama pants with a matching top and a long-knit cardigan. It's as though she came up to my place in a rush with no time to change. She places fried bacon on a plate and cracks two eggs into a pan. The eggs sizzle in the leftover bacon grease.

"Where's Robbie?" I ask, scanning the living room.

"He came down and got me about twenty minutes ago. Said he had to go into work early and didn't want to wake you." She lifts a brow. "But I think he was just embarrassed and didn't want to face you."

I take a seat at the island counter. "You think?"

Debbie nods and flips the eggs. Two pieces of bread pop out of the toaster. "Oh yes. That wasn't like Robbie at all. He's always the one that keeps you and Maya out of trouble. Not the other way around." She raises a brow.

"I don't know what got into him. He kept ordering beers and shots for him and Tyler."

Debbie slathers butter onto the toast and pours orange juice into two glasses. She slides one to me along with my morning pills. I toss them in my mouth and wash them down with a gulp of OJ.

"I think he's just worried," Debbie says.

"About what?"

"Losing you."

My face crinkles in confusion. "Why would he think he's going to lose me?"

"Because when you figure out which of these guys you love, you'll spend your time with him. Maya has Anthony. You'll have your man, and it'll leave Robbie as the odd one out." Debbie places a fried egg on each plate along with some bacon and toast.

"I wouldn't do that."

I study my hands, fiddling with my fingernails. I don't understand why Robbie would ever think I'd stop being friends just because I was in a relationship. Have I done that before? When I was in one of my short flings? I hope not. Or maybe he thinks it'll be different this time, but I would never stop being his friend over some guy, no matter what.

"I know. But Robbie is a worrier, always has been, which is why he's so good at being an actuary." She laughs as she places a plate and fork in front of me. Steam rises from the eggs.

"But I had boyfriends before. Did Robbie act like this then?" I pick up a piece of chewy bacon and bite off a chunk of it.

Debbie dives into her plate. "No, but it's different this time."

Humph. Even Debbie thinks it's different this time.

"How?" I look to her.

"Well, you were going to tell one of these guys you loved them and that you wanted to be with them before your accident. You've never told a man you loved them before."

"What?" I squint. "That can't be right. You and Maya said I had past relationships that lasted nearly a year. I would have said it to one of them."

"Nope, you never did. Some people throw around the word *love* like it's another word for *potato*, but not you. You've always held it close to your heart, only reserving it for family and your closest friends."

"That's probably why my relationships never lasted. I can just imagine me responding to 'I love you' with *And I like you* or *Thank you*."

Debbie snickers and constructs an open-face sandwich with toast, bacon, and a fried egg. She bites into it and chews it slowly, savoring it.

"What about Robbie?"

She wipes her mouth with a napkin. "What about him?"

"Has he had any serious relationships?"

Maybe Robbie and I are alike in that sense, and that's why he's worried because I'll be leaving him behind—the last member of the perpetually single and occasional fling-y relationship club.

"He has, but he always finds some silly reason to break up with them or why they're not right for him," Debbie says, taking another bite.

"Like what?"

"One girl he broke up with because she didn't think *The Office* was funny. Another he ended it because she didn't drink coffee." She taps her finger against her chin. "Oh, and the most recent relationship deal breaker was because the girl only ate chicken tenders and french fries."

"It sounds like Robbie's the problem." I bite into my toast and sip my OJ.

"Yeah, but I did agree with him on the chicken tender girl. He brought her to one of my dinner parties, and she DoorDashed McDonald's when she realized chicken and fries weren't going to be served." She shakes her head.

"Robbie's the one that said he was going to make sure I found out which guy I loved before my birthday so we didn't have to go through with our silly pact, and now he's getting drunk and acting weird because he's worried he'll lose me. I don't get it. Am I supposed to just be single until he finds someone too?" I let out a heavy sigh. But I can see where he's coming from, I suppose. I think it'd be hard for me if he had a serious girlfriend and I was the only one of the three of us without a significant other. No one wants to be last in these situations.

"No, and don't worry about Robbie. He'll come around. He always does. Your only concern is getting better and following your heart."

I lower my head because I do feel bad for him, but also because I'm confused about my own situation. "That's what I'm trying to do," I say.

"As long as you're trying, that's all that matters. You said Tyler joined you last night?" Debbie asks, changing the subject. "How'd that go?"

"Awkward because of Robbie." I shrug. "But Tyler was really nice about it. I thought for sure Robbie had scared him off, but we're still on for our date today. He's taking me axe throwing," I say, eating a piece of bacon.

"Axe throwing? Back in my day, dating was dinner and a movie. Axes weren't thrown until the end of the relationship."

"He assured me we wouldn't be throwing them at each other," I say with a laugh. Wiping my hands off on a napkin, I pick up my plate.

Debbie immediately extends her hand out. "All done?"

"Yeah, thanks."

She takes the plate and smiles. "And you left your two bites like you always do."

A look of confusion comes over me. I didn't even realize I did that again. Must be muscle memory or something, but I don't know why I do that. Maybe Debbie knows. "Robbie mentioned the two-bite thing too. Is there a reason I do that?"

She inhales a quiet, deep breath. "You started it when you were recovering in the hospital after the car accident." Her eyes develop a sheen like she's about to cry, but she blinks it away. "I think it was a way for you to cope with the sudden loss of your parents. Anytime you ate, you always left two bites on your plate, one for each of them."

A tear rolls down my cheek, and a pain settles in my belly. I breathe through it, letting it subside. It's a good thing, I remind myself. Not remembering why I always leave two bites behind but still doing it makes me feel like the love I had for them and they had for me is stronger than any stolen memory. But regardless, I still want to remember.

Debbie lends a sympathetic look and places her hand on mine. "Oh, sweetie. I didn't mean to make you cry."

"You didn't. I just . . . I just wish I remembered them." I lower my head and chew my bottom lip to stop it from quivering.

"You will, honey, and deep down, I think you do. It's why you leave the two bites." Her hand squeezes mine.

"That's right. But Robbie keeps eating them." I let out a laugh mixed with a cry.

"He does that because it became more of a sad reminder for you rather than a sweet remembrance. At some point, seeing the food left on your plate stopped helping you cope, and Robbie noticed how it was affecting you, so he started eating your last two bites, and then it just became a cute thing between you two."

"That's sweet," I say with a sniffle. It's like he knows what I need without even asking.

"Knock, knock," Maya calls out. I hear her shoes kick off and the door close behind her. Her feet pound up the stairs.

"Hey," I say, wiping my eyes before turning around to face her.

"Good morning. Want some breakfast?" Debbie asks.

Maya's face brightens with delight. "Yes, I'm famished."

She joins us at the counter, taking a seat beside me. Debbie busies herself at the stove, frying up another egg and dropping a piece of bread in the toaster.

Maya bumps her shoulder against mine. "I heard you had an interesting night."

"Who told you that?"

"Robbie. I'm supposed to be doing secret recon to figure out what he all said and did and whether or not he should be embarrassed." The corner of her mouth lifts.

"Doesn't sound very secret to me," Debbie says, flipping an egg in the pan.

"Robbie knows I don't do secrets, so it's his fault for asking me." Maya chuckles and regards me with a raised brow. "So, what should I tell him?"

I could say that he and I need to talk about some of the things he said last night. Like when he admitted to remembering the pact. Or at least I think he did. He said it under his breath, but I'm pretty sure that's what I heard. But then Debbie's words come back to me. Robbie's just worried about losing me, and I don't want to do anything to push him away or make him feel worse than he already does.

"Tell him we had a fun time and there's nothing to be embarrassed of."

Maya pulls her phone from her pocket and starts typing out a message. "Is that the truth or just what we're telling Robbie?"

"Just what we're telling Robbie."

"You can tell him I'm mad at him." Debbie throws a glance over her shoulder. "He told me my porch was uneven."

"The audacity!" Maya hits "Send" on her phone and sets it down on the counter.

"That's what I thought. I take great pride in my home," she says with a nod, not noticing Maya's sarcasm. Debbie slathers butter on the toast and plates the rest of the food.

Maya and I exchange a smile.

"Orange juice?" she asks.

"Yes, please."

She sets the plate and a glass of OJ in front of Maya.

"Thanks, Debbie. You're the best."

"I know," she says with a small smile before cleaning up the kitchen.

"Robbie was wasted last night?" Maya chews on a piece of bacon and glances at me.

"Yep. He was kind of grilling Tyler too, and I barely got him home in one piece. And then . . ." I pause. "Never mind."

Maya's eyes bulge, and her forkful of egg lingers midair, hovering in front of her mouth. "What? Tell me."

I bite my lower lip, deciding whether or not to tell them about Robbie being kind of flirty toward me. Maybe it wasn't flirty. No, it wasn't. He was just drunk. But he did undress in front of me and flexed his pecs and muscles. But that could have been unintentional. Sometimes muscles just flex, right?

"It's nothing," I say, sipping the rest of my orange juice.

Maya points at me. "You're biting your lip."

"So."

"That's your tell."

"I don't have a tell," I argue.

"Yes, you do," Debbie says. "You bite your lip when you lie."

"So, spill." Maya eats a hunk of her toast.

"Fine. I think Robbie was being a little flirty with me."

Debbie pauses her cleaning and whips her head in my direction. She leans over the counter, propping her chin up on her hands, waiting for me to say more.

"It was nothing," I say, flicking my hand.

"We'll be the judge of that," Debbie says. "Go on. Tell us more."

I glance to Maya and then Debbie. They both stare at me, waiting for me to spill. "He mentioned the pact, and I think he said he didn't actually forget about it."

"Did he say that?" Maya asks.

"I don't know. I think so. He also said maybe the pact wasn't silly."

"Aww," Debbie says.

"I told him he was right about it being silly." I glance at my hands and then back at Debbie and Maya. "And then I reminded him what he said about us not being good together anyway. And he said he says a lot of things."

"That sounds like flirting to me," Debbie says with a nod.

"It's borderline flirting," Maya adds.

"Your generation is too used to communicating via emojis. You wouldn't think it was flirting unless there was one of them eggplants thrown in."

Maya squints. "How do you know about the eggplant emoji, Debbie?"

"It was an accidental discovery when I tried eharmony."

"You online dated?" I ask.

She nods. "It's impossible to meet a man in person anymore. They aren't at the grocery store because of DoorDash. They're not out shopping because of Amazon. I had no other choice."

"What I don't understand is how you learned about the eggplant." Maya chuckles.

"Well, I had the eggplant emoji in my bio because it's one of my favorite foods, and let's just say I received a number of inappropriate photos," Debbie says with a smirk.

"Debbie!" I laugh.

"What? It was an honest mistake. How was I supposed to know your generation has sexualized eggplants? Don't even get me started on the peach and taco emojis." Her eyes dart between Maya and me.

Maya and I trade smiles.

"So, as I was saying, Robbie was definitely flirting," Debbie says.

"He also undressed in front of me," I blurt out. I feel my cheeks redden, and I slap a hand over my mouth, wishing I hadn't let the words escape.

Debbie's brows raise so much, they practically touch her hairline.

Maya's mouth drops open and her voice goes up two octaves when she speaks. "You saw Robbie naked?"

"No, he was wearing boxers . . . well, boxer briefs."

"Those are the tight kind, right?" Debbie looks to Maya for confirmation.

Maya nods. "So, you saw him half-naked in Saran Wrap underwear?"

"Just regular underwear."

Maya and Debbie share a knowing look.

"What did he do after that?" Maya asks.

"That's when he said the whole maybe-the-pact-wasn't-silly thing."

"Told ya, he was flirting," Debbie says.

Maya gestures to me. "I would have known that too if Peyton hadn't left out the part about him being naked."

"Half-naked," I correct. "Besides, I'm sure I've seen him in his boxers before, so maybe that part isn't a big deal." I glance at each of them for verification, since I don't remember what I have and haven't seen of Robbie.

Maya nods. "You've seen him in swimming trunks. I don't know about underwear."

"And he was really drunk," I add.

Debbie gives a coy smile. "But they say drunk words are sober thoughts." She wets a rag under the faucet and wipes down the counter and stove top.

"So, you think Robbie was flirting with me?"

Debbie and Maya nod.

I groan, letting my shoulders slump.

"I think you need to worry less about Robbie and more about the guys you're actually dating." Maya places her hand on my shoulder.

"Maya's right," Debbie says as she wrings out the washcloth and hangs it over the faucet. "Even if Robbie was flirting, if something was ever going to happen between you two, it would have already. You've been friends for over a decade. Like I said earlier, I think he's just worried about losing you, and it's got him confused."

Maybe Debbie's right. Robbie made it very clear that he and I would not be good together and that we've always just been friends. He said he didn't want to jeopardize our friendship and even agreed to help me figure the guys out so we didn't have to go through the original pact. This whole thing has us both confused. That's all. And I'm extra confused without my memories. I need to focus on Tyler, Nash, and Shawn. I got hit by a car trying to tell one of them I loved them. That's gotta be true love, or at least something like it.

"Okay," I say. "Enough about Robbie. What should I wear on my date with Tyler tonight?"

"Finally, we get to talk about something important." Maya smirks.

Debbie collects her empty plate and washes it. "Something that shows the girls off," she says, gesturing to my chest.

"Debbie!" I cross my arms over them.

"What? One day you're gonna be tucking them into your waistband, wishing you had shown them off when they were perky and young."

I snicker.

"Debbie's right. Give them the glory days they deserve," Maya says.

I unfold my arms and look down at myself, back at Debbie, and then Maya. "Fine, I'll wear something a little low cut. Just a little."

"And what about your date with Shawn?" Debbie asks.

"I think we're going to a fancy restaurant because he texted me telling me to dress to impress." I scrunch up my lips. "But I don't know what to wear. I have a couple dresses, but I might have worn them on our previous dates since they've always been at nice restaurants."

"Good thinking because you definitely wouldn't want to show up in the same dress you already wore. That's embarrassing," Maya says.

Debbie purses her lips together. "I'm sure he'd understand with the amnesia and whatnot."

"It's already been decided." Maya nods. "We'll go shopping tomorrow for a new dress."

I bump my shoulder against Maya's. "This feels like an excuse for you to go shopping."

"It is," she says with a laugh.

CHAPTER 12

I glance over my shoulder at Tyler. He's leaned against the chicken wire fence wall behind me, the one that separates the axe-throwing area from the bar. My eyes skim over him. From his silky dark hair pulled back in a bun, to his broad shoulders, to his long, muscular legs. He's dressed casually, blue jeans and a dark-green shirt that hugs his pecs and biceps tightly. He smiles. It's warm and flirty.

"You got this," Tyler says.

"I know," I say, even though I don't mean it.

Debbie told me to act confident even if I'm not because real men are drawn to confidence. She also told me to cross my arms under my chest to ensure my cleavage is at peak elevation. But I'm going to ignore that piece of advice.

I toss him a smile before turning back and focusing on the target. The axe-throwing area is covered in plywood with a large bull's-eye painted on the wall about ten feet in front of me. A man to my side whips his axe. It hits the center of his target with a thud. He throws his arms up in the air and cheers. A group of people behind him clap and holler. I take a deep breath, make sure my toe is on the line where the employee showed us to stand, and bring the axe above my head, gripping it with two hands. I focus on the bull's-eye. When I'm ready, I hurl the axe, letting it fly out of my hands. It spikes the plywood to the right of the center.

"I did it," I squeal, clapping my hands.

Tyler wraps his arm around my waist and pulls me into him, practically picking me up off the floor. "I knew you would," he says.

I grin and feel a whoosh of butterflies floating and flapping around in my stomach. "Your turn."

His gaze lingers on me. I notice specks of yellow in his green irises, and I wonder if I noticed them before. Tyler lets his hand drop from my shoulder and puffs up his chest. I lean against the chicken wire fence. Now it's my turn to watch him. His large hand grips the axe handle, and he rips it clean from the plywood with ease. Retaking his position, Tyler throws a smile over his shoulder before he hurls the axe. It hits the bull's-eye right in the dead center.

I dash to him, giving a double high five. "Want me to pull the axe for you?" he asks.

"Yes, please."

I slide my phone from my pocket and record him walking to the target and ripping the axe from it. It's all very dramatic but I think he's trying to impress me. It's working because I am impressed. I quickly send the video to Maya with the text, Date is going well. Thought you'd enjoy this.

She immediately responds with I'm gonna need to take Anthony there followed by the red sweating-face emoji with the tongue out. I giggle and pocket my phone just as Tyler turns to walk back to me.

"Think you can hit the center this time?" he teases while handing the axe over. The corner of his lip perks up.

"Oh yes," I say with a confident nod.

"Wanna bet on it?"

I tilt my head, looking up at him. "What do you have in mind?"

Tyler taps his finger against his chin. "If you don't hit it, you have to give me a kiss right here," he says, pointing to his cheek.

I raise my brow. "Oh, you're betting against me?"

"No, never. Because if you hit it, you have to kiss me right here." He taps his finger against his lips.

"Smooth, Tyler."

He grins.

"But you've got yourself a deal."

His grin widens as he backs away. "Get up there and hit that bull's-eye."

I toe the line, raise the axe over my head, and fling it at the target. Surprisingly, it hits dead center. I jump up and down with joy. When I turn around, Tyler is standing right behind me with the biggest smile on his face.

"You must really want to kiss me," he says in a sultry and teasing voice.

"I guess I do." I shrug. Our eyes meet and we stare at one another for a moment before leaning in. His lips are warm and soft, practically melting into mine. His hands press against my lower back as he draws me in closer. My skin tingles and my heart rate quickens. I can't help but compare his kisses to Nash's. His are passionate and hungry, where Nash's are sweet and gentle. When we pull apart, we're both beaming.

"We should make more bets like that," Tyler says.

I pat my hand against his chest playfully. "I don't mind winning," I tease.

"And I don't mind losing." He bends down and plants a quick kiss on my lips. "Want to get out of here?" he whispers.

I smile up at him and nod.

Tyler pushes his front door open and flips the light switch. A dog bark echoes from deep in the apartment. His place is open concept and modern with white walls and chrome finishes. Most of his furniture is made of dark cherrywood—the TV stand, coffee table, and kitchen stools.

I wonder if he built them himself. The couch is plush and covered in throw blankets and pillows. Despite the modern appearance and floor-to-ceiling windows, Tyler's apartment is cozy and warm.

"Toby," Tyler calls out as he places a large, hot Neapolitan-style pizza on the island counter. Dog nails click along the hardwood floor, and a moment later a golden retriever trots in. His tail wags as he runs to Tyler. Toby jumps up, his paws landing on Tyler's stomach. Tyler rubs his ears and tells him he's a good boy. When the dog notices me, he jumps down and runs to my side, smelling my shoes and pressing his body against my legs. I pet his head and scratch his chin.

"Good boy," I say. "Oh, you like the chin scratchies?"

"He loves all the pets, scratches, and rubs," Tyler says. He kicks off his shoes and hangs his jacket on a wall hook. Turning back to me, he asks, "Can I take yours?"

I nod and pull it off, revealing my V-neck long-sleeve top. When he finishes hanging it up, he gestures to his home. "So, this is the kitchen and living room."

"I like it," I say.

"I know. That's what you said last time," Tyler says with a small smile.

I pull my lips in and nod, unsure as to how I should respond. Toby barks.

"Someone knows their dinner is late," he says. "Come on. Let's get you some food, boy."

Tyler walks to the pantry and scoops dog food into a dish. He brings it to the sink and quickly splashes it with water before setting it down on the floor. Toby sits and waits for permission.

"Okay," he says, and the dog dives mouth first into his food dish.

He clasps his hands together. "Now, time to feed you."

I let out a laugh and walk a couple of steps into the apartment, surveying the place, searching for familiarity, but there is none. I wish I could remember being here. Actually, I wish I could remember being anywhere before the accident. Tyler pulls two plates from the cupboard and offers me something to drink. I tell him water's fine. He pours a glass of water, pops the cap off a beer for himself, and flips open the pizza box. It's a margherita pizza. The gooey cheese glistens, and the smell of fresh basil wafts in the air. We serve ourselves, and I follow him into the living room, grabbing a seat on the couch.

"How is it?" Tyler asks after I take my first bite.

"Really good." The cheese stretches a few inches in length before finally splitting off from the slice.

"Excellent," he says, biting into his.

Toby joins us in the living room, lying down directly in front of us. He stares at me, and then at Tyler, and then at me again.

"Ignore him," Tyler says. "He's trying to figure out which one of us is most willing to give him scraps."

I give the dog a sympathetic look. "Sorry, Toby."

Toby watches Tyler. "He knows it's me." He laughs and tosses a hunk of crust. Toby catches it in his mouth and chews happily.

"He's got you pegged."

"Yeah." He smiles. "He knows I'm a big softie. Who could say no to that face?"

Drool hangs six inches in length from Toby's right jowl.

"Only a monster could." I chuckle and toss him my crust. He catches it in his mouth and chews. When he's finished, he barks once.

"What was that for Toby?" I ask.

"That's him saying he approves of you."

"Oh really? Because the last bark meant he was hungry."

"Okay, you got me," he says, standing from his seat. "His after-dinner bark means he wants to go outside." Tyler leashes Toby at the front door and tells me he'll be right back as they leave the apartment with Toby wagging his tail the whole way.

My phone buzzes. It's a text from Robbie. **Hey, just checking when you'll be home?**

I stare at the text for a moment. Do I bring up the night before? Ask him if we're okay or if he's okay? No, I don't want to embarrass him, and I don't want to push him away or make him feel bad. He already left this morning without telling me. Besides, Maya and Debbie told me my focus needs to be on the guys, not Robbie, so I respond with, Soon.

A message pops up from him, saying, Okay, see you soon, with a smiley-face emoji.

I pocket my phone and set my plate on the coffee table. The apartment door swings open, and Toby comes running in. He leaps onto the couch and lays his head on my lap, nudging his snout into me. I smile and scratch his ears.

"That's actually his seal of approval," Tyler says with a laugh.

I run my hand along his soft fur. "Did you train him to do that?" I raise my brow.

"Maybe." He makes his way to the couch and sits down on the other side of Toby, patting him on his back. "How did you enjoy axe throwing?"

"Better than I thought I would."

"Good." He nods. "I had fun with you."

"Me too," I say.

His eyes linger on mine, and he licks his top lip like he's readying himself to kiss me. Toby jumps up from the couch and leaves the room, his nails clicking all the way down the hallway.

"Where's he going?"

Tyler scoots closer to me. "He knows how to read the room." Smiling, he leans in and plants his lips on mine. His hand caresses my cheek as he kisses me, making my skin tingle once again. I wrap my hands around the back of his neck, pulling him closer. Our mouths move in tandem, opening and closing. Tyler wastes no time. His hands move to my side and lower back. I lean even more into his body, and all of a sudden I'm straddling him. His fingers press into my skin beneath my shirt, running up and down my back, sending shivers. Debbie was right. This was the top to wear. My hands skim over his broad shoulders and firm pecs, following the grooves and ridges of his muscles. His fingers curl under the hem of my shirt, and he starts to lift it, but for some reason I pull away.

"Sorry," I say.

His eyes open. They're clouded with confusion, staring back at me. I tuck my chin in. "I know you told me we've been intimate before but . . . I wanna take it slow. Without my memories, it's just different for me now."

He pushes a piece of hair out of my face, tucking it behind my ear. "You don't have to apologize, Peyton. We can take it as slow as you want." His fingers brush along my cheek.

I give him a small smile as I slide off his lap, retaking my seat beside him. I love that he's patient with me. Robbie's words come back to the front of my mind. *If any of these guys cared about you, they'd wait until you're better.* And Tyler is doing just that.

It's around midnight when I push open the door to my townhome. I creep slowly up the stairs, careful not to wake Robbie. I told him I'd be home soon hours ago, but then again, I was on a date, and I have to focus on figuring out who I love, not on Robbie. Tyler and I ended up watching *13 Going on 30*. I picked it because Robbie said it was his favorite, but then I spent the whole time thinking about him while I was cuddled up next to Tyler. I should have picked something else; however, I really enjoyed it, and I can see why it's his favorite.

"Look what the cat dragged in," Robbie says.

My shoulders jump, and my head whips in the direction of his voice. He's stretched out on the couch with a book in hand. The lamp set on the side table provides ample light for his reading.

"Jeez, you scared me, Robbie."

"Sorry," he says, closing the book. He sets it on the coffee table and gets to his feet, stretching his arms over his head.

I pull off my jacket and hang it up on the coatrack. "What are you still doing up?"

"Waiting for you."

I squint. "Why?"

"Just wanted to make sure you got home okay. I thought you'd be home hours ago. But I guess we have different definitions of *soon*." He walks into the kitchen and pours a glass of water.

"I guess we do."

He slides the glass to me. "Must have been a good date then?"

"It was," I say, sipping the water.

Robbie leans against the counter with his arms folded across his chest. "Good. I'm glad to hear that." There's no enthusiasm in his voice, so I doubt he actually feels that way. I think he's mad at me for having to wait up, but he didn't need to.

I give him a peculiar look but quickly relax my face before he notices. His feelings flip every day. Yesterday, he was flirting-ish with me and telling me he was wrong about our original pact being silly. Granted, he was drunk, but still. He also said I should end it with Tyler, but now he's glad to hear my date with Tyler went well. Pick a lane, Robbie. My mind goes back to what Debbie said about him. He's confused and scared he'll lose me, so I deliver a sympathetic look.

"Why are you looking at me like that?"

"Like what?" I contort my face into a neutral position, trying to appear casual.

Robbie cocks his head. "Like you feel sorry for me."

"I do not feel sorry for you."

"You're looking at me like you do."

"Robbie, I really don't know what you're talking about."

His shoulders drop, and his gaze falls to his feet. It takes a few moments before he lifts his chin and stares back at me. "I'm sorry about last night."

"There's nothing to apologize for." I drink the rest of my water and place the glass in the dishwasher.

"No, there is." He takes a step toward me. "I shouldn't have gotten drunk or grilled Tyler. I know this whole situation is hard enough on you without me adding to it. So I am sorry."

"Did you mean it?" I ask, studying his face.

"Mean what?"

"What you said last night?"

"I don't remember what I said." He shrugs and briefly breaks eye contact. "So probably not."

I consider reminding him and asking how he feels about our marriage/relationship pact or if he had really forgotten it, but instead I leave it in the past just where he wants it. Debbie's words spring to the front of my mind. *Even if Robbie was flirting, if something was ever going to happen between you two, it would have already.*

"I'm going to bed," I finally land on.

He delivers a tight smile. "Good night, Peyton."

"Night, Robbie," I say as I turn on my heel and head down the hallway. He lets out a heavy sigh, stopping me in my tracks. I pause to listen. He whispers something to himself but I can't make it out. My phone vibrates. I slide it from my pocket and on the screen is a text from Tyler, reminding me of where my focus and attention needs to be. I type out a reply and walk toward my bedroom, leaving Robbie alone in the kitchen.

CHAPTER 13

When I wake up the next morning, I notice Robbie's side of the bed is made, and I'm not even sure if he slept in it last night. Axe throwing really took it out of me. As soon as my head hit the pillow, I fell asleep, so I never heard him come in. I wonder if he's even here or if he pulled a fast one like yesterday, making for a quick exit. After I get ready for the day, my nose guides me to the kitchen, following the scent of freshly brewed coffee.

Robbie is seated on the couch with a mug in one hand and a book in the other.

"Hey," I say.

"Good morning," he says, not taking his eyes off the page.

I pour myself a cup and sit in the plush chair next to the couch. "Did you come to bed last night?"

The steam rises from the coffee as I bring it to my lips and cautiously sip.

"No, I slept on the couch."

My brow puckers. "I told you I didn't want you to sleep on the couch, Robbie. You're too tall for it."

He peers over his book. "I didn't want to wake you."

"What time did you go to bed?"

"Not sure." He shrugs. "I think closer to 2:00 a.m."

"What were you doing up so late?"

"Nothing. Just couldn't sleep."

Robbie's dressed in a pair of blue jeans and an L.L.Bean sweater. His hair is intentionally messy on top, and his blue eyes are laser focused on the book he's reading. They move left to right and top to bottom.

"Are you okay?" I ask.

He cracks a smile and closes his book, setting it on the end table beside him. "Yeah, I'm fine." Robbie sips his coffee. "What's on the agenda today?"

"Well, Maya and I are supposed to go shopping for a dress. I have my date tonight with Shawn."

My phone vibrates just as I finish speaking. It's a text from Maya. I type out a reply and hit "Send."

"Scratch that," I say.

"What?"

"Maya can't make it today. Anthony surprised her with a couple's spa day for their anniversary. She said he's had it planned for a while and couldn't reschedule."

Robbie scrunches up his face. "I'm sorry."

"It's all right." I shrug. "That's really sweet of Anthony. I mean, I don't remember him, but he seems like a good guy."

"He is. You'd like him. No, you do like him," Robbie says. "They're great together. Anthony is like Maya, quick-witted and able to give her shit back."

"I think that's what she needs," I say with a laugh.

"Oh, it is. She chewed up and spit out all her past boyfriends. They couldn't keep up with her." Robbie smiles and sips his coffee.

"I'm glad she has someone like him in her life."

He stands and pulls his phone from his pocket. "I gotta make a quick call," Robbie says, disappearing down the hallway.

I glance out the glass door that opens up to the balcony. The sky is a bright blue, almost the same shade as Robbie's eyes. There's not even a cloud in sight. The sun's rays seep in through the windows, creating a soft glow over the apartment.

"It's settled," Robbie says, reentering the living room with a big grin plastered across his face.

"What's settled?"

"You and I are going dress shopping."

"Don't you have to work?"

"Not anymore. I called in."

"Robbie, you didn't have to do that."

"I know, but I wanted to, and I told you I'd help you find a dress if you needed one." He folds his arms across his chest.

"I'm sure I can find something in my closet to wear," I say.

"Nope, I already texted Maya, and she said you need a new dress." Robbie raises his chin. He's clearly pleased with himself and all the angles he's covered. "You're not getting out of this, Peyton."

I can't help it when the corners of my lips slowly curve up, crinkling my eyes. "Fine," I say.

Standing in front of a dressing room mirror, I turn side to side, examining myself. A red dress with thin straps hugs my body tightly (too tightly), stopping right at my knees. It has a sweetheart neckline and a high split, accentuating my bust and legs. I toss my long hair back so I can see the full picture. Debbie would approve, but I don't feel comfortable showing off a body I'm not all that familiar with. When I look at myself, it's like I'm looking at an old friend I've lost touch with.

"I'm not coming out," I announce.

"You have to," Robbie shouts from the other side of the dressing room door. Well, it's not a door. They're floor-to-ceiling gold-velvet drapes dividing the dressing room from the sitting area. Maya recommended this boutique and told Robbie that I'd for sure find something here to wear for my date. Two more dresses are hung on a hook ready for me to try on, but I think they're all a bit too flashy for me.

"It's too much," I yell.

"Like cost-wise?" he asks.

"No, looks-wise."

"I'll be the judge of that. Come on out," he says in a singsong voice.

I let out a sigh and pull open the drapes. The large metal rings clink together as they slide across the curtain rod. Robbie is seated on an oversized armchair with a high back. His face lights up, and he stands as soon as he sees me. I don't know how, but his eyes are even bluer. It's like they change shades of blue based on his mood. Navy blue when he's grumpy or feeling down, and sapphire when he's happy.

"Wow," he says. His mouth parts, and his gaze moves over me from my head to my toes. "You look amazing."

My cheeks warm at the compliment, and I get the feeling that I'm not good at accepting praise. Glancing at the floor, I tug at the sides of the dress, pulling it down for length and up at the neckline.

"It's not me," I say.

"It should be." Robbie clears his throat and scratches the back of his neck.

I walk to the trifold mirror and stand to the right of him for a better view. Robbie takes a couple of steps forward, so he's a just few feet behind me. His eyes never leave my reflection. I turn side to side but I just don't like it. It's obvious I don't see myself like he sees me.

The tall, wispy shop owner rushes into the room with a pile of dresses draped over her arm. Her dark hair is pulled back in a sleek bun. She wears a black jumpsuit and a customer-service smile.

"That looks amazing on you, Peyton," she says.

"Thanks."

"But in case that doesn't work, I have all of these." The woman gestures to the clothing she carried in. "I'll just hang them up in your dressing room."

The deep smile lines around her mouth are evidence of her upbeat and positive personality. We're the only ones in the store, and it's clear she's eager to make a sale. She hangs them up and then tells us she'll keep looking as she disappears through the door toward the front of the store.

"We're gonna be here for a while," Robbie teases.

I turn away from the mirror and stare back at him. "I'll pick something quick, just not this," I say, glancing down at the dress.

He folds his arms in front of his chest and smiles. "Hey, take your time. I've got all day."

I toss him a smile and walk back into the dressing room, closing the drapes behind me. I quickly change out of the dress and slip on a black one. It's also formfitting, with a square neckline and thick straps. It stops a couple of inches above the knee. It's a little tighter than I'd like, but at least it has more of a classic look. I stare at my reflection, turning side to side. I think I like it.

Robbie picks his head up when I push open the drapes, and I'm met with the same reaction the red dress got from him. Wide eyes and a parted mouth.

"You're beautiful," he says. "I mean, the dress is." His cheeks flush. "I mean, you're beautiful in that dress." He shuffles his feet, dropping eye contact for a moment.

I squint at him in the mirror but then relax. "Thanks," I say.

My gaze glides between my reflection and Robbie's. I notice his mouth curving into a grin.

"What?" I ask, staring at him through the mirror.

"Nothing." He shrugs.

"Why are you grinning?"

Robbie slips his hands into the front pockets of his jeans and rocks back on his heels. "I'm just happy to see you happy."

I smile back and nod. "This is the dress."

"I think it is too." Robbie pulls his lips in. "Shawn's a lucky guy," he says in a low voice as he walks back to his chair.

I'm not sure if I'm supposed to respond and agree that he is lucky or say I'm the lucky one, so I don't say anything at all. Instead, I just return to my dressing room, sliding the drapes closed without another word.

My heels click along the hardwood floor. They're strappy wedges, only a couple of inches high. Any higher, and I was sure I'd biff it. A simple gold chain necklace with a round pendant hangs from my neck, paired with a set of gold studs. My hair is full of large curls, and my makeup is the same as how I've been wearing it the last couple of days—simple, except this time, there's an extra coat of mascara and a layer of mixed brown eye shadows on my lids.

"Wow, look at you," Robbie says as I enter the kitchen. I stop and glance down at myself. The black dress was the right choice. It hugs me in all the right places, it's comfortable, and it feels like me. Straightforward and forgettable (like my memories).

"Thanks," I say, setting a small gold purse on the counter. I transfer some items from my everyday bag to it. "What are your plans for the night?"

He leans against the counter. "Going to Maya's comedy show."

"Oh, she has a show tonight?"

"Yeah, practically every Friday night. Whenever she can book a gig, she does. I haven't been able to make one in a while, so I'm looking forward to it. She said she's got a whole new set."

"I wish I could go," I say with a slight frown.

"We can go together . . . another time when you're free."

My frown disappears at his offer. "I'd like that."

"When's Shawn supposed to be here?"

I check the clock on my phone. "Any minute now."

Robbie pulls a beer from the fridge. "Are you excited?" he asks, popping the cap off and taking a swig.

"Yeah, and also a little nervous. It's my last first date . . . again." I chuckle.

He laughs and nods. "No need to be nervous. Just be yourself."

"Yeah . . . but I'm not entirely sure who that is."

"Yes, you do, Peyton. You've been yourself around me the past few days. You may not remember who you are, but you're still you."

"Thanks for being here for me this week," I say, delivering a half smile.

He tips his beer in my direction and says, "That's what friends are for."

We stare at one another, and I swallow hard. Only the sound of my phone ringing steals my attention.

"It's Shawn," I say, picking it up.

Robbie's eyes seem to darken to a denim blue. He walks to the couch and plops down while I take the call.

"Hi, Shawn," I say into the phone. "Are you here?"

"Hey, I'm really sorry, but I've gotta reschedule our date. I have a family emergency." He's out of breath, and I can hear traffic whooshing past him in the background.

"Oh no. Are you okay? Is your family okay? And don't worry about it. We'll reschedule."

A car horn blares. "Yeah, I'm fine. Sorry, I'm just rushing to the hospital now. I'll text you when I know more."

"Okay. Take care and let me know if you need anything."

The phone clicks off. My shoulders slump, and I stand there for a moment before turning back toward Robbie.

"What's up?" he asks.

I set my cell on the counter. "Shawn canceled. He has a family emergency."

Robbie jumps to his feet. "What happened?"

"I don't know. He didn't say, but I hope everything's all right."

"Yeah, I hope so too."

I fiddle with my nails and then the pendant on my necklace, sliding it back and forth. I can't help but be disappointed. I was really looking forward to my date with Shawn, and I worry I'm not going to get the chance to get to know him. I glance down at my dress and heels. I guess I'll save these for our rescheduled date.

"Hey, Peyton," Robbie says.

"Yeah," I say, lifting my head.

"Do you want to come with me to Maya's comedy show?"

"I'd love to," I say. All of a sudden, I'm not disappointed anymore.

A smile spreads across his face. "Perfect. It's a date." He scratches the back of his neck and stammers. "I mean . . ."

"I know what you mean." I smile back.

CHAPTER 14

A large man with a receding hairline and thick brows speaks into a microphone. The bright spotlight follows him as he paces the stage. "Our next stand-up comedian is a Chicago native. You may know her from the viral video where she completely destroyed a douchebag heckler—legit chewed him up and spat him out."

Even though the room is dimly lit, I can see Robbie roll his eyes. He's seated next to me, only a few inches away. I bump my shoulder into him. He shakes his head but grins. Zanies is an intimate comedy club with rows of small tables packed tight. We're seated in the front row, just a short distance from the stage.

The announcer continues. "Trust me. You don't want to mess with her. She throws an insult like Mike Tyson throws a punch. Please welcome to the stage the hilarious Maya James."

Robbie and I go nuts cheering and clapping while Maya emerges from the back and jogs up the steps. The man hands the mic over with an encouraging nod. She's wearing the red leather jacket she told me I bought for her, and the color of her lips perfectly matches it. She exudes confidence in her black skinny jeans and combat boots. Under the spotlight, her skin glows and her curly hair shines. When she spots Robbie and me, she nearly squeals but keeps her cool composure. Maya raises her chin as she takes in the applause and readies herself for her performance.

"Thank you," she says. "Thank you. That's exactly what I was expecting." The audience eats up her deadpan delivery.

"My best friend was hit by a car last week, but miraculously she's here tonight." The crowd claps. "Which part are you all clapping for?" Maya regards the audience with suspicion. The clapping is replaced with laughter. "Don't worry, the car's fine."

I knew she was planning a set about me and my *situation*, and I've been dying to hear the jokes she came up with. It'll be a nice reprieve laughing about it rather than living it—like a little comedic vacation from my life.

"She is too. Mostly, except for the amnesia." She pauses and paces the stage. "Yep. That's right. She doesn't remember anything. Not even me, which I find hard to believe given how famous and successful I am." Maya grins. "I can't even go to my own dentist without being recognized, and my landlord, don't get me started on him. He's been harassing me for months for an autograph. I keep signing stuff for him, but he says it needs to be at the bottom of a check. Fans are so particular these days." People laugh and clap. "So, anyway . . . it's been a tough time for me. I know she has amnesia or whatever, but we've been friends for over ten years, and she just forgot about me. How rude."

Maya stops pacing and stares at the audience. "And I don't care what the doctors say, I will not accept brain trauma as an excuse. Our friendship bracelets from college say FRIENDS FOREVER, not FRIENDS UNTIL WE GET INTO A CAR ACCIDENT AND FORGET THE OTHER PERSON EXISTS."

The crowd roars. Maya winks at me, and I laugh even louder.

"You all ever seen the movie *Overboard*, where the woman gets amnesia and the contractor that she was mean to uses it as a way to get revenge by making her become a maid and a babysitter?"

Many people in the crowd yell out "Yes."

"It's quite the opposite experience for my friend. Instead of all that, three of her Tinder dates showed up at the hospital declaring their love for her. What kind of Disney shit is that?"

Maya turns on her heel and walks across the stage. "So, now she gets the joy of first dates with each of them again, being wooed and swooned, them listening intently, hanging on to her every word, holding doors open, and sending her gifts, all in an attempt to win her over." Several of the women in the crowd make an *aww* sound. "I know, ladies. It's so sweet. Doesn't it make you just wanna jump for joy . . . right in front of a moving vehicle?" The crowd explodes with laughter.

Maya walks to the mic stand and peers out at the audience. "And they say fairy tales don't exist." She shrugs. "The dented hood of a 2010 Chrysler Sebring begs to differ."

Her set continues for another fifteen minutes. She's cool and confident, commanding the stage for every second of it. There's never a lull, as every joke she tells lands with the audience. My cheeks hurt, and the muscles in my stomach are sore from laughing. It feels like I've done a hundred sit-ups. I smile up at her, completely in awe.

"That's my time. Thank you, everyone. I'm Maya James." She waves at the audience. People clap and whistle as she hands the mic to the announcer and leaves the stage.

"She was amazing," I say, turning to Robbie.

"She was." He adds a generous tip and signs the receipt, closing up the book.

"What do I owe you?"

Robbie waves a hand at me. "Nothing. My treat."

"Thanks."

He slips his coat on and helps me into mine. "Want to go meet Maya and Anthony for a bit?" he asks as he adjusts the collar on my jacket.

"I'd love that." I nod.

"Follow me," he says, leading the way. I walk behind him, staying close in the crowded club. He sticks his hand out, and I grab it. Robbie smiles over his shoulder for a brief moment before returning his focus to navigating us through the crowd and toward the exit.

We grab seats at a bar two blocks from the comedy club. It has all the features of a typical dive bar—neon signs, a jukebox, pool tables and dartboards, cheap drinks, and furniture that hasn't been maintained. Robbie pulls two more stools over to the high-top table and places his jacket on one of them. I put mine on the other, saving them for Anthony and Maya.

"Want something to drink?" Robbie asks.

"Just a club soda with a slice of lemon."

"You got it."

He walks to the bar and finds a space to wedge himself in. The place is packed with people cutting loose on a Friday night. It's loud with chatter, and a classic rock song plays on the jukebox.

"Looks like you need some company," a man with thin lips and buzzed blond hair says. Without an invitation, he takes a seat on the stool next to me, Robbie's seat. He reeks of too much cologne mixed with rum, and he gives me a crooked smile as he props his elbows on the table.

"That seat's taken," I say, leaning away from him.

"Well, it isn't right now."

I roll my eyes and don't respond, but he doesn't take the hint and just keeps talking. "So, you got a man?"

I glance over at the bar. Robbie's back is to me, and he's busy ordering drinks from the bartender.

"Yeah, three of them," I say.

He waggles his eyebrows. "Three? Sounds like you need a man that can keep up with you."

I shoot him a disgusted look, turning my nose up.

"What's your name?" he asks.

"Doesn't matter."

He moves in closer, and I strain to lean farther away from him. "I'll tell you mine if you tell me yours."

"I don't care what your name is."

Robbie places four drinks on the table and raises his chin, squaring up with the guy. "Is there a problem here?"

"No problem here. This one's just playing hard to get," the man says with a laugh.

"No, I'm playing get the hell away from me."

"You heard her." Robbie strolls around the table, closing the distance between himself and the guy.

The creep stands and scowls. "She's a slut anyway."

Without hesitation, Robbie throws a fist right into his jaw. It makes a crunching sound. I hope it's from the man's chin and not Robbie's hand. The guy stumbles backward, shaking his head. His face reddens, and his eyes burn with anger as he charges at Robbie. Instinctively, I jump from my seat and try to pull Robbie back. The last thing I want is for him to get hurt defending me. Another man jumps in, wedging himself between me and Robbie. He's at least six foot four with a dark complexion and broad shoulders. One of his arms is the equivalent of two of Robbie's. The large man steps in front of Robbie, putting distance between him and the creep.

"You want a piece of him"—he gestures to Robbie—"you're gonna have to come through me first."

I let out a sigh of relief, knowing the large man is on our side.

The creep squints, sizing up the man, but it doesn't take more than a second for him to realize he stands no chance. He backs up and scurries out of the bar. The large man turns toward Robbie and grins.

"Perfect timing, Anthony," Robbie says, putting out his hand. They shake and pull one another in for a half hug with a pat on the back. This is Maya's Anthony. I can't help but smile, knowing she has a guy like him by her side.

"Didn't mean to sound so corny." Anthony laughs, mocking himself. *"You're going to have to come through me first."*

"Only you can pull off that type of ridiculous smack talk." Robbie chuckles.

"You caught me off guard. What was that even about?"

"He was harassing Peyton." Robbie gestures to me. Goose bumps cover my arms. I can't believe Robbie jumped to defend me without even a thought.

I give a small wave as Anthony turns to face me. He pulls me in for a hug and practically lifts me up off the floor. "Peyton! I'm so glad you're okay."

"Hi . . . me too," I say as he releases me.

Anthony grins, revealing a set of pearly white teeth. "Oh shoot. Sorry, forgot about the amnesia." He chuckles. "I'm Anthony, Maya's boyfriend."

"I've heard a lot about you."

"Hopefully all good things."

"Only good things." I nod.

"Maya's outside." He gestures toward the door. "Her mom rang right as we were coming in, so she's just taking the call quick."

Robbie hands Anthony a pint of golden-colored beer.

"Thanks, man."

They clink their beers together and chug. Robbie's hand clasps the glass, putting his red and swollen knuckles on display. I didn't realize how hard he hit the guy. I slip away to the bar and ask for a cup of ice and a rag. The bartender smiles and hands them over. "Tell Robbie no more throwing fists tonight," she says.

"You got it." I nod, returning the smile. Dumping the ice into the rag, I fold it up, creating a makeshift ice pack.

"Let me see your hand," I say to Robbie.

He holds it out, palm face up. I turn it over and press the rag ice pack onto his inflamed knuckles, causing him to wince.

"Sorry," I whisper.

Goose bumps cover his forearm, probably from the ice. "Thanks," Robbie says. His eyes are like sapphires.

"No, thank you for standing up for me." I smile up at him. "You didn't have to do that."

His face turns serious. "Yes, I did."

"What's going on over here?" Maya plops down next to Anthony. She leans in and kisses him on the lips, lightly brushing her nose against his.

"Robbie punched someone," I say, still pressing the ice pack against his knuckles.

Maya's head swivels to Robbie. "You what?"

"He was harassing Peyton."

"I came in right after Robbie punched him. Told him he'd have to come through me," Anthony says, puffing out his chest.

She laughs and pats Anthony on the shoulder. "You really said that?"

"It came off way scarier in the moment," he says with a nod.

"It's true. I was shaking in my heels," I tease.

Anthony chuckles and gulps his beer.

"I'm sad I missed it. I could have used a good laugh." Maya smirks.

Robbie pushes a drink toward her. "Here you are. I got you a vodka soda."

"Just what I needed," she says, sipping from the straw.

"Speaking of good laughs, you were incredible tonight," I say to Maya.

Her forehead puckers. "Hopefully it wasn't too much for you?"

"Not at all. It felt good to laugh about it. Life's too short not to laugh at yourself." I smile.

Her face relaxes with relief.

Anthony bumps his shoulder into her. "And it's nice to have a break from her making jokes about me."

"And her forcing me to heckle her," Robbie adds.

"I appreciate all of your contributions to my comedy material." Maya glances at each of us. She pauses and raises a brow at me. "Wait, aren't you supposed to be on a date with Shawn tonight?"

"Yeah, he canceled. Said he had a family emergency." I shrug and sip my club soda.

Maya leans back in her chair. "What happened?"

"I don't know. He didn't say."

"Do you have another date scheduled with him?"

I shake my head. "He told me he'd text me."

Maya presses her lips together, moving them side to side. "Sounds like he's not entirely invested. You should probably cut him."

"Maya! I'm not eliminating him because he had a family emergency."

Robbie pulls the ice pack from his knuckles and clenches and unclenches his fist. He tosses me a grateful smile before swigging his beer.

"Don't listen to Maya. She'd be single if it wasn't for me." Anthony snickers.

Maya pokes him in the side. He squirms in his chair, leaning away from her. The two laugh and playfully tickle one another. Finally, he grabs her hand and holds it while she rests her head against his shoulder, beaming up at him. Robbie was right. They are really cute together. What they have is what I want, and I hope I find it.

"What about the other two guys?" Anthony asks.

"I had a great time with both of them. They're very different from one another. Tyler's more outgoing, but he's playful and we have great chemistry."

Robbie gets up from his seat and says he'll grab us another round. He moseys over to the bar, flagging down the woman working it.

"You were saying." Anthony gestures to me.

I refocus my attention on Maya and Anthony. "Yeah, where was I? Oh yeah, the guys. Nash is really sweet, and he's an incredible cook. He's a little shy, but I got to see another side of him on our date when we were cooking at his restaurant."

"Sounds like you got some good ones to choose from." He nods.

My eyes land back on Robbie. He's leaned over the bar, chatting with the pretty bartender. She tosses her head back and laughs.

"Yeah, I guess I do," I say.

CHAPTER 15

Stacked across my arms are two bouquets of colorful flowers and a large cake from a local bakery. A reusable bag full of groceries hangs from one shoulder, tapping into my side as we walk.

"Are you sure you got all that?" Debbie glances over her shoulder at me.

"Yep," I say, stumbling behind her.

Debbie has her hands full with several bags of the heavier stuff like bottles of wine, which she said she wanted to stock up on. She's far stronger than she looks.

"Thanks for helping me run these errands," she says.

"What's all this for anyway?"

Debbie pushes the crosswalk signal. It beeps, and we stand at the corner waiting to cross the street. We're just two blocks from home.

She stares at the light, waiting for it to change. "Retirement party for a friend of mine."

"Oh, that's nice of you. Is it someone you worked with at the hospital?"

"Yeah," she says. As soon as the light turns, she starts off across the street. "Did that boy ever reschedule another date with you?"

"Not yet, but he checked in and said all is well with his family emergency now."

Debbie glances back at me. "Did he say what happened?"

"No, and I didn't ask. I figured maybe it was personal, and if he wanted to tell me, he would."

She turns left on our street and tosses a sympathetic glance over her shoulder. "What about the other two? Do you feel stronger about one over the other?"

"I don't know, maybe, but I'm trying to be sure I make the right choice . . . and by that I mean whichever one I was dead set on before the accident."

She purses her lips together. "Don't overthink it. You're following your heart, not solving a math equation."

I stare straight ahead, careful to not trip over any uneven sidewalk. Her words tumble around my brain. Have I been overthinking it? I've been so scared of making the wrong choice that maybe I haven't been focused on making the right choice.

When we reach our house, she holds the courtyard gate open for me. "It's unlocked, so you can head right in," Debbie says as she stops to check her mailbox.

I make my way up the steps, careful not to drop the cake, flowers, or grocery bag slung over my shoulder. At the door, I struggle with the handle. First, I try to turn it with my hip, then my foot. Finally, I extend my hand from beneath the cake and quickly grip and spin the handle, pushing the door open. The lights turn on before I can hit the switch, and a crowd of people yell, "Surprise!"

Startled, my shoulders jump. The flowers fall first, the cake flips out of my hands, splatting against the floor, and the grocery bag slides off my arm, its contents spilling out. There's a collective gasp, followed by whispers.

"Whoops. Should have planned that better," Maya says. She slips past everyone and approaches me as I bend down to clean up the mess.

Robbie joins us on the floor and helps flip the cake right side up. Thankfully, it's still in the box. "I got it," he says to me.

"Hey, girl," Maya says, collecting the flowers. She picks up several of the loose petals and stuffs them into the bouquet bag.

"What is all this? And who are all these people?" I whisper. I quickly scan the room but only recognize a few of them—Anthony, Nash, and Tyler. The other six or so, I have no idea who they are.

"Surprise!" Debbie yells from behind me.

I glance back at her. Her smile fades and forms into a straight line. "Maya, I told you she was coming in first."

"Yeah, but you didn't tell me you had her loaded up like a mule. You were supposed to distract her, not make her run all your errands."

"It's called killing two birds with one stone," Debbie huffs.

"Can someone tell me what is going on?" I ask again, this time more firmly.

Maya grins. "It's a surprise party."

"But my birthday isn't for another five days."

"It's not a birthday party. It's a *yay you're out of a coma* party." Her grin widens as she gets to her feet.

Robbie scoops up the mangled cake while I grab the bag of spilled groceries.

"Your coworkers, suitors, and friends are all here to celebrate your consciousness." Maya uses the mangled bouquets of flowers to gesture to the room of people.

They all stare at me, clapping and cheering. Smiles are plastered on each of their faces. I awkwardly wave and clear my throat. "Hi, everyone. Welcome to my surprise coma celebration."

Several people chuckle. I scan the room, hoping my memories will come flooding back as I peer out at them, but they're strangers to me. Tyler and Nash stand next to Anthony. They smile at me. I know Maya planned this whole thing so she could really talk with the guys and size them up, because there is no such thing as a *you're out of a coma surprise party*. I briefly glance over at her and wonder what else she has up her sleeve.

"Umm . . . I'm glad to be conscious," I add.

"We're glad you are too," an older woman with a sleek bob haircut says. "And we miss you at the office."

Several other people echo her sentiment.

"I miss you all too . . . I think." An awkward laugh escapes me.

"She hasn't lost her sense of humor," a woman around my age calls out.

Robbie shuffles the cake box to one hand, palming it. He wraps his arm around my shoulder. "Peyton's going to get her heart rate back down to normal, and then she'll be back out to mingle," he announces to the room and seals it with a wide grin.

Everyone laughs and claps, and then they go back to mingling.

"Thank you," I whisper to Robbie.

He leads me through the crowd of people. I exchange smiles and hellos with many of them as I follow him through the hallway and into the kitchen.

"For the record, the party was not my idea," Robbie says, setting the cake on the counter. He flips open the box, revealing a janky mess. Most of the frosting is smeared or stuck to the top of the box. "I tried to talk Maya out of it but—"

"I'm stubborn," Maya interrupts as she enters the kitchen. She places the flowers next to the sink and turns toward me with a smile. "How else was I going to size up these guys?"

I point at her. "I knew that's why you planned this."

"But." She holds her finger up. "I know you've been struggling with figuring out who you love, so Robbie, Debbie, Anthony, and I are here to help. It's a win-win."

"How are you going to help?" I ask, throwing my hands on my hips.

"I've already got Anthony grilling them."

"Maya!" I groan.

"I mean talking to them. He's a great judge of character." She raises her chin. "And Debbie will be able to sniff out the liar too."

"That's right," Debbie says, strolling into the kitchen. "I got a nose like a bloodhound for lies."

Robbie takes the bags of groceries from her and starts putting them away.

I gesture to the cake, wine, and flowers. "Wait, is most all this stuff for my surprise party?"

Debbie nods.

"You told me it was for a retirement party!"

She lifts her chin and smirks. "And you didn't even realize I was lying. That's why you need me to figure out who the liar is."

My hands slip from my hips. There's no getting out of this. It's clear Debbie and Maya have their minds made up. Plus, everyone is already here. It'd be rude if I just left.

Debbie stands in front of me, staring into my eyes. "We want to help. That's all."

I sigh. "Fine," I say. "But please no more surprises."

She gives a firm nod in agreement.

"Hey," a voice from behind me calls out.

Debbie's face lights up, and she turns me around so I can see the person attached to the voice. Shawn fills nearly the entire doorway. I didn't realize how tall he is. I guess because the last time I saw him I was laid up in a hospital bed. He smiles, but it's not the big, bright smile I witnessed before. It's small. Actually, it's barely there. His face isn't clean shaven either. It's scruffy like he didn't have time to shave.

"Hi, Shawn." I smile.

"Can I talk to you?" His eyes bounce around before landing back on me. "Privately."

"Yeah, sure," I say, and I follow him down the hallway. He veers off into a guest room and closes the door behind me.

I turn to face him. "How are you doing?"

"I'm good," Shawn says, but he wears a serious look, one that says, *I'm not good.*

Although he's standing four feet away, it feels like we're miles apart. Things have clearly changed since I last saw him, and I'm not sure why or how they could have.

"There's something I want to talk to you about."

"Okay." The word comes out slowly.

"I've been lying to you."

I take a step back. My mouth slightly parts. He's *the liar.*

"No. Actually, I've been lying to myself." Shawn's gaze falls to his leather oxford shoes and then climbs back to me. "For a long time now."

"I don't understand," I say.

He runs a hand over his face. "I've always been one of those people searching for the next best thing. In work, relationships, life, everything. Heck, I even order oysters anytime they're on a menu because they're considered the best, but I don't even like them."

Oysters, I think to myself. I'm reminded of the notes I found in my planner. "That's why I wrote down oysters," I say out loud, not meaning to.

His brows push together. "What?"

"Never mind." I shake my head. "You were saying."

He lets out a deep breath before he continues. "Peyton, I was engaged before, and I broke it off because I thought to myself, what if there's someone out there who's better for me? I know, it's terrible. But now I know there's not, because the best person for me has been there all along."

"I'm not sure I understand."

"The family emergency I canceled our date for." He lowers his chin. "It was my ex-fiancée. She had a health scare, and I was still listed as her emergency contact, so the hospital called me. Just the thought of losing her . . ." Shawn sighs and his eyes well up with tears. "It made me realize how much I still love her. Actually, I never stopped loving her."

"Is she okay?" I take a small step toward him.

The tears fall but he smiles through them. "Yeah, she's great," he says, wiping his face. "I'm really sorry, Peyton. If I had known before, I wouldn't have led you on. Honestly, between your accident and her health scare, it made me realize I've been wasting my time chasing life rather than living it." He lowers his head. "I feel so bad to do this to you now, especially with everything you've been through."

I place a hand on his shoulder. "Shawn, it's okay. I know what it's like to not know who your heart belongs to. It's an awful feeling, but I'm really glad you figured it out. And I'm happy for you . . . for the both of you." Tears fall from my eyes too. Not because I'm sad, but because I'm truly happy for him, and I want what he has—clarity. I want to be so sure of the person I love that the very thought of them makes me smile and cry at the same time, just like Shawn is right now.

He stares back at me. "I didn't mean to hurt you."

"You didn't." I smile up at him. "If anything, you've helped me."

Shawn wraps his arms around me and we hug. "I'm really sorry," he whispers.

"There's nothing to be sorry about. Thank you for being honest with me and yourself."

When we pull apart, he's still smiling. "I just listened to my heart for once."

Listen to your heart. I repeat the words back in my head. They're familiar, and this moment almost feels like déjà vu. But not entirely. Just the message, not the messenger. He takes a couple of steps back and wipes at his eyes again.

"Take care, Peyton. I hope your heart steers you right."

We share a smile as he leaves the room, and then he's gone, and I'm down to two boyfriends. I walk to the dresser and glance at the mirror hung above it.

"Hey," Maya says, poking her head in. "Did Shawn just leave?"

I wipe away my smeared mascara and take in Maya's reflection. "Yeah, he broke it off with me."

I'm not sure I can even qualify it as a breakup since I don't remember dating him.

"What?" Maya practically yells. "I'm gonna kick his ass."

"It's fine," I say, turning to face her. "Really. It is."

She delivers a sympathetic look and pulls me in for a hug. "He's an idiot," she says.

"No, he's not. He's just following his heart."

"Same thing." Maya takes a step back, surveying me. "Are you okay?"

"Yeah. I actually think I'm a little relieved." I let out a laugh.

"Why?"

"Because now it's down to two, and I think Shawn was the liar, so I don't have to worry about that now. But he wasn't just lying to me, he was lying to himself."

Her eyes go wide. "Wait, what if it was him? What if he was the guy you were running to the night of your accident?"

"It wasn't."

"How do you know?"

"I can just feel it."

Maya lets out a sigh and rubs the side of my arm. "If you're not up for your coma party, I can have Anthony kick everyone out."

"It's fine. I think it's just what I need."

It's a couple of hours later, and I'm waving goodbye to my work friends as they walk down the steps of the porch. My boss tells me to take as much time off as I need. One of my coworkers begs me to come back as soon as possible because she's bored to tears without me.

They yell out "Bye" and "Take care" and "See you soon." A few of them get into their vehicles and drive off, while others leave on foot.

I spent most of the party chatting with them in an attempt to learn a little more about myself. I don't feel like I learned much, though, because I was so focused on trying to remember each of their names, how long I've worked with them, and what their jobs are. But it was fun to get to know the work side of me.

When I reenter the house, Tyler catches my eye. He smiles at me from across the room. Debbie taps him on the shoulder and points to a floorboard. She steps on it to show him that it's loose. He smirks and bends down to take a closer look. Poor Tyler. I'm pretty sure he spent nearly the entire party fixing random things around the house.

I spot Nash, Robbie, and Anthony out on the balcony, sipping from Solo cups and chatting. Robbie grins when he sees me, and I return it.

"Time for a party game," Maya declares, strutting into the living room. She opens the balcony door and beckons with her hand. "Guys, get in here."

They all stand and file into the living room.

"I hope it's spin the bottle," Debbie says, waggling her brows. She plops down in her chair and sips at her heavily poured wineglass.

I snicker and take a seat on the couch. Robbie selects the spot next to me, and Anthony situates himself on the other side. Nash and Tyler sit across from us in folding chairs, forming a sort of circle.

"The game is two truths and a lie," Maya says, standing in the center of the room. "You say three things about yourself. Two of them have to be true, while the third thing is a lie. The rest of us guess which is which, and then we continue clockwise around the circle. Any questions?"

I squint at her. "How am I supposed to be able to play this game?"

"Robbie, Debbie, and I will play for you. Between the three of us, we know everything there is to know about you."

I roll my eyes and lean back in my seat. Robbie bumps his shoulder into me and smiles.

"Any other questions?" Maya asks. When no one speaks up, she takes her seat next to Anthony. "Tyler. I'm randomly picking you to go first."

He cocks his head. "How is that random?"

"Because I said it was. Now, go." She points to him.

"Maya," I warn.

"I mean, please proceed," she says.

Tyler props his elbows up on his knees and leans forward in his chair. "Hmm. Let me think. I've never traveled outside of the country. I have a twin brother. And I'm a Green Bay Packers fan."

"I thought this game would be much spicier." Debbie brings her wineglass to her lips and takes a big gulp.

I stifle a laugh.

Robbie snaps his fingers. "Twin brother is the lie."

"No way. It's the never traveling outside of the country. That's the lie," Maya says.

"You better not be a Green Bay Packer fan in Bear country," Anthony teases.

"Peyton, what do you think?" Tyler asks. The corner of his lip perks up.

I glance to my side at Robbie and then back at Tyler. "I'm with Robbie. I don't think you have a twin brother."

Tyler presses his lips firmly together and nods. "That's right."

Robbie holds up his hand for a high five. Our hands splat together, and then he points at Tyler. "We got you pegged," he says.

"Easy to have him pegged when you did a deep dive on him," I tease.

He shrugs and laughs, while Tyler's face is serious, almost more of a pensive look, with a creased brow and tightened eyes. I smile at him, but he doesn't return it. Instead, he takes a long sip from his Solo cup.

"Nash, your turn," Maya says.

Nash sits up straight in his chair and sips his drink.

"Make this one spicy," Debbie says.

He rubs his arm, his fingers brushing over the colorful tattoos. "I lived in France for a year. I've been on TV. And I went on a date with a celebrity." His face remains stoic when he finishes speaking.

"Damn. I can't believe two of those are truths," Anthony says with a husky laugh. "You're a cool guy, Nash."

Nash shrugs like he's being modest, but a small smile creeps across his face.

"You got him pegged too?" Tyler directs his question toward Robbie.

Tyler and Robbie lift their chins and lean forward in their seats, almost as though they're challenging one another. I didn't think this was supposed to be such a serious game.

"I think I do," Robbie says. "The date with a celebrity is the lie."

"My bet is on the TV show." Maya sips her drink.

"What do you think, Peyton?" Nash looks to me.

I tap my finger against my chin, pondering for a moment. "Dating a celebrity is the lie."

"That's right," he says with a nod.

"Wait, what TV show were you on? It couldn't be my *Bachelor* shows." Debbie squints and leans forward in her chair, trying to get a better look at him. "I for sure would have recognized you."

Nash cracks a smile. "No, I wasn't on one of those dating shows. I was on *Chopped*. It's on the Food Network."

"I love *Chopped*. Did you win?" Anthony's voice is full of excitement.

"No, came in second place. I got cut because I forgot to plate one of the ingredients."

"Dang. That's the worst. Sorry, man," Anthony says.

Nash nods. "It is." He sips his drink.

"All right, Peyton's turn," Maya says.

I whip my head in her direction. "No, I'm not playing."

"I told you, me, Robbie, and Debbie will name your three."

I sigh and eyeball the guys. Tyler tilts his head and folds his arms over his chest. It's almost like he doesn't want to be here. I smile at him, but either he doesn't notice, or he ignores it again. Nash props his foot up on his knee and gives his attention to Maya, waiting for her to speak. He seems to be having a better time than Tyler.

"I'll go first," Debbie says. "Peyton is the kindest person I know, and if any of you hurt her, I'll . . ."

"Debbie," Maya pipes in. "That is not how you play. It has to be something true or false about her, not how you feel followed by a threat."

Her forehead puckers. "But it is true."

"I'll go first," Maya says, letting out a sigh. "Peyton is terrified of spiders."

"I am?" I ask.

Maya shrugs. "Now, you go, Debbie."

"Hmm, let's see." She taps her nail against her wineglass, and when she thinks of one, her eyes light up. "Oh, I got it. Peyton is a terrible singer."

"Isn't that subjective?" Nash asks.

Debbie shakes her head. "Not at all. One time when she did karaoke, the DJ shut her mic off. That's how bad she was." She chuckles and leans back in her chair.

I quietly hum to myself to see if she's right. It sounds good in my head.

"Are you humming?" Maya asks.

"No," I lie.

"The bad singing is definitely true," Tyler says with a smirk. "That is too specific of a story for it not to be true."

Debbie raises a brow. "Or I'm a good liar?"

"Robbie, your turn." Maya gestures to him.

He readjusts himself in his seat. "Whenever Peyton finds a coin on the ground, if it's tails up, she flips it over so the next person that comes along next will have good luck." Robbie glances at me and gives a small smile.

Tyler chuckles. "That's the lie."

"I think it's the being scared of spiders," Nash says.

Both Nash and Tyler look to me for the correct answer. "I don't know," I say with a laugh.

"Nash is right." Robbie nods. "The fear of spiders is the lie."

Tyler grimaces at him, while Nash smiles and sips his drink.

"Am I really that bad of a singer?"

"Oh yeah, the worst." Debbie chuckles. "Who needs a refill?" she asks, holding up her wineglass. Tyler and Nash raise their cups and get to their feet.

Robbie pats my knee and whispers, "I like your singing. Because it's similar to mine. Our karaoke duets sound like a couple of stray cats yowling and meowing for scraps of food." He cracks a teasing smile.

I nudge him with my elbow. "Are we really that bad?"

"Oh yes. It's like punishment for the other patrons."

We both laugh.

"Hey, Peyton," Tyler calls out. My laughter extinguishes as I look to him. He stands in the entrance to the hallway with knitted brows and wandering eyes that zip between Robbie and me.

"I've gotta go," he adds, gesturing to the front door.

"Everything all right?" I ask, while getting to my feet.

"Yeah, just gotta let Toby out." He looks down at his wrist even though he's not wearing a watch. "It's been a while."

"Okay. Let me walk you out."

He nods but doesn't make eye contact with me. I think he's mad, and I don't know why.

Out on the porch, I thank Tyler for coming and tell him I had a good time. He says, "Yeah," but doesn't echo my sentiments.

"Are you free this week for a date?" I ask.

He runs a hand over his face, glancing away for a moment. "Is it with you?"

I pull my chin in. "What do you mean?"

Tyler takes a step back and shoves his hands into his pockets, blowing out a gust of air. "When I agreed to do whatever this is, I thought I'd be dating you."

"You are."

"It doesn't feel like it. It feels like I'm dating a committee. You have Robbie doing deep dives on us, and Maya's arranging gatherings so she can size us up. Plus, I spent the whole party fixing things around Debbie's house rather than spending time with you. It just doesn't feel like you're the one making the decision."

"But I am. They're helping me figure things out," I argue.

Can't he see how difficult and baffling this is for me? I have no memories. It's like I'm sitting in a classroom 24-7 learning about myself. I don't get it, though. On our last date, he said he'd be patient, so I don't understand where this change in attitude came from.

"Robbie's deep dive." He shakes his head. "If you wanted to know things about me, why didn't you just ask?"

"I don't know . . . It's confusing. Because I don't know what we've talked about and what we haven't talked about."

"And I understand that. I knew what I was getting into when I agreed to date you again. At least I thought I did. It's just—" He groans. "This isn't what I had in mind."

"I'm trying," I plead.

"I get that, but I guess I didn't think it would be a difficult decision for you to make. I thought you would know how strong our connection is . . . well, was." He sighs and his gaze veers off toward the street.

"Are you saying you don't want to date me anymore?"

"No. I don't know. I just . . . I have to go." Tyler's mouth forms a hard line. I notice his eyes have a sheen to them, but he turns away from me and jogs down the steps of the porch before I can get a better look. "I'll text you," he calls over his shoulder as he heads toward his car.

"Tyler," I yell, but he doesn't respond. He doesn't even look back at me.

I instantly feel sick to my stomach. *What am I doing?* He's right. I should just know who I love. I should know who my heart beats for. I should know who I have the strongest connection with. This shouldn't be such a difficult decision to make because I've made it before. And if I don't figure it out soon, I'm not going to have anyone left to love.

CHAPTER 16

My eyes sluggishly open. I blink several times, adjusting to the light. There's a weight on me, something draped over my stomach. I glance down and see that it's an arm, attached to Robbie. His skin is warm, and it feels like I'm nestled up next to a fireplace, all cozy and safe. His body is pressed against mine like he's the big spoon, and I'm the little spoon. We didn't fall asleep like that, so I wonder at what point in the night the pillow wall got completely dismantled. Maybe subconsciously Robbie was trying to comfort me because he knew I was upset. I played it off like I was fine, but he knew. I think he assumed it was because of Shawn bowing out. But it wasn't. It was what Tyler had said. I grab my phone and quickly check my messages. He still hasn't texted me.

Sitting up, I cautiously lift Robbie's arm, sliding it off me. He doesn't move when I slip out of bed. He just lies there, almost purring as he sleeps.

In the kitchen, I brew a pot of coffee. It's the first one I've made post-amnesia—but somehow I remember how to do it. Grind the beans. Fill the reservoir with water. Add a filter with the ground coffee. And turn it on. My gaze bounces to the fridge and then to the stove. I wonder what else I can do. The house is quiet, so I know Robbie's still asleep. Perhaps I'll surprise him with a breakfast sandwich. Something simple like egg, cheese, and bacon. He's been doing so much for me, and I think it'd be nice to try to do something for him.

I race around the kitchen, collecting the ingredients. I click on the burner and drop four slices of bacon into the pan, then slice two English muffins and pop them into the toaster. The scent of the nutty coffee fills the room, and I inhale it.

As I wait for the bacon to buckle and curl in the frying pan, my mind goes back to yesterday. I've made a mess of everything. Maybe I should have listened to Robbie and waited until my memories came back before I started dating again. I clearly wasn't ready, and I don't know what I was thinking when I agreed to go through with all this. Well, I do. I figured my heart would just know. That's its job. To love and to pump blood. That's it. I glance down at my ticker and scowl at it for only doing half its job.

My phone buzzes against the counter, and the screen lights up. It's a good-morning text from Nash. He left shortly after Tyler did, leaving me with a kiss on the cheek and plans for another date. He didn't seem upset like Tyler did, so maybe I'm doing this whole dating with amnesia thing half right. But I really need to figure out who I was running to before the accident, and I need to do it soon. Before it's too late . . . if it's not already.

I scroll to the last message Tyler sent me. It was from yesterday morning. He said he missed me. I said I missed him too. But nothing since then. I consider texting him, a casual and light message, like *good morning* or *how are you*. But he said he'd text me, and he made that clear. I think he needs space, time to mull it all over. I knew this would be hard on me, but I didn't consider that it would also be hard on the guys. I pour myself a cup of coffee and wince. It's still too hot to drink.

Three loud beeps screech throughout the house. My shoulders jump and the mug of coffee slips from my hand, crashing onto the hardwood floor. Shoot! Smoke pools above the burning bacon, and I rush to the stove, turning off the burner.

"Peyton!" Robbie yells. His footsteps pad down the hallway, and he suddenly appears, dressed in only a pair of pajama pants. His panicked eyes zoom to me, the stove, and the smoke alarm above the kitchen table that's raging with three long, loud beeps over and over. He pulls open the balcony doors and then grabs a throw blanket from the couch, waving it near the alarm. The smoke dissipates as he fans it toward the open door. I'm just standing here, leaning up against the counter, frozen. Finally, the alarm shuts off. He catches his breath and tosses the blanket back on the couch.

"What happened?" he asks.

I feel like a deer in headlights. "I was trying to make you breakfast."

"Well, are you all right?"

I look down at the spilled hot coffee and broken mug beside my feet.

"Stay right there," he says, dashing toward the hallway. A moment later he returns with a towel, diving onto his hands and knees to clean up the mess I've made.

"Sorry," I say.

Robbie glances up at me. "No need to be sorry. It was just an accident."

The bread pops out of the toaster. It startles me, and my shoulders jump again.

When the spilled coffee and broken mug is cleaned up, Robbie gets to his feet and grins. "So, what'd you make me?"

"Umm, burned bacon and a toasted English muffin," I say, glancing at the stove and toaster.

"My favorite," he teases, and I can't help but smile. My shoulders finally relax and I let out a deep breath. He leaves the kitchen with the dirty towel in hand, and I pour him a cup of coffee, careful not to drop this one. The washer kicks on, and a moment later Robbie is standing in front of me. He's thrown a T-shirt on and his hair is now pushed back, rather than going in all directions. I hand the mug over.

He slowly sips his coffee, but he doesn't wince like I did. Must have a higher pain tolerance. "Still upset about Shawn?" Robbie asks.

I busy myself by scrubbing out the pan in the sink. "I was never upset about Shawn."

"Oh, then what was wrong?"

I scrub the pan harder, deciding whether to tell Robbie about Tyler. I know what he'll say. He'll tell me I shouldn't have dated until I was feeling better. He'll tell me I should break it off with him. But maybe I want him to say those things. Maybe I need to hear them so it'll light a fire under me and stop me from waffling on the decision.

"I think Tyler may have bowed out too."

"What? Why?"

"He left pretty upset last night." I rinse the pan, set it in the drying rack, and turn to face Robbie. "Didn't like that you had done a deep dive on him or that Maya had arranged the party so she could size them up."

His brows shove together. "But we're helping you."

"That's what I said. But he felt like if I had questions I wanted answers to, I should have just asked him. He said it seemed like I wasn't the one making the decision."

"That's ridiculous," Robbie scoffs. "You have a brain injury—of course your friends are going to help you."

"But maybe you all are helping a little too much." I dry my hands off with a dish towel and pour myself a cup of coffee.

He tilts his head. "Is that really what you think?"

"I don't know. I just feel like I should know who I love and maybe I'm overthinking it because you all have so much to say about the guys. It's confusing. And Tyler is hurt that I still don't know who I love." I sip slowly.

"Oh, so he's mad that you didn't just pick him right away." Robbie rolls his eyes.

I let out a sigh and stare into my mug. "I guess he was really confident in our connection, so he assumed I would be too and that I would just know in my heart."

"So, Tyler's out?"

"I don't know." I shrug. "He said he would text me."

"You should be done with him," he says earnestly.

"What? Why? I'm not ending it with Tyler."

"You should. If he's not willing to be patient and understanding of your situation, he's clearly not the one for you. You deserve better than that, Peyton."

"Oh, stop. Tyler has every right to be upset. His feelings are just as involved as mine are. And I should have been spending my time getting to know each of them rather than focusing on deep dives from you and Maya." My eyes narrow, and I don't even mean for them to.

"Sorry you wasted your time on me."

"That's not what I meant." My face softens. "It's just been a lot, and I'm trying to figure it out without hurting anyone or getting hurt myself."

"This is exactly why you should have never done this whole dating-again thing in the first place. Rather than focusing on you, you're worried about their feelings. I told you it would be too much, especially given your injury."

"You can't protect me from everything, Robbie."

"I'm not trying to. I just think if any of these guys truly cared about you, they wouldn't be pushing you to make a decision."

I knew that's exactly what he would say. He thinks he knows what's best for me. But this isn't all about me. There are other people and their feelings involved.

"I just need you all to give me space to figure it out."

"I'm only trying to help you, Peyton. You don't exactly have the best track record when it comes to dating, and I don't want you to end up in another relationship with some jerk."

"I think you're the last person that should be giving any advice on relationships, Robbie," I scoff.

He cocks his head. "What's that supposed to mean?"

"You've never been close to telling anyone you loved them. You break up with girls over stupid reasons like what shows they like or what they eat. So, of course for you, any reason is a good reason to break up with someone. You've never loved anyone, so you can't possibly know what you're talking about." I stomp into the living room.

Maybe I'm being unfair to Robbie, but how dare he bring up my dating history when his isn't any better. I can't process all my emotions right now, and he's not making it any easier on me. I feel like I'm being pulled in too many directions and everyone wants something different.

His footsteps follow behind.

"And what would you know about love, Peyton? You don't even know who you love."

I turn to face him. "Yeah, you're right. I don't know who I love, but I know I do. I can feel it in my skin, in my fingers, in my heart. And I know it's worth fighting for. It's worth the mess and the confusion and the frustration. It's worth being sick over. Hell, I got hit by a car for it, and I'm not just going to throw it away because you think I should." By the time I'm done speaking, I'm standing only six inches away from Robbie, glaring up at him.

He stares blankly.

"What, Robbie? What is it?"

"All I ever wanted was for you to be happy. That's it."

"I think what you want is for me to be miserable just like you, Robbie." I regret the words as soon as they leave my mouth, but I'm frozen. They hang in the air for a moment too long, and it now it feels like it's too late to pull them back. You can't just unsay something.

His jaw clenches like he's chewing on the things he wants to say out loud. His Adam's apple rocks up and down, and his eyes become glassy.

"Well, I hope you find out who you love then." Robbie steps back. "Because I wouldn't want you to end up like me."

I want to apologize and tell him I didn't mean it. I'm just confused, and I'm taking it all out on him because I know he'll take it. It's not fair to Robbie at all, but I don't know how to go back, and I don't know how to explain how I'm feeling. The words get stuck in my throat. I'm frustrated with him for being so wishy-washy on this whole dating thing. One day he's against it, the next he's for it. He likes Tyler and then he doesn't like him. It's all so complicated, and I don't know how to uncomplicate it.

Robbie grabs his belongings without saying another word. The stairs creak as he descends them, and the front door opens and closes. I let out a heavy sigh. I'm the one who accepted Robbie's help. I agreed to the new pact. I asked for his opinions. I wanted him to be protective of me. So, it's not all on him. It's on me too.

CHAPTER 17

I haven't seen Robbie in two days. He hasn't texted or called. I sent him a message saying I was sorry. The three little dots popped up over and over like he was typing, but nothing ever came through. I've been staying at Debbie's the last two nights. I would have just stayed home alone because I don't think I need anyone watching me. But maybe I do because I keep screwing everything up. Robbie told Debbie he was going to be busy with work for a while, so someone else needed to take nights. I went along with his lie and didn't tell Maya or Debbie about our fight. Debbie knows something's up. She's got a sixth sense for that, but she doesn't pry.

Tyler hasn't texted me either. I think he and I might be done. The only guy I have left in my life is Nash. I haven't told him that, but maybe I will right now. Nash smiles over his shoulder at me as I take a seat at a table in a small Italian restaurant. It's cute and cozy. They hand-make pasta in the front window, and it's counter service only. The floor is covered in alternating black and white tiles, almost like an illusion, one you could get lost in.

Nash orders at the register. He's dressed in a white button-down, a navy-blue suit jacket, and a pair of khakis. I haven't seen him dressed so nice before. I stare at the back of his head. A colorful tattoo peeks out from behind his collar. Was he the one I was running to? I try to picture it. Me running as fast as I can toward him. His bright hazel eyes.

Tattoo-covered arms. Sharp jawline. I can picture it, but I don't know if it's a memory or just something I'm imagining right now.

When he's finished ordering, he carries a tented sign with an order number back to our table. He smiles at me again. It's a small one. I force a smile back. I am happy he's here with me, but I'm unhappy about everything else. Most of all Robbie. How did I lose a friend in all this? My phone sits face up on the table. I glance at it, hoping a message will appear. But it doesn't.

"What did you order?" I ask.

Nash takes a seat across from me and unfolds a napkin in his lap. "It's a surprise."

I hope it's better than my last surprise, and by that I mean the party where not one but two guys broke it off with me.

"I'm glad I could finally take you out on a date at night," he adds.

"Me too." I sip water, while my eyes wander to the other couples seated at their tables. They're engaged in conversations, staring intently at one another, laughing, and eating, like nothing else around them matters.

I think that's what love is supposed to look like. Your person completely in focus while the world melts around you. My gaze swings to Nash. Everything around him is as clear as he is.

"Nash," I say.

"Yeah."

"Are you upset that I haven't made a decision yet?"

His brow creases. "No, why would I be?"

I readjust the napkin in my lap. "Do you feel like I should have just known who I loved?"

"What do you mean?"

"Like, did you think our connection was so strong that it had to be you?"

He tilts his head to the side. "I knew I felt strongly about you, but I didn't know if you felt the same way. I mean . . . I hoped you did."

I search his face like I'm trying to find an answer to a question I already know the answer to.

It couldn't have been Nash. Even now, he's not entirely sure how I feel about him, and I don't know either. There's no way I was running toward him the night of the accident, and I think I've known that since our first date. I chalked it up to him being shy or nervous, but really our connection just isn't strong.

His face changes, almost turning downward as if he knows what I'm thinking, knows he's not the one. Tyler felt so deeply about us that it hurt him that I couldn't feel it too. But I could. I knew the stronger connection was with Tyler, but for some reason I couldn't say it out loud. I couldn't end it with Nash and Shawn and commit to him. I don't know why, but it has to be Tyler. He was the one I was running to.

"I'm sorry, Nash."

He pulls his lips in and nods like he already knows what I'm going to say.

"You're an amazing man, truly, one of the good ones. You deserve someone that's going to love you with every ounce of their being." My voice cracks. "But you weren't the guy I was running to the night of my accident, and I'm really sorry it's taken me this long to figure it out."

Nash leans across the table and rests his hand on mine. "It's all right, Peyton. There's nothing to be sorry about."

"Are you mad at me?"

"Not at all. My mom might be when she finds out I'm not bringing a girl home for Christmas again." He chuckles. "I may have been a little presumptuous and told her about you." His cheeks flush. "If you're free, maybe you can pretend to be my girlfriend."

I smile. "I think I've got enough tropes in my dating life for this year."

"Next year then."

We laugh, and he squeezes my hand gently before pulling away.

"What are you waiting for?"

I give him a quizzical look.

"You should go. Go tell him how you feel."

"Are you sure?"

"Yeah. I'll be all right. Plus, I'm famished, and their plates are pretty small here." He smirks.

"Thanks for being so great, Nash." I stand from my seat and slip on my jacket. "Some other girl is going to come into your life, and she's gonna feel like she won the lottery when she meets you." I smile and turn on my heel to head for the door.

"Hey," he calls out.

I stop and glance back.

"It's like I'm one of those coins you turn over for someone else to find," Nash says with a smile. This time it reaches his eyes.

My knuckles rap against the door three times. I'm not even sure he'll answer. Footsteps pad on the other side, growing louder. Dog nails click against the hardwood floor. The door swings open, revealing Tyler dressed in sweatpants and a white tee. His hair is pulled back in a low bun with a few flyaway strands floating in the air like he's just woken up from a nap. His eyes widen. It's clear he's startled by my unexpected drop-in. Toby barks once, but as soon as he recognizes it's me, he wags his tail and whimpers.

"What are you doing here?" Tyler asks.

I stare back, imagining I'm running toward him as fast as I can, so fast the world is a blur around me and all I can see is him. Those green eyes that I know I've gotten lost in. His perfectly trimmed beard, cut close enough to see how strong his jaw and chin are. Those wide shoulders and muscular arms. His long dark hair with strands as soft as down feathers. I can picture it. It's him. It's Tyler.

His hand clutches the door, like he's not sure whether to open it farther or close it on me.

"I broke it off with Nash," I say.

"Really?" His gaze dances around my face.

I nod. "Really."

The corners of his mouth quiver. "So, it's me. I'm the one you were running toward."

"Yeah, it's you. It has to be you."

Tyler blows out a gust of air and smiles so wide, I think his lips might split. All of a sudden, I'm wrapped up in his arms, my face pressed against his chest. His heart races like he's just finished running a marathon. I inhale, breathing in his scent, a mix of sawdust and citrus. He kisses the top of my head, and then tucks his hand beneath my chin, lifting it so our eyes meet.

"I knew it was you and me," Tyler whispers.

He leans in and kisses me, first soft and gentle, then with more passion, like I'm the oxygen he needs to breathe. I kiss him back. Our mouths open and close. My hands run over his chest, settling around his neck. He picks me up in one fell swoop, my legs wrapping around his waist. The door closes behind us, and our lips never part as he carries me toward his bedroom.

CHAPTER 18

"Well, well, well. Look who's back from her trek of triumph," Maya says with a smirk.

I place a hand over my eyes and peer up at the porch as I push open the courtyard gate. Maya and Debbie are seated next to one another in rockers. They both grin at me as I make my way up the steps. I'm still dressed in last night's clothes. My hair's tied up in a high ponytail. I tried my best to push my makeup back into place, but I'm sure I look more like a Picasso painting.

"I thought it was a walk of shame," Debbie says.

Maya shakes her head. "Nah, that's outdated. We celebrate our carnal conquests now. No shame in that game."

Debbie nods in agreement and glances at her watch. "Whew! Getting home at nine in the morning. Must have been a good date." She gives a teasing smile.

My cheeks feel ablaze. I rub my face and sit down on the concrete-and-brick seating wall that lines the porch.

"How's Nash?" Maya waggles her brows.

"I broke it off with him."

They glance at one another and then back at me. "Then who were you with?" Debbie asks.

"Tyler."

Maya lets out a low whistle. "And you stayed the night?"

"Yeah . . . but I didn't sleep with him."

"Bullshit," Maya says.

"No really, I didn't."

"I would have." Debbie laughs.

Maya and I exchange a small smile.

"I told him I didn't want to until I had my memories back." I glance down at my feet. "I only have a week's worth of memories with Tyler, but I want to have all of them."

"I think that's sweet," Debbie says.

"So, he's the one?" Maya asks.

"Yeah."

Debbie rocks in her chair. "And how do you feel?"

"Relieved."

"Really?" She knits her brows together.

"Yeah," I say. What's wrong with being relieved? Maybe that's not the right word, or that's just the emotion I'm feeling right now. I am relieved.

Maya and Debbie share another look. "I'd think you'd feel elated, warm and fuzzy, euphoric, excited," Debbie says.

"Yeah, relieved is something you feel after going to the bathroom or finishing up a long day of work or getting out of a speeding ticket," Maya adds.

"I do feel all those things. But mostly, I feel relieved that I finally figured it out." My eyes swing between the two of them. Debbie moves her lips from side to side, while she studies my face. Maya, too, watches me carefully.

"I'm happy," I say, sealing it with a large smile. *I am,* I reassure myself. This whole thing wasn't a normal courtship. It wasn't boy meets girl and they fall in love. It was girl meets three guys. Girl gets amnesia and forgets about the three guys. Girl dates all three guys again, narrows it down, and finally figures out who she loves. So of course my emotions are going to be mixed and all over the place. The situation calls for complicated feelings.

They stare at me for a few moments before they finally relax their concerned faces and smile. Debbie stands from her rocking chair and embraces me with a hug. "I'm glad you're happy. Tyler seems like a great guy."

"Did your memories come back then?" Maya asks.

"No," I say.

"Then how did you know it was Tyler?"

"Because I knew it wasn't Nash. We just never had that strong of a connection. He's amazing but he's not the one. And Tyler felt so strongly about us. There was never a doubt in his mind that it was him I was running toward."

Maya frowns. "Poor Nash."

"Wait, do you think I should have picked him?"

"No. You said he's not the one. I just really liked him," Maya says.

"Me too," Debbie adds. "He was so sweet. He even emailed me his chicken noodle recipe after the party last night because I kept raving about it." She smiles fondly and reaches for my hand, squeezing it once before releasing it.

I fiddle with my nails. "I felt really bad breaking it off with him, but he was so nice and understanding, and he didn't make me feel any worse than I already did. Actually, he made me feel better."

"I wonder if he's into cougars." Debbie raises her brows and chuckles.

"Debbie!" Maya says.

"How do you even know what that is?" I ask.

"Another online dating mishap," she says with a smirk.

A laugh escapes us.

Maya eyeballs me. "What's next for you and Tyler?"

"He's taking me out to dinner on my birthday."

"Nice." She smiles.

Debbie holds a finger up. "Oh, that reminds me. I got something for you." She disappears inside her home for a moment before emerging with a small box wrapped in green paper. A white bow adorns the gift with a sealed envelope tucked underneath it.

"Here," she says, handing it to me.

I take it from her and look down at the envelope resting on top. *Peyton* is written on the front of it. I know immediately that it's Robbie's handwriting. I don't know how I know that but I do. It's a little sloppy but still legible.

"It's from Robbie." Debbie tightly smiles. "He dropped it off this morning. With how busy work has been for him, he wasn't sure he'd be able to get it to you before your birthday." She says it like she doesn't believe that's the truth.

I feel my heart race like it grew feet and started running, pounding against my rib cage. My stomach flips, and I blink back tears. I should have never said what I said to him. I didn't mean any of it. I was just feeling emotional and disoriented. And now I feel so awful and sad. I miss Robbie, and I'm mad at myself for how I spoke to him.

Maya leans forward in her chair. "Are you going to open it?"

"No, I'm going to wait until my birthday."

She groans and waves her hand at me. "You're no fun. I wanted to see what it is."

"Knowing Robbie, whatever it is, it'll be very thoughtful," Debbie says.

I hold the present a little tighter. It's so neatly wrapped, like he took his time with it, making sure it was perfect. A frown settles on my face. As much as I want to rip it open, I don't feel like I even deserve whatever's inside of it . . . even if it's a piece of trash.

CHAPTER 19

Tyler's texts says he's five minutes away. I give myself a once-over in the mirror, making sure my makeup is blended and my hair is volumized. It's in ringlet curls, which took me hours, but it gave me something to do. I take a step back and check out how my new outfit looks—a white long-sleeve bodysuit with a sweetheart neckline and a pair of high-waisted black leather leggings. It was a birthday gift from Maya. I think it's more her style, but I'm getting used to it. I readjust the gold necklace wrapped around my neck. It's simple and delicate with a heart pendant that rests right beneath my collarbone. It was a present from Debbie, and it came in one of those nice jewelry boxes with the felt lining. I knew right away she spent more than she should have on it. When I told her it was too much, she said, "There is no such thing."

I smile at my reflection. "Happy birthday," I say to the girl staring back at me. It's strange. I've lived thirty-two years, but I only have two weeks' worth of memories, and I have no idea how I got here.

The perfectly wrapped present set on the kitchen counter catches my eye. I said I'd open it on my birthday, but it feels wrong to unwrap it without Robbie here. My feet carry me toward it. I pull the card from the gift and flip it over in my hand. On the back of the envelope reads, *Open last*.

I smile. Of course Robbie would have instructions on how to open his gifts. I unwrap the box. Inside, I find a charm bracelet adorned with coins—a mix of pennies, nickels, and dimes. There are fourteen of them spaced evenly around the chain. It jingles when I pick it up. I wrap the bracelet around my wrist and clasp it. The coins dance against one another as I wiggle my hand. My gaze returns to the envelope. I tear it open and slide the card out, scanning over the words Robbie handwrote.

> Peyton,
> You've turned over so many coins, leaving good luck for others. I hope you don't mind that I collected some of them for myself, fourteen to be exact, one for each year I've known you, because they've been the luckiest years of my life. Happy birthday.
> Love,
> Your friend, Robbie

By the time I finish reading the card, I can't see the words anymore. My eyes fill with tears and my bottom lip trembles. I don't deserve this. I don't deserve him. A single tear drops onto the card, landing on the word *love*. The ink spreads, and I quickly wipe it away. Holding up my wrist, I admire the charm bracelet, the thoughtfulness of it, the planning that went into it, and the time it took him to make it.

Pulling my phone from my purse, I stare at the lit-up screen. I want to call him, but I don't think he'll pick up. So instead, I send a text.

> Thank you for my gift, Robbie. I love it, and I wish you would have been here when I opened it.

I hit "Send." The three little dots pop up immediately. He's typing.

> I'm glad you like it. Happy birthday, Peyton.

There are no emojis. No exclamation points. Nothing. I let out a sigh and type another message.

> I'm sorry about our fight. I didn't mean what I said. I was just frustrated, and I took it out on you. You didn't deserve that. You've been here for me this whole time, and I'm so lucky to have you in my life.

He texts back, I'm sorry too. I'm the lucky one.

His message brings a smile to my face. I type out another because I don't want our conversation to end. A text from Tyler pops up telling me he's here, but I swipe it away so I can finish my text to Robbie.

> And good news, we don't have to worry about the pact anymore. Lol. I finally figured it out, and I'm so sorry I blamed you for me not knowing who I love.

The three dots pop up and then disappear and pop up again and disappear. Another message appears from Tyler. I swipe it away. Finally, a message from Robbie comes through.

> Congrats. Hope you're happy.

I let out a heavy sigh, rereading the four words over and over again. They're short and impersonal. He didn't even ask who I picked. Isn't he at least curious? Robbie's the one that said he would help me figure it out. He said he would make sure I picked the right guy just to prove he wasn't trying to sabotage our pact. And now he doesn't even care who it is. I type out an angry message but then I erase it. Then I type a message riddled with questions. I delete that one too. Then I write up a snarky one, saying I am happy. Thx. Remembering what Debbie said,

I erase that one too and instead reply: No matter what, you'll always be my friend, Robbie.

He's just scared of losing me, and I know fear can bring out the worst of us. The three dots pop up and a text from Robbie lands on my screen.

I know.

I hope it wasn't just a flippant message and that Robbie truly knows that I'll always be in his life. He might be upset and scared now, but I'll prove it to him.

I text Tyler, saying I'll be right out.

The charm bracelet full of coins jingles as I slip on my jacket. They're supposed to be lucky but right now I feel anything but.

I'm seated in a booth at a small sandwich and soup shop in the West Loop. The walls are covered in a hodgepodge of old street signs, and Tyler stands at the counter ordering for the both of us. We're the only ones here aside from the employees. He fills up two Styrofoam cups at the drink station and returns to our table.

"Here you are," he says, handing me a cup and sliding into the booth across from me. He pops a straw in his and sips.

I give him a small smile.

"Happy birthday," he adds.

"Thanks." I unwrap my straw and stick it in the drink.

"Sorry, I wanted to take you somewhere nicer than this, but with the short notice, I couldn't get reservations at any of the restaurants I had in mind." Tyler tilts his head.

"That's all right. I don't care where we eat," I say, and I mean it. I force myself to smile because I want him to know that I mean it and that I'm happy to be here with him, even though I'm feeling sad about how things are with Robbie right now. I never wanted to lose him as a friend over this whole thing.

A middle-aged man wearing an apron sets a basket in front of each of us. He nods and tells us to enjoy before strolling back behind the counter. There's a bag of Lay's potato chips and a Reuben sandwich in mine. Tyler doesn't hesitate to pick up his meatball sub and bite into it. He moans as he chews.

"Dig in." He gestures to my food, while still chewing his own.

I take a bite and wait until my mouth is free of food before speaking. "It's really good," I say.

"I knew you'd like it."

"How did you know I'd like it?" I raise my brow.

Tyler shrugs and cracks a smile. "Because it's the best. Everyone likes it." He takes another large bite.

I press my lips together and force the corners of them up. We continue eating in silence and making eye contact intermittently. He finishes before I do.

I clear my throat and wipe my mouth with a napkin. "You said when I told you that I had ended it with Nash that you knew it was you and me that were supposed to be together."

"That's right." Tyler sips from his straw.

"How did you know?"

"Because we're good together."

I pluck the last few chips from the bag and toss them in my mouth, chewing slowly.

"There's a bar around the corner. We should go there after," Tyler says, pointing in the direction of where it's located.

I slightly nod.

"They've got a great beer selection," he adds.

"Oh, well, I can't have any alcohol yet. Doctor's orders."

"More for me then." Tyler chuckles and sucks from his straw. It makes a slurping noise, signaling there's no more liquid left. He shakes the cup and sucks again, making the same grating sound. "I'm gonna get a refill," he says, sliding out of the booth.

I place the rest of my sandwich back in the basket, leaving the last two bites behind. I remember what Debbie told me about them and why Robbie always eats them. It brings a smile to my face and an ache to my heart. I wish he were here now.

"You look really pretty," Tyler says, retaking his seat with a freshly topped-off soda.

"Thanks."

He gestures to my outfit. "I like this style."

I glance down at myself. "Maya got it for my birthday. It's not really me, but I told her I'd wear it tonight."

"She's got great taste."

My fingers touch the pendant of the necklace, moving it side to side on the chain. "And Debbie got me this."

"Cute," he says.

I hold out my wrist, and the coins clang against one another and shimmer in the fluorescent light. He clearly took the time and care to polish each one. "And this was from Robbie."

Tyler leans forward, getting a closer look. "That is exactly why men shouldn't pick out jewelry." He chuckles to himself and sucks up his sugary soda.

I frown, pulling my wrist back toward me. I place my hand in my lap, hiding it from Tyler's view. "He actually made it himself."

His shoulders vibrate as he talks through his laughter. "I can see why he's an actuary and not an artist."

"I like it." I take a deep breath and raise my chin. "Besides, it's the thought that counts."

He glances at his watch and then back at me. "At least I know your expectations aren't too high," Tyler teases.

I think he's joking but maybe I'm not in a laughing mood. I force a smile anyway. The corners of my lips quiver from the strain, but I hold it.

"Are you all done?" he asks.

"Yeah." I push my food toward him. "Do you want the rest of my sandwich?"

He stands from his seat. "Nah, I'm full." Grabbing the basket, Tyler walks it to the garbage can and empties it. The last two bites fall into the trash. He tosses the plastic basket onto a stack and turns to me. "Ready to head out?"

"No," I say without even thinking. It just comes out fast and hard like it had a jet engine powering it: 3 . . . 2 . . . 1 . . . blastoff.

Tyler gives me a quizzical look. "Oh, are you still hungry? I can get you something else." He gestures to the chalkboard menu above the counter.

I shake my head. This doesn't feel right. In my gut and in my heart, it just doesn't. There's still an ache there, as though it's longing for something. I meet his gaze. He appears just as confused as I am. I imagine myself running. The muscles in my legs explode. The cold Chicago air fills my lungs as I gasp for more of it. My heart races, pounding against my ribs. Even though I'm staring right at Tyler, I can't picture him.

He waves a hand in front of my face like he's trying to pull me from a trance. "Peyton, you all right?"

I blink several times, snapping out of it. "It's not you," I say.

His thick brows nearly become one. "What do you mean?"

"You're not the one I was running to that night. It can't be you."

Tyler cocks his head and takes a step toward the table. "What? You said it was me." He speaks in a low voice.

"I know, but I was wrong."

"Did your memories all of a sudden come back?"

"No, I still don't remember. But I know it wasn't you."

"How?" His eyes become slits, and I'm not even sure he can see me.

225

"The man I was willing to risk my life for just to tell him I love him would finish my sandwiches." As soon as the words leave my mouth, I know how silly they sound, but deep down I know they're not silly to me.

"You think I'm not the one because I wouldn't eat your leftovers? That's what dogs are for, not boyfriends."

"It's more than that." I raise my chin. "I can't put it into words, but I know it in my heart, and I don't need my memories to recognize you're not the one I love."

"Wow." He takes a step back and runs a hand down his face, pulling at his skin. "You're a real piece of work, Peyton."

"I'm sorry. I wish—"

"Save it," he interrupts, flicking a hand at me dismissively. "I don't need to hear this speech again."

"What do you mean *again*?"

He lets out a heavy sigh, looking away for a moment before meeting my gaze. His eyes are clouded with frustration. "You broke it off with me the night before the accident," he scoffs.

"What? Why in the hell did you show up at the hospital claiming to be my boyfriend if I had already broken up with you?"

"I came there to win you back, and then when I found out about the amnesia, I figured it was an opportunity for me . . . like fate."

"That's not fate. That's lying. That's taking advantage of someone. That's being a horrible person," I yell. I can't believe he would do something so low. How did I not see it?

He takes a step back. "I am not the bad guy here. You're the one that led me on, Peyton. You showed up at my place the other night telling me you loved me and that I was the one for you. And now you're just breaking it off willy-nilly."

"I didn't remember breaking up with you the first time," I seethe.

Tyler shrugs. "That is not my fault you didn't remember."

"But it is your fault you lied to me about it." I raise my chin a little higher.

This is why I've been so confused. Tyler has been straight-up lying to me the entire time, manipulating me. He was clearly the one I told Debbie about, the one I said I was going to break up with because I kept catching him in little lies. Turns out, I did end it with him. He just didn't tell me. I wonder what else he lied about.

Realization sets in, and I scowl at him. "Wait, did we even sleep together?"

His shoulders slump the tiniest bit, but I notice it. "In a technical sense, yes," he says with a firm nod.

"What does that mean? 'In a technical sense'?"

"You fell asleep, and we slept next to one another."

"Oh my God. You said we slept together, Tyler. What is wrong with you?"

"Dang, that's messed up," the man behind the counter pipes in, shooting a glare at Tyler.

"Nothing is wrong with me. I was just trying to show you how strong our connection was . . . is." Tyler reaches for my hand, but I swat it away.

"Don't. We're done . . . again." I turn and head for the exit.

The man behind the counter tells me to have a good night. I tell him the same.

"If you walk out that door, Peyton, then we are never, ever getting back together." Tyler points a finger at me, then crosses his arms over his chest and purses his lips. I can't tell if he's delusional or if his ego is so big that it sucks up all the air around him, leaving his brain deprived of oxygen.

"Good," I say, throwing open the door and stepping outside into the cool Chicago night air. It closes with a thud behind me, and I'm right back where I was before the accident.

CHAPTER 20

I consider texting Maya, Robbie, and Debbie and telling them what happened. I know they'd drop everything to be here for me. Well, maybe not Robbie right now. No, he still would. But I don't contact any of them. I think I just want to be alone. I pull my jacket tightly around me as I aimlessly walk the lit-up streets of Chicago. Cars and buses whiz by. Horns blare intermittently, signaling impatience and frustration. If I had a horn, I'd be blowing the hell out of it right now. I pass several couples holding hands, leaning into one another, exchanging whispers and smiles. I can't help but feel jealous. How did I go from having three boyfriends to none in the span of a week? Technically, two. But three if you ask Tyler. How was I so sure who I loved before the accident and now I have no idea?

I wait for the WALK signal to change at an intersection and look up, taking in the shimmering skyscrapers that appear to puncture the dark sky. There's a full moon tonight, set high and proud, begging to be appreciated. The light changes, and I cross the street. A large man stands at the corner, dressed in sweatpants and an old, oversized jacket. He holds a sign torn from a cardboard box that says, DOWN ON MY LUCK. ANYTHING HELPS. His skin is weathered, but his eyes are kind.

Without even a thought, I pull the rest of the cash I have from my purse and extend it to him. He smiles and tilts his head, glancing at my hand.

"It's all I have," I say.

"I know, Peyton. You always give all you have." His grin widens as he accepts the cash.

I'm taken aback. I scan his face, searching for a memory, but there isn't one. I'm about to ask him how he knows my name, but he speaks before I do.

"Did you ever tell that boy you love him?"

"I'm sorry, what?"

His shoulders rise and fall as he shakes his head. "Oh, you don't remember me. I don't blame ya. I'm not all that memorable of a person. Have a good night." The man nods and turns on his foot.

"No, wait. It's not you. I don't remember anything," I explain. "I was in a car accident two weeks ago and all my memories are gone."

He turns back with a peculiar look. "Are you yanking my chain?"

"No," I say. "I got hit by a car before I told him I loved him."

"Damn, and I thought I had it bad." The man rubs his jaw. "I'm Hank, by the way." He extends his large, calloused hand toward me.

"Nice to meet you . . . again," I say, shaking it.

"Likewise." He glances around and then back at me. "What are you doing out here alone?"

"I just broke it off with a guy and told him I didn't love him." I laugh.

"Well, I can tell you don't love him," he says.

"Really? How?"

"Last time I seen you, you were crying because a guy told you he loved you, and you told him you didn't love him back. But you clearly did. This time, there's not even a glimmer of a tear in your eyes." Hank smiles. "That's how I know."

"I was crying?"

"Oh yes, like a newborn baby." He laughs. "I told you; you had clearly let your mind speak for your heart. You were so scared that it would end that you never let it begin. But like I said before, it's better to live with a broken heart than to never let anyone into it in the first place."

My brain starts to tingle like it's been poked or prodded, and a dizzy spell comes over me. I feel as though I could fall right to the ground. Hank notices and places a hand on my shoulder, keeping me upright.

"You all right?" he asks.

The dizziness passes quickly, and my mind becomes so sound and strong that I'm almost confident I could fly if I really wanted to. Goose bumps cover my skin, and it's not because I'm cold—it's because I'm alive. I can finally see it . . . the night of the accident. The memory that was stolen, the one I've been chasing this whole time, plays out right in front of me, like a private viewing. I don't know how I ever forgot it. I blink several times, staring back at Hank and those kind eyes of his.

"Yeah."

"You sure?" he asks.

"I remember," I say. "I remember who I love."

I nod several times, grinning like the Cheshire cat, but instead of falling down the rabbit hole, I'm finally climbing out of it. I can't believe how long it took me to see what was right in front of me. Tears burst from my eyes all at once, as though my heart is pumping them right out of my body. They stream down my face, but I don't wipe them away.

"Then what are you waiting for? Go. Go tell him."

"Okay, okay. I'm going to tell him. Thank you, Hank." I wrap my arms around him.

Hank hugs me back. "Thank you, Peyton."

We break our embrace and share a smile.

"All right, go." He pats me on the shoulder.

I turn from him, and the muscles in my legs explode as I take off in a full sprint. My lungs suck in the cold night air, and my heart bangs inside my chest.

"Don't get hit by a car this time!" Hank yells out with a chuckle. His words echo through the streets of Chicago.

I laugh and cry as I run, a melding of emotions reserved only for when the heart gets to speak for itself. My shoes pound against the pavement, each step carrying me a little closer to where I should have been all along. At the intersection, the signal changes to Do Not Walk. Remembering what happened last time and determined to not end up being Tyler's girlfriend again, I stop and wait for it to change. Traffic whooshes by as I catch my breath. I slide my phone from my purse and quickly send a text to Maya, telling her who I love, just to be safe.

She immediately replies with, I know.

I smile and stow my phone away. The light changes, and I take off again, faster this time. I'm scared I'll be too late, that he'll have moved on or had a change of heart after I broke his.

I throw open the doors to the building and rush to the elevator. My fingers hit the Up button repeatedly, but it doesn't move. I can see it's stuck on one of the higher floors. A sign beside a closed door that says Stairwell catches my attention. I suck in air and bolt through it, taking the stairs two at a time. I'm beyond exhausted, but I won't stop until he's standing right in front of me, hearing my heart finally tell him the truth.

My knuckles rap against his door, fast and furious. Maybe he's not home. But I don't care, I keep knocking anyway.

Finally, the door swings open, and there he is standing before me with a look of bewilderment. He's crystal clear and completely in focus. But all around him is a blur, like Monet himself painted his world. I've stared into those blue eyes a million times, and somehow, I didn't see what was right in front of me. The love of my life, and the reason all the other ones didn't work out. It's because they weren't him. They weren't Robbie.

"Peyton," he says. His face is full of concern, and I realize I probably look like a madwoman. I ran nearly a mile to get here, crying and laughing the whole way.

"I remember," I say.

"You remember what?"

"You. You told me you loved me. I remember."

His cheeks flush, and he lowers his head like he's embarrassed or something. "Yeah, then you also remember you said you didn't love me back, that we were just friends." When he picks his head up, I can see the pain in his eyes, and I feel so bad for ever hurting him to begin with. They're glassy, just like they were the night of my accident—the night I lied to him.

"I know. But it wasn't true."

He sighs and shakes his head. A tear falls from the corner of his eye, and I step toward him, wanting to put it back. I don't want to be the reason for it. Robbie holds his hands up, halting me. "Peyton, no. You're just confused. I'm telling you. You don't love me. You made it very clear that night. You said it more than once."

"But you were the one I was running to when I got hit by the car, Robbie."

He shakes his head again. "No."

"Yes." I nod, taking another step forward. He drops his hands, but I can tell he still doesn't believe me. I don't blame him, though, given how much I hurt him when I lied.

"I remember. It was you, Robbie. It was always you. And I was too scared to love you because I didn't want to lose you. I'm not scared anymore. I'd rather love you for a minute than love anyone else for a lifetime."

He stares back at me. Unblinking, his eyes search mine as though he's waiting for the other shoe to drop, for me to take it all back. But I won't. My heart belongs to Robbie whether he accepts it or not. Even if right now he says it's too late, and my heart breaks in two, half of it will always be his.

"I love you, Robbie. I've loved you since the night we made that pact back in college, and I'm sorry it's taken me so long to realize it." My bottom lip trembles, and tears spill out. He doesn't say anything.

He just stares. I'm not even sure he's hearing what I'm saying, or if he even cares to hear it. I think I might be too late. How could I have not known? These past two weeks, I've felt such a closeness to Robbie, an undeniable connection. Waking up next to him was like watching the sunrise, and falling asleep beside him was like falling into a dream. I never needed my memories to love him—I only needed them to remember I did.

Robbie's hand slips into the pocket of his joggers. I don't know what else to say to make him believe me. And I don't know if he ever will. But he has to. I've wasted too much time already. He pulls his hand from his pocket, holding it out in a fist, palm up. Does he want me to bump it? Play rock, paper, scissors? Kiss it? I'm not sure what to do or what to say.

He slowly unclenches his fist, revealing a penny. It lies in the center of his palm, tails face up.

Robbie cracks a grin, and I realize what he wants. I flip the coin over in his hand and smile back at him.

"You found this penny on campus our freshman year of college and handed it to me right before I had to take a final exam, one I was sure I was going to fail. You said it was all the luck I needed, and I've carried it around ever since. But I don't need it anymore." His gaze meets mine. "Because I have you."

The memory comes rushing back, playing out before me like a movie. I can't believe he kept it all this time.

"But you failed that exam," I say through laughter and tears.

"Well, it's not a magic penny." He laughs.

I stare into his blue eyes, never wanting to look away. His gaze intensifies, and his face turns serious. This time we don't let anything stand in our way. He closes the distance, unzipping my jacket and pushing it off my shoulders. It slides down my arms and falls to the floor. My hands run over his chest and shoulders, wanting to touch every part of him, making up for all the time I could have spent loving him. His arms wrap around me, pulling me into him. My charm bracelet jingles as I slide my hands around the back of his neck. We stumble and giggle, shuffling a couple of steps into his apartment—the kitchen, to be exact.

Finally, his lips meet mine. It's where they should have been all along. His kiss is warm and passionate and explosive, like nothing I've ever experienced before. It makes the world around us fade away, the big bang of our lifetime.

It's electric.

No, it's better than that.

It's magic.

CHAPTER 21

Two months later

"Almost ready to go?" Robbie calls out from the living room.

Well, actually, *our* living room, as of last week. I spritz perfume on my neck and give myself a once-over in the mirror. I smile at the girl staring back at me because I know who she is now. She's the reflection of the life I've lived, the people I've loved, and the memories I've carried with me. She's my mother and my father. She's my friends and my foes. She's my failures and my successes. I may not remember everything about her, but I don't need to in order to know who she is. Nearly all my memories have come back. They didn't pop into my head all at once. Unfortunately, that only happens in the movies. They've returned a few at a time, like pages of a diary sent through in the mail. I feel as though I've lived my life all over again the last two months, remembering and savoring each morsel of it, both the good and the bad.

I clasp the charm bracelet around my wrist and straighten it out. The coins jingle against one another. Hearing it brings me back to the first time Robbie and I kissed. My body immediately reacts to the sound. Goose bumps cover my skin, and my heart races like I'm right back in that kitchen. It's a memory not even amnesia could take away from me. I'll always remember that night because it lives in my heart.

Robbie's arms wrap around me. They feel like home. He leaves warm kisses on my skin as he nuzzles my neck.

"We're going to be late," he whispers.

"I mean, if we're going to be late anyway, we may as well be really late." I turn to face him. My eyes flick from him to the bed, and I give him a devilish grin.

Robbie follows my gaze and smiles. "You're bad."

"Only because you're so good."

He leans in and presses his lips against mine, pulling me into him. Our bodies melt into one another as we kiss and undress and tumble onto the mattress.

It's a half hour later when we arrive. Robbie holds my hand as we walk up the steps of the porch, careful not to slip on ice or snow. I remember the night I had to practically carry him up these stairs. He was too drunk to stand, and I almost didn't get him home. I smile at the memory.

"What's got you smiling?" Robbie asks, glancing over at me.

"Nothing." I laugh. "You wouldn't remember anyway."

He squeezes my hand and smiles. "Think we're the last ones here?"

"Definitely not. Maya's always running fifteen minutes late," I say.

At the door, I don't knock because it's home.

"Hello," Robbie and I call out as we step into Debbie's house.

We pull off our jackets and kick off our shoes.

"It smells amazing," Robbie says.

"Yeah, it does. It smells familiar actually, but I can't place it."

Footsteps pad along the hardwood floor, growing louder. Debbie appears in the living room dressed in a red top and black leather pants. Her hair is pinned up, and her lips are painted red. Christmas music plays softly from a speaker.

"There you two are," she says, holding out her arms for a warm embrace.

I hug her tight and apologize for being late.

"You're actually right on time. We're just setting the food out," she says, wrapping her arms around Robbie.

"Debbie, where did you get that outfit?" I ask.

She turns slowly and laughs. "Oh, this old thing. Maya got it for me. She said I need to spice it up since I'm dating again."

Robbie and I chuckle.

"Of course she did," I say. "And where's your date?"

"He's in the kitchen. Maya and Anthony are in the dining room."

I exchange a look with Robbie. "We're the last ones here."

"Technically, yes. But that's because I told Maya it was a half hour earlier so she'd be here on time." Debbie smirks. "Come in." She beckons with her hand and leads us down the hallway.

In the dining room, Maya and Anthony are seated next to one another. She immediately jumps from her seat and runs to hug me.

"You put Debbie in leather pants," I whisper into her ear.

"Guilty," Maya says. "She complimented mine one day and said she wished she would have had the gall to rock them when she was young, so I bought her a pair."

"Honestly, she's pulling them off better than I did." I laugh.

"So, how's living with Robbie?" Maya tilts her head in his direction.

I glance over at him. He and Anthony shake hands and do that half hug / half pat on the back thing. They laugh and walk to the buffet, where a half dozen open bottles of wine are set out. Debbie sure knows how to throw a dinner party.

"It's the best," I say to Maya. "I couldn't imagine falling asleep without him next to me."

"Being in love has made you corny." She chuckles.

"It really has."

"I'm glad you two are finally together. Took ya long enough." She pats my shoulder.

"I know. Sometimes you can't see what's standing right in front of you."

"All right, someone get this girl a drink and a lobotomy," Maya teases. "She's speaking in limericks."

"Peyton," a deep, familiar voice calls from behind me. I turn to find Hank dressed in a quarter-zip sweater and a nice pair of slacks. He doesn't look like he did the night I met him, but everything else about him is still the same. From his kind eyes to his infectious smile to the warmth his very presence exudes.

"Hi, Hank. How are you?" I hug him tight.

"I'm great. Feeling like the luckiest man in the world," he says.

Robbie extends glasses of red wine to me and Hank just as we break our embrace. They greet one another, and Hank and I clink our glasses together.

"How are you liking your new home?" I ask.

He peers up at the ceiling and back at me with a small smile. "To be honest, I haven't been spending a lot of time up there."

Hank's been staying at my place for the past seven weeks. I spent every night sleeping over at Robbie's, so it made sense to offer it to him since it wasn't being used anyway. It officially became his home a week ago, when I moved out. Robbie got him a job at his company working in the sales department. He's only been there for a little over a month, and he's already one of the top sales associates. I'm not at all surprised. He sold me on following my heart, something I'd never done.

Debbie carries in a basket of fresh baked rolls. She walks up behind Hank and plants a kiss on the side of his cheek. He and Debbie developed a friendship, which quickly blossomed into a relationship. I wasn't surprised.

"Oh, let me help you with those, honey," Hank says, taking the basket of rolls from her.

"What did I do to deserve you?" Debbie beams.

He leans down and gives her a quick kiss on the lips. "I could ask myself the same question."

She blushes and turns toward the table, addressing the room. "All right, everyone take your seats. The caterers are ready to bring the food out."

Hank and I exchange a smile and a nod, our way of thanking one another for being the reminders we needed to follow our hearts and to love as long as we live. Robbie and I take a seat next to each other, across from Maya and Anthony. Debbie and Hank sit at the head of the table on either end. Robbie's hand finds mine. It always does. I don't even have to glance over at him to know that he's smiling, just as I am.

"You got a caterer, Debbie?" Maya asks.

She nods. "Yes, I did. Now that I have a boyfriend, my time is rather preoccupied." Debbie winks at Hank. He returns it and sips from his glass.

The door off the dining room swings open, and a woman around my age enters. She's petite with dark hair and light-brown eyes. She carries a tray of canapés and smiles at each of us as she places it in the center of the table.

"Hi, everyone. I'm Maddie. To start, we have bacon-wrapped dates stuffed with goat cheese on the left and scallion and chive flatbread on the right. Your soups will be out shortly," she says with a nod.

We thank her, and everyone immediately dives in, serving up plates and passing them around as she leaves the room.

"This is incredible, Debbie," Anthony says, biting into a bacon-wrapped date.

A moment later the door swings open again, letting out a high-pitched squeak.

"Good evening," a voice calls out. I immediately recognize it.

I turn to find Nash, dressed in a black chef jacket. He holds a serving tray lined with bowls of his homemade chicken noodle soup. That was the familiar scent.

We smile at one another.

"Debbie. You hired Peyton's ex to cater this dinner?" Maya furrows her brow.

"Why wouldn't I? He's the best chef in the area, and he's barely Peyton's ex. No offense, Nash," Debbie says.

"None taken." He chuckles.

"It's fine," I say. "It's really good to see you again, Nash."

"Likewise." He walks around the table, setting a bowl of soup in front of each person. When he gets to Robbie and me, he pauses. "Are you two together?"

We smile and nod.

Nash grins back. "Good. Honestly, when I saw you both interact at that coma surprise party Maya made up, I wondered how you two weren't together. I'm glad it all worked out."

"I appreciate that, man," Robbie says.

"What about you, Nash? Are you seeing anyone?" I ask.

He walks to the head of the table, holding the empty tray against his chest. "Actually . . ." Nash points toward the door. "I'm taking Maddie to my family's Christmas next week."

We all swoon and clap. The attention makes his cheeks redden.

"Lucky girl," Debbie says. "If Hank hadn't come into my life, I was going to hit you up."

Maya and I burst out laughing.

"Lucky for me too." Hank grins across the table at Debbie.

Nash puts a hand up. "Don't get too excited for me. We're just pretending to date for my mom's sake. It's my gift to her, except it's fake, but she won't know that. And she'll have one holiday not worrying about how single I am or trying to set me up."

"I bet you two end up together," Debbie says. "Those pretend-dating plans always lead to marriage. That's actually how I got my first husband. Turns out the reason he was so good at pretending to be my boyfriend was because he was a natural-born liar. But hopefully she's not one of those."

Debbie lets out a snicker, and we laugh with her.

"Yes, let's hope that's not the case," Nash says. "I'll be in the kitchen prepping your next course. Please enjoy the chicken noodle soup." He nods and ducks out of the dining room.

"I always liked him," Robbie says.

"Me too," I say. "He's one of the good ones."

"You know who's not?" Debbie squints. "That Tyler fella. He sent me an invoice for 'fixing' my sink." She makes quotation fingers around the word *fixing*.

Maya's mouth drops open. "He didn't!"

"He did."

"Did you pay it?" I ask.

"Heck no. But I did send him an invoice for that sandwich I made him." She smirks.

"I'd pay a hundred dollars for one of your sandwiches," Robbie says.

"And that's exactly what I billed him for." She gives a firm nod.

"That's my girl," Hanks says.

Debbie smiles fondly at him. "Before we dive into our soups, let's have a cheers," she says, holding out her glass.

We do the same and look to her. "Cheers to making new memories," she says.

"And not forgetting the old ones," Maya quips, glancing at me with a teasing smile.

We laugh, clink our glasses together, and tip them back. My eyes shift to Robbie, and I smile as Hank's words come back to me—the ones he said the night of my accident.

Follow your heart. It'll never steer you wrong.

Robbie is proof of that.

ACKNOWLEDGMENTS

First, I want to thank my readers. I have the best readers in the world (not you, Scott), and it's because of all of you that I get to do what I love. If this is the first book you've read by me, thank you for taking a gamble on a new-to-you author. If you've read one of my thrillers previously and have crossed over into the rom-com genre, thank you for joining me on this journey.

Thank you to the entire team at Montlake for taking a chance on me writing in a new genre! Special shout-out to Anh Schluep for reading a couple of my other books and trusting that I could write romance. You saw my potential when no one else had, and if it weren't for you, I may have never written a rom-com—or at least not for a very long time. Huge thank-you to my developmental editor, Charlotte Herscher, for your invaluable insight and feedback. You made this book so much better!

I always have a couple of people read my work before I send it off to my agent or editor just to ensure it's not a total dumpster fire. Thank you to Cristina Frost and Bri Becker for taking one for the team and reading the first draft of this. Also, I'm sorry.

Thank you to my agent, Sandy Lu, for championing my work regardless of the genre and for supporting me both on and off the page!

Finally, thank you to my husband, Drew, a.k.a. "past tense of Draw," for being the inspiration for Robbie's character. I couldn't write a love story if I didn't have one with you.

ABOUT THE AUTHOR

Photo © 2022 Katharine Hannah

Jeneva Rose is the *New York Times, USA Today*, and Amazon #1 bestsell-ing author of *The Perfect Marriage, The Girl I Was, One of Us Is Dead*, and *You Shouldn't Have Come Here*. Her work has been translated into more than a dozen languages and optioned for film/TV. Originally from Wisconsin, she currently lives in Chicago with her husband, Drew, and her English bulldog, Winston. When she's not writing, you can find her bingeing reality television shows and calling it "research." For more information, visit www.jenevarose.com.